SURVIVAL ISOLATION

MW01135263

A BUNKER 12 NOVEL

BOOK THREE: CONTROL
The third installment in the post-apocalyptic saga

A vicious madman has kidnapped Finnian Bolles' brother, Harper, and is holding him as bait in a deadly game of wits. But Finn's chances of rescuing his twin from a fate worse than death are quickly thwarted when someone close betrays him in a selfish bid to gain their own freedom . . . as well as information about the cure to the deadly disease that has decimated mankind, the Flense.

Meanwhile, the other survivors of Bunker Eight hope to find the elusive and possibly nonexistent twelfth bunker, their only link to the cure. Their search leads them deep into Wraith-infested territory hundreds of miles away. But will they find what they're looking for in time to save Finn and his brother? And if they do, will it be enough to save themselves and the rest of Humanity, too? Or will their efforts be rewarded in the most terrifying way imaginable?

Make sure to look for the companion series
THE FLENSE

Hundreds die in a fiery train crash in northern China. A cargo ship smuggling refugees is lost to calm seas off Libya. Entire villages in Ghana are abandoned overnight.

Contracted by a prepper group to investigate a series of seemingly disconnected global tragedies, a young medical reporter, Angelique d'Enfantine, uncovers a disturbing pattern: each event is preceded by the sudden spread of a mysterious ailment and is followed by the appearance of a man dressed in black and silver who witnesses claim is the devil himself.

Each event is more grisly than the last. As the risk to her life grows, Angel begins to doubt that the tragedies are harbingers of an impending biblical catastrophe, but rather practice runs conducted by a fanatical organization bent on global annihilation. Could her sponsors be using her to advance their own paranoid agenda?

The story begins in China . . . .

Scan for more information:

website: http://www.tanpepperwrites.com
email: authorsaultanpepper@gmail.com

CONTROL

BOOK 3 OF THE BUNKER 12 SERIES

SAUL TANPEPPER

BRINESTONE PRESS

PUBLISHER'S NOTE

This book is a work of fiction. Names, characters, places, and incidents either are the product of the author's imagination or are used fictitiously, and any resemblance to actual persons, living or dead, business establishments, events, or locales is entirely coincidental.

Published by Brinestone Press
San Martin, CA 95046
http://www.brinestonepress.com

Copyright © Saul Tanpepper, 2017

Set in Garamond type
Cover credit and interior design K.J. Howe Copyright © 2017
Images licensed from Depositphotos.com

ISBN-13: 978-1-54-257026-8
ISBN-10: 1-54-257026-3

Not even the immune

are safe

CHAPTER 01

FINN PEELED OPEN HIS EYES AND SQUINTED THROUGH the dusty glare on the windshield. There were more trees here, which meant they were getting close to the compound.

The front end of the truck dropped into a deep rut, jolting him as he turned to wipe away the grit on his face, and his cheek slammed into his shoulder. A grunt of pain rose from his parched throat, hit the rag stuffed inside his mouth, and went no further.

What's another bruise? he thought crossly. *Just one more to add to all the rest.*

His neck was stiff, and his head felt like it was covered in sheet metal that a jackhammer was trying to punch holes into. Moving any part of him at all sent crackles of pain down his spine and into his legs. Yet he forced his head around and blinked away the blurriness until the figure behind the steering wheel sharpened into focus.

Seth Abramson didn't turn at the sound of Finn's cough. He gave no indication he even knew Finn was awake. He kept his eyes glued to the road ahead, his head and shoulders hunched forward in intense concentration. The claws of his fingers endlessly curled and uncurled around the steering wheel.

They passed over an especially rough patch of road, and the truck rattled so violently that Finn thought it would shake itself apart.

Bastard must be aiming for the potholes.

An alarming rattle had developed somewhere in the truck's undercarriage. It came and went without rhyme or reason, like a metaphor of his own precarious existence.

He grunted again, trying to catch the man's attention. When that failed, he pulled his hands up, forgetting for the moment they were bound. The rope securing his wrists and ankles was cruelly short, and the ache in his back flared, threatening to completely unravel his frayed nerves. Another muffled plaint rose in his throat; this one made it past the gag.

But still, Seth ignored him.

A few choice words came to Finn's mind. He turned back to the window at his side and tried to calm himself down.

The trees were mostly pines now, rather than the scraggly oak and desert scrub from earlier, and they were growing more densely up ahead. Their numbers would continue to increase with the ascent to Adrian's compound. First came the rise, then the broad forested plateau. Then, in the center of it, the remote fishing and hunting refuge the madman had turned into a sick and twisted playground of torture.

Almost there.

He could feel the seconds fleeing away. He tried to usher forth some hope that this latest twist of fate would somehow play out in his favor, that he would walk away from this alive and unscathed.

But all he could muster was an unshakable sense of dread. It spread over him, suffocating him with the hard truth of his situation. Adrian would never keep his word. Come nightfall, they would all be prisoners in his demented little game.

And all because of one selfish decision made by the man sitting beside him.

Finn flashed on the scene of the bodies scattered on the roadway that afternoon, Bix's among them. All the gunshot wounds and blood drying in the harsh sunlight. And he wondered why so many had to die. Why did there have to be so much killing all the time?

He hated that this was their new reality.

He imagined his brother saying how every life was precious, every individual a treasure.

Was Harper even still alive?

Focus, dammit!

He needed to keep his wits about him, but how was that even possible when such thoughts kept crowding in?

What would he look like now? How might he have changed over the past three years?

Focus!

Seth ground the gears as he downshifted, and the transmission coughed in protest, bucking them in their seats. From the back came a pair of startled cries, Bren and her mother sitting on the wooden benches in the bed of the truck. Finn wondered how they were doing and what they must be thinking. Did they feel betrayed by what Seth had done? Would they ever be able to forgive him for what he was doing now?

As before, Mister Abramson made no acknowledgment he'd heard the cries. He stared at the road ahead, shifting when the engine whine grew excessive. The only movement his eyes made were to the occasional check of the scribbled map impaled onto the dash with a bloodstained hunting knife. The markings Finn had made on the paper weren't very accurate, but they hadn't needed to be. The route was straightforward. There weren't that many passable roads this far north.

Finn glanced over and checked the gauges. The tank was low, the temperature high, once more nudging into the red.

Earlier, Seth had turned on the heater to draw hot air away from the radiator, and that helped stop the engine from overheating. But the dry blast from the vents left them both baking, searing the membranes inside Finn's nose and throat until he gagged against the cloth gag Seth had shoved into his mouth. His stomach rebelled. He feared he'd be sick, but he also doubted Seth would remove the rag.

He won't let me choke. He needs me alive. It's the only way he gets what he wants.

And what was that? What exactly were the man's motivations anyway?

He hates you, hates that you're with Bren. He loves seeing you like this, tormented and terrified.

Enough to risk his own family for it?

At last Seth looked over, as if he'd sensed the loathing rolling off Finn, and out of the corner of his eye Finn thought he saw a grim smile creasing the corner of the man's mouth. Seth nodded once, then returned his attention to the front without saying a word.

They had entered the forest surrounding Adrian's compound. If Finn found any comfort from that, it was in knowing that the end was finally near, and it was too late to change anything now.

CHAPTER

"STOP RIGHT THERE!"

Three men materialized from out of the shadows fifty feet ahead and spread out over the road, blocking their way forward. As a unit, they raised their military style rifles, braced the stocks against the hollows of their shoulders, and aimed at the windshield.

Two more men emerged from behind trees on either side. They quickly hopped onto the truck's running boards, rocking the cab slightly with their weight, and banged loudly onto the roof with the butts of their pistols.

"Stop the truck *now*," the man outside Finn's open window ordered. Finn recognized him as one of the men from Adrian's barn fights, one of the more fanatical participants loudly shouting for salvation, when what they all wanted was blood and violence. He also remembered the man was one of the first to flee in the chaos after Bix killed the infected killer their friend Nami had been turned into.

"Stop right now, before I put a bullet into your brain."

Seth braked to a stop about twenty feet from the men on the road. He looked over at Finn, but if he harbored any doubts about his decision, they were carefully masked.

Little late for that now anyway.

"Out of the truck!" shouted the man. He thrust the pistol past Finn's nose and aimed it at Seth's head. "No, not you, asshole! You stay right there behind the wheel. I mean the boy. I need to inspect the package."

"Where's Adrian?"

"Shut up!" The man tried Finn's door handle, but it wouldn't open.

"It's broken," Seth said. He was struggling to keep his voice calm and steady, but there was an unmistakable quiver in it now. "The latch is jammed. Got shot back there during the gunfight. Besides, he's all tied up. He can't move."

"I don't give a crap! I told him to get out!" He pulled futilely on the door, getting angrier by the moment.

"The deal was we exchange Finn for the brother. No one's going anywhere until I see him," Seth said. "He promised." He tilted his head down and to the right, redirecting the man's gaze to the gun pressed into Finn's side. "He wants this one alive. Think about how disappointed he'll be if you make me shoot him. Give me Harper and we leave."

"You might want to rethink that, shithead," the man standing beside Seth growled. His breath stunk so badly, even Finn could smell it from where he sat on the other side of the truck.

There was a shout from the back — Missus Abramson calling for Bren — and Finn's heart nearly stopped when he heard Adrian ordering her to shut up. The madman appeared below Seth's window dragging Bren by the arm, the sharp edge of a knife pressed against the tender skin of his girlfriend's throat. Rage flooded through him. He wanted to scream, to lash out, but he could barely move as it was.

Don't lose it! Stay calm.

"What I wanna know is, what kinda idiot drags his wife and kid to a prisoner exchange?" Adrian drawled. He wrenched Bren around, who squealed in panic. She tried to pry his meaty fist off her throat, but he was too strong. Her face was a pale moon in the gloom beneath the forest canopy, her eyes wide with terror. "Y'all are stupid to bring them here."

"I couldn't just leave them behind. Besides, you promised if I did what you said, you wouldn't hurt us. Well, here he is. I brought him just like you wanted. Now give us Harper and we'll be gone before—"

"I said *both* boys. I only see one."

"You said Bix was optional. You said you'd be happy with him dead or alive. Well, he's dead. And you can blame your men for it."

"*My* men?"

"There was a lot of gunfire when the boys ambushed us. Your men were shooting wildly. You had to expect—"

"Liar!" Bren spat at her father. She tried to lunge, but couldn't break free. "You shot him! You killed him! You would have killed them all if you could!"

Adrian raised his eyebrows at Seth.

"Does it matter who did the actual shooting?" Seth said. "The boy's dead either way."

Adrian coughed. "It makes a difference, because y'all had no right to take his life. He owed me! The deal was—"

"It was necessary. I would never have been able to get away with Finn otherwise."

"Yer lyin."

"Look, your men underestimated those two boys— *you* underestimated them. And now your men are all dead because of their mistake. I wasn't going to take the same chance."

Adrian mulled this over for a moment.

"Finn's the one you really want anyway."

"Y'all shoulda brought the little brat's body, then."

"I left it for the vultures to pick over," Seth spat. "Him and all the others. He deserved it, for all the trouble he's caused me."

"You bastard," Bren shrieked at her father. She tried once more to break out of Adrian's grip. "How could you? I hate you!"

"I did it for you!" he shouted back, loud enough that it startled the man standing beside him, causing him to fall off the step and onto the road. But rather than hopping up again, he backed away from the truck, swinging the rifle nervously around like he expected to be attacked.

The other men mirrored his actions.

Finn knew Seth had seen it, too, and they both knew it meant the woods weren't secure. The deadly creatures Finn had had a hand in liberating from inside the compound during his escape several days earlier hadn't all been captured or killed.

The same creatures that had killed Adrian's sister, Jennifer, and set the madman on this path of vengeance.

"Bren, listen to me, honey," Seth said, his voice breaking with emotion. "I did it for you and your mother, for your safety." He turned his attention back to Adrian. "Please, don't hurt them. Let her go. You said you were a man of your word."

Adrian didn't move. The hard look on his face neither acknowledged nor denied the claim.

The man standing beside Finn stepped down and circled around the front of the truck. "Sir, we shouldn't stay here too long. It's starting to get dark. We should at least move inside the perimeter."

At last, Adrian nodded.

"Please, just give us Harper, and we'll—"

Adrian signaled his man with a nod, who stepped over, wrenched the driver's door open, and yanked Seth out. A blast filled the cab, popping Finn's eardrums. He blinked in shock, as the burnt gunpowder pinched his nostrils. The pistol tumbled from Seth's grip and landed in the space beneath the steering wheel, a wisp of smoke curling up from the barrel.

Finn looked down at his side, expecting to see blood pouring out of him. But there was no wound. The slug had punched a hole into the seat beside him, just inches from his leg.

Seth fell in a heap on the roadway, yelling in surprise. Bren screamed and tried once again to break free of Adrian's grip, but whether she meant to help her father or attack him herself wasn't clear. One of the men stepped between them and pointed his rifle at Bren. He pushed Seth down with his foot and ordered him not to move as he frisked him for more weapons.

"I suspect you ain't told me the whole truth," Adrian calmly said. "So, we're gonna have to have ourselves a little chat."

"I've told you everything!"

"Jackson, you and Frasier take the women to the house. Search them. Y'all know what to look for."

He shoved Bren toward the man standing in front, then gestured to another. "Pierce, y'all get in and drive."

"Where?"

"Take the boy to the barn. Check him over good when y'all get there, then tie him up, just like we discussed. Tear the truck apart."

He glanced down one last time, signaling for Seth to stand up. "I am a man of my word," he said. "Once I get what I need, y'all will be free to go."

CHAPTER
03

"WHERE ARE THEY TAKING MY WIFE AND DAUGHTER?"

"Y'all should really just learn to relax a little," Adrian said, waving to a plastic lawn chair and instructing Seth to sit down. "Especially if everythin y'all said is true."

He pulled another chair off a heap of debris and set it upright, brushing the thin film of soggy ash off the surface before sitting down. "Yer ladies are safe for the time bein. Ain't no one gonna hurt them."

"They need to be with me."

"I don't think y'all want them to see this. I suspect they's a bit perturbed by what they's imaginin already."

"We weren't planning on sticking around to see anything," Seth said. He leaned forward. "Look, I honestly don't care what you do to Finn. Frankly, the boy's been a goddamned thorn in my side for the past three years, and—"

"What about yer daughter? Anyone can see she has feelins for him."

"She's too young to know what she wants," Seth growled menacingly. "She's only ever had one boyfriend, him. She doesn't know any better."

Adrian leaned back and crossed his arms. He had a smug grin on his face. "Yes, I suppose she's led a sheltered life, livin inside that bunker of yers while the outside world changed. But one thing ain't never gonna change, and that's how much a child can hate a parent who betrays them. Yer willin to accept that?"

"She's my daughter. You don't get to tell me how she feels. You know nothing about us."

Adrian shrugged and turned his gaze over to the truck, where two of his men were wrestling Finn out of the cab. The boy was putting up a good fight, but he was too tightly trussed up to get away.

"Where is Harper Bolles?" Seth asked again. "Just give him to me and we'll be on our way."

Adrian pretended not to hear. He was enjoying watching the men wrestle Finn over to the stump of the post he'd once kept the ferals chained up to. The top was snapped off high above their heads, and one of the barn walls had collapsed, bringing down the roof. Most of the charred wreckage had been cleared away, but he'd kept the post right where it was in expectation of this very moment. Two thick lengths of chain were anchored about waist high into the wood with heavy bolts.

"We checked his pockets, sir," Pierce said. "Nothing on him."

At last, Adrian turned to Seth, his face hard and stoic. "And nothin on this one, neither?" he asked the men.

"He's clean, boss."

They threw Finn to the ground, and one kneeled on his neck while the other removed the cloth bindings from his ankles and replaced them with the iron shackles. Finn had a hard time breathing, and looked like he might pass out.

"Be careful with him, you fools!" Adrian scolded. "I need him conscious."

The ropes were sawed from his wrists. Then he was flipped roughly over onto his stomach so the cold metal bracelets could be snapped onto his arms. The chains were ratcheted taut and locked into place.

"Should I ungag him?"

Adrian nodded.

"He might scream."

"I'm countin on it. Now, take the truck. Check it over good, like I said."

"It needs fuel," Seth said.

Adrian chuckled, but he nodded at the man, dismissing him. "Fill it up once yer done checkin on the jennies. Make sure they's all topped off for the night."

"Yes, sir. But are you going to be okay here by yourself?" He glanced uncertainly into the woods. The sun had dipped below the tops of the trees, leaving only a few glints of sunlight peeking through the trunks.

Adrian shrugged. "I done built this place. Course I'm sure. Now go on."

The men didn't need to be told a third time. They gathered their weapons and climbed into the truck. The engine roared to life. A moment later, the taillights disappeared into the gathering gloom.

Finn struggled to get to his knees. The chains were too short for him to stand, so he knelt. To Adrian's disappointment, he didn't cry out or beg, though he did glance nervously around him, especially at the darkness in the surrounding woods. There was no hiding the terror in his eyes.

Adrian glanced back at the man, who refused to turn around and make eye contact with the boy he had just betrayed.

He feels guilty. Good, I can use that.

He stood up and walked over to the part of the barn still standing and flipped a switch attached to the wall, sending power to a pair of floodlights at opposite ends of the clearing. He watched Finn raise an arm against the glare, though he kept twisting his head around, searching in vain for the ferals.

Adrian chuckled and flipped a second switch. It had no obvious effect, except to him. Then he made his way along the wall to a door for one of the smaller stables. It had once housed a sow and piglets, but they had all died when the ferals escaped, some trampled, some starved, and some flayed and partially consumed.

Moving with calculated slowness, well aware of the eyes now focused on him, he inserted a key into a large iron lock holding the door secure. The mechanism sprang open with a loud snap just as a hiss sounded from inside.

He heard the plastic chair fall over as Seth Abramson sprang to his feet in surprise, but it was already too late. With a grimace of disgust, he allowed the door to burst open, and watched as the blood-soaked figure of his sister lunged out of the darkness inside.

CHAPTER

DESPITE THE RECENT CHANGE IN WEATHER, JONAH hadn't expected the water to be as cold as it was. The chill reached deep into his chest, where its steely fingers cinched tight around his heart. The iciness seeped into his marrow, eliciting shivers so forceful he feared his body might just curl itself into fetal knot and refuse to function.

The worst part was how cold it felt on his newly shaved scalp. He wasn't used to it.

That's the least of your problems right now.

He tried to focus on the dark outline of the adjacent shore and not about how he was probably going to end up infected before the night was out. Or dead.

If you're lucky.

And all because he couldn't just walk away like he should have done already. He'd certainly had enough chances over the past couple of weeks.

Next time. This is it. If I get out of this, I'm done.

He always knew, from the moment he met Finn, that it was never going to end well between them. They were just two very different people.

What was it his brother always told him? Never get close to anyone?

Unless they've got a cherry ride you can chop.

An unconscious grin of reminiscence creased his face, but it was fleeting, as another spasm wracked his body. He tried instead to focus on his breathing.

There was a soft, wet *plop* some thirty or forty feet away, the sound of something entering the water. He peered out into the deepening mist, but saw nothing.

Just a frog. Or a turtle.

Well, the frogs were certainly loud enough. Them and the crickets. It was like they were trying to cram in as much living as they could before winter set in.

He angled silently away from the sound, kicking with his feet, and hoped it was in the right direction.

Another splash, closer this time, though still small. Just a little *plink*. The sound a toe might make dipping in to test the water. The image was fraught with enough possibilities to make his heart race.

He spun around, splashing.

"Quiet, Jonah!"

With the thickening mist, the shore had been diminished to a faint gray outline beneath the darker charcoal shades of the charred trees beyond. The blaze was recent enough that the air still stank. Much of the canopy had burned away, leaving the forest draped beneath a network of dead branches and a few leaves too stubborn to die or let go. He could hear them rustling in the breeze.

Down here at ground level, however, the air was deathly still and cold enough that it drew a ghostly pall from the water. It would soon erase everything from view, save what was right in front of his face.

"Getting harder to see."

He glanced over at Eddie. The man's pale arms were like thick, pale tentacles rising up out the inky water, his fingers gripping the other corner of the rowboat like tangled knots.

"Yeah, this mist is really something," he replied. The fog was beginning to curl about them. "I don't like it."

"Works to our advantage," Eddie said.

There was a louder splash. Jonah's throat closed and he froze. The lakeside chorus went silent.

"Just a fish," Eddie said after a moment. He was close enough that Jonah could feel his warm breath on his face. "We're almost there. I can see the dock now, just ahead. Doesn't look like it's guarded."

"Must be nice having superhuman eyesight," Jonah said.

He hated that he was so dependent on his own senses, mediocre by comparison to Eddie's. The occasional telltale knock of another rowboat nudging against a wooden dock brought unsettling images of infected creatures beneath the black surface. He half-expected an army of killers to rise up all around them at any moment.

Eddie didn't immediately respond to the taunt. He kept nudging them forward with each silent flutter of his feet. When he finally did speak again, his voice was tinged with worry: "I can't tell if my abilities are fading."

"They're not," Jonah said. "Believe me, you're . . . ."

Eddie glanced over, waiting for him to finish.

Jonah didn't think the word *unnatural* would ease his friend's anxiety.

"They seem just as strong as ever," he finished.

That is, a hell of a lot stronger than any normal human being's should be.

"It's just that," Eddie said, struggling to express himself, "I don't know. Sometimes I worry they'll—"

He stopped suddenly and turned back in the direction they had come, listening. But the night was still, and when the desperate mating songs of the summer's last frogs recommenced, he turned back and resumed their swim.

"You picked out those guys back there on the road," Jonah reminded him. He was breathless from the cold and the numerous false alarms, but also because of the rush of memories from that afternoon. "Had to be a couple miles away, yet you knew they were there."

"One mile," Eddie countered. "One and a half at the most."

* * *

It all happened so quickly— the deadly confrontation with Adrian's men was barely over and they were still in shock when Seth admitted Adrian had taken Harper to his compound. The argument that followed was getting heated.

In the middle of it, Eddie pulled Jonah aside to inform him they were being watched. "Don't look, but we're not alone."

Jonah's hand went instinctively to the gun tucked into his waistband, but Eddie stopped him.

"No. Act normal."

"Where?"

"Other end of the valley, where this rocky ridge curves around to the north. Not sure how many there are. Two people, maybe three."

"You saw them?"

"I can smell their horses. Heard a whinny and at least one human voice."

Despite Eddie's warning not to look, Jonah stole a glance up the distant arête. But he saw no sign anyone was there. "That's like two miles away."

"The valley acts like a funnel. Sounds carry well on the wind. Smells, too."

"You're sure?"

"I thought I'd seen something earlier, while we were driving, but with everything happening, I got distracted. Pretty sure they've been shadowing us for a while now, possibly since we left the bunker."

"You think it's this Father Adrian character?"

Eddie shook his head.

"I think whatever it is he wants to do to the boys, he wants to do it on his own turf. That's why he's not here and why I don't think he'd be satisfied to watch from a distance. It also explains why it was so easy for the boys to gain the upper hand here. These men are killers, yet with all the opportunities they had, they never shot at Finn or Bix, not with any intention to kill. I'll bet they were ordered not to kill them."

Jonah glanced over at Finn, who was shouting that no one had any right to stop him from rescuing Harper. "I don't need anyone's help. I'll take the pickup truck. The rest of you head on back to the base. Go find Bunker Twelve, if you can. I'll catch up with you after."

"No, you won't, Finn," Bix said, chiming in for the first time. "Gimme those keys."

"Don't stop me, Bix."

"I'm not. I'm driving. Remember? You can't drive stick."

Eddie placed a hand on Jonah's arm. "I think the success of this little encounter has made Finn overconfident in his abilities. He can't see that Adrian's counting on that. He wants him to feel invincible. If he goes, he'll be walking into a trap."

"So, we don't let him."

* * *

The sudden bump of the rowboat against the reeds jolted Jonah back to the present, and he nearly cried out in surprise before remembering where he was.

The rotting pilings loomed up out of the darkness beside him. Eddie was already pulling himself out of the lake onto the dock. The water poured off of his pale, hairless skin in sheets, pattering noisily onto the wood. He stood for a moment, panting and trembling. Then, planting his bare feet firmly on the deck, he crouched and reached into the boat for the bundles of dry clothes they had stashed inside.

"You okay?" Jonah asked. "You look a little shaky."

"I'm fine," he whispered back, "just a little sore from riding that damn horse for so long." He reached down to offer Jonah a hand up. "Come on. Let's go rescue Finn."

CHAPTER

SHE ATTACKED ADRIAN THE MOMENT HE STEPPED AWAY from the door, digging her fingernails into the soft flesh of his face and tearing strips of skin away. An unearthly screech erupted from her mouth. Two men immediately appeared by his side and pulled her off, but not before she sank her teeth into his shoulder.

Adrian didn't move. There was no emotion on his face, neither surprise at the unexpected attack, nor anger or horror. He raised a hand to his ruined face and dabbed gingerly at the scratches. He seemed mesmerized by the sight and feel of the blood on his fingertips, as if he had never seen such a wondrous thing before. Or perhaps he was simply astonished that he could be made to bleed at all.

"Bren!" Missus Abramson cried out in horror. She wrenched her arms out of the grip of the man holding her and hurried over to her daughter, pulling her into her arms and casting hateful glares at Adrian and her husband standing behind him on the threshold.

Adrian rubbed his bruised shoulder and grimaced. He shuddered to think what might have happened if the girl had bitten through his jacket. The human mouth was a filthy cesspool of germs. And the mouths of little girls were especially nasty.

He refused the cloth offered to him and instead let the blood dribble down his cheeks. He stared at the two women for a moment, giving them time for the news of Finn's sentence to fully sink in, to get over the shock of knowing the truth so they could dispense with the futility of hope.

At the same time, he understood the chasm that existed between them and the man standing on the threshold behind him, though it mattered not at all to him one way or the other in the grand scheme of things.

"I want to see him," Bren said, sobbing into the crook of her mother's arm. She raised her head, and tears streamed down her cheeks. "I want to see him."

"Too late for that, young lady," Adrian said. "Y'all should have said yer goodbyes already."

She glared past him at her father, but neither of them spoke a word to the other.

"We ain't finished our discussion," he said. "The sooner we do, the sooner ya'll can leave. Course, it'd be inhospitable of me to let y'all go in the dark of night. Tain't safe out there, so I would suggest y'all consider stayin on till mornin."

"We're not staying another minute longer," Seth growled. "Give us Harper and our truck, and we'll be on our way."

"Well, see'n as how it's my diesel they's puttin in it, I'd say y'all are still in my debt."

"We have a couple guns. You can choose from them."

Adrian dismissed the offer with a wave of his hand. "Humor me. There are a few things I ain't yet gotten from y'all."

Seth's eyes narrowed suspiciously. "What?"

"First, I just can't figure why yer so keen on the brother. Why is he so important? Why do y'all want him so badly?"

"I feel responsible for him."

Adrian snorted. "Y'all sure that's what it is?" He kept glancing back and forth between him and Bren, as if trying to figure out if the father had considered whether the brother might be a suitable replacement for his daughter's boyfriend. Finally, he shrugged and ordered both women to their feet.

Seth stepped between them. "What are you going to do?"

"I can't have them around," he replied. "They's too emotional, too much of a distraction. Women are like that. My Jenny was like that, buttin her nose in where it didn't belong. We needs to get to the heart of this matter without nitpickin every little detail to death."

"I'll show you emotional!" Bren screamed, and pushed away from the man pinning her down. She demanded once more to be taken to Finn.

Adrian raised an eyebrow. "See? That's what I mean. Now, please, it's done. Time to let the men talk now."

"Pig!"

He gestured toward one of the overstuffed armchairs and directed Seth to sit down in it. Then he turned to the men and ordered them to take the women to the hold. "Guard them well." He locked eyes with Seth, giving him a chance to protest, but he didn't. "They'll be safe till we're finished up here."

"Finn saved your life!" Bren screamed at her father. "He didn't have to stop Eddie from throwing you off the walkway!"

"Bren—"

"And I'm sorry I came back for you. I should have let you rot inside that place! *I hate you! I hate you!*"

"Bren, no," her mother moaned. She placed her hands on Bren's face and tried to force her eyes toward her own. "Please, look at me. He did it because he loves you. He wants us to live."

"He killed Bix, Mom! He shot him and killed him just like he killed Doc Cavanaugh and Mister Bolles! And all the rest of them, too! He did this! And now he's killed Finn!" She collapsed to the floor, as if the weight of the truth suddenly became too much to bear. "Oh god! I can't— I can't do this anymore!"

"He's not . . . . Finn isn't . . . ." Mister Abramson began, but his words lost energy and he didn't finish.

Adrian shifted uncomfortably, unsure for once what to say or do. It was unseemly, the scene playing out before him. Sure, the girl had every right to be angry. He didn't even blame her for attacking him. In fact, he pitied her— not for the decisions he'd made, but for the ones her father had.

But he was tiring of all the drama. It was time to get serious.

"Take them," he said.

He watched as the men pulled the women kicking and screaming out the door.

"I need two things," he told Seth. "Give them to me, and y'all will be free to leave, just as I promised. The first relates to the boy's brother."

Seth pursed his lips, then nodded. "And the second?"

"The second is the other boy's body."

"Bix? I told you we left him behind."

"I need to know for sure yer tellin the truth. If'n y'all are, then y'all can go, unharmed."

Seth didn't answer for several seconds. Finally, he nodded.

CHAPTER

JONAH TUCKED HIS SHIRT INTO HIS JEANS FOR unrestricted access to his weapons. He was still shivering, though it wasn't as bad as before. The air retained a trace of the day's warmth, enough to stave off the chill, but now that night had fallen it was quickly leaking away.

"Here comes the second boat," Eddie whispered, and leaned over the edge of the dock as the bow appeared out of the mist. He nearly overbalanced, but managed to catch himself from tumbling back into the lake. The sound of the splash would have been disastrous, ending their rescue attempt even before they'd gotten started. "Other side," he whispered. "There's more room over there. We don't want to get in each other's way when it comes time to leave."

Harrison Blakeley appeared from behind the boat and pulled himself out of the water and onto the dock.

Jonah handed him his bundle of clothes, but instead of getting dressed, Harrison immediately set about unloading the supplies, arranging them on the deck beside one of the equipment duffles.

"You might want to cover your head," Jonah told him. "You're practically glowing in the dark there." He was trying for humor, but it came out sounding forced.

Eddie glanced up at Jonah's pale scalp and chuckled. "Speak for yourself."

Jonah stepped over to the shore and stared out into the woods. He thought he saw a faint glimmer of light through the trees, but it winked out when he tilted his head and he couldn't seem to relocate it.

"You sure you heard someone?" he asked, when Eddie shuffled over.

"Yeah, off to the left there, maybe a couple hundred yards away. Two voices."

Once more, Jonah wished he possessed the man's heightened senses. This stumbling around in the dark and not knowing who was where and whether they were aware of them was for the birds.

"I'm going to do a quick scout," Eddie said, stepping past Jonah. "You stay put until we're ready."

"I'll come with you."

"Not this time, Jonah."

"I'll keep up."

"Sure you will."

He could hear the amusement in Eddie's voice. It was a funny thing, the way one's emotions could alter one's voice so that you could actually *hear* someone smiling or frowning, even if you couldn't see them.

But he knew Eddie was serious as well. The last time Jonah offered to accompany him, he'd only slowed him down.

* * *

"Here!" Eddie shouted, slapping his palm on the roof of the truck cab. "We're out of sight now. You can pull over, Hannah."

Jonah glanced reflexively at the rocks to his left, but the outcropping where Eddie had pointed out the men and their horses was lost to view, hidden by the bluff of weathered granite they had driven past. He turned to check the road behind him, half expecting to see the bodies to be gone — all of them — but they were still there, just mounds of dirty, bloody clothes that were already drawing the attention of vultures circling overhead. The two remaining horses had galloped off and were now grazing in the shade beneath the road sign where Finn had earlier staged his ambush.

The large military cargo truck was already gone, having raced away over the next rise on its way to Adrian's compound. Seth had wasted no time escaping during the chaos that followed the shooting.

"Park behind there in the shade," Eddie instructed his daughter. He hopped deftly over the side and onto the shoulder. Jonah pulled up on the motorbike and killed the engine.

"Think they saw what happened?" Harrison Blakeley asked.

"I'm counting on it."

"And do you think they're still there?"

"I'm guessing not, but we need to be sure."

Jonah set the bike's kickstand and hopped off. "I'll come with you."

"It'll be faster if I go alone, "Eddie said, hitching the rifle over his shoulder. He propped his foot up on the bumper to tighten the laces on his shoes. "I can be there and back in under ten minutes."

Jonah shook his head. "Too risky. If they're on the move, then they might catch you by surprise."

"If they're on the move, they're heading northwest to shadow Seth."

"I can cover you."

Eddie snorted. "Seth's not going to waste any time getting to the compound. Why don't you work on getting those horses?"

"We can't get to them until we know for sure they're gone. You'll be safer with a backup."

Eddie frowned. "Are you doubting my abilities?"

"No. Look, Eddie, you may be fast and strong, but you're still just one man."

"And you're not going alone, Daddy," Hannah said. She pulled the bandana off her face so he could be sure and see the determination on it. "Take Jonah with you."

"Let the girl drive and she suddenly thinks she's in charge," Eddie said. He sighed. "Fine. You win, honey." He turned to Jonah. "Think you can keep up?"

Jonah glanced up the slope. "Sure, no problem," he said, trying to sound confident.

They ran along the base of the bluff, which wasn't so bad as it was partially shaded. After several hard minutes of rock hopping Eddie was as fresh and energized as he had been at the start. Jonah tried not to show how winded he was becoming, but once they began to climb, he found himself flagging.

Eddie reached the top first and had to wait. He crouched behind a worn boulder and advised Jonah to catch his breath.

"I can keep going. I'm good."

"You're not good. You're making too much noise." Eddie lifted his nose and sniffed the air.

"Am I making too much smell, too?"

"Yes, since you asked." He shook his head in frustration. "Damn sunlight's right in my eyes. And the wind's shifted away. I can't tell if they're still there."

They resumed the climb, skirting the rise and skipping awkwardly over the irregular terrain. It was slower going, but it afforded Jonah an opportunity to fully catch his breath again. Eddie tried not to show his irritation at the slow pace, but only a blind man would miss the impatience in the man's face.

The berm eventually curved around and dropped level with the higher ground, stripping them of protection and forcing them out into the open. But when they arrived at the spot where Eddie figured the men had been hiding, it was deserted.

"Maybe there wasn't anyone here after all," Jonah said.

Eddie pointed at the scuffed up dirt about fifty feet away on the hard pan. "Horse tracks. No, they were here, all right, but now they're gone."

Still unconvinced, Jonah squinted over the rocks down to the road. "Unless they've got your miracle eyesight, there's no way they could see what was going on down there from this distance."

Eddie reached down into a crack in the rocks at their feet, prying them loose and tossing them away before extracting a small olive green plastic disk. "Binoculars." He placed the lens cover in Jonah's hand, who flipped it back to the ground. "They were here. They must've left as soon as Seth took off with Finn."

He clapped a hand on Jonah's shoulder. "And so should we."

Jonah wiped the sweat from his face and nodded.

"Maybe next time I say I'm fine, you'll believe me."

CHAPTER

07

ADRIAN LET OUT A SHRILL WHISTLE, THEN SHOUTED through the door leading to the back of the house: "I can hear y'all in there! Come on out!"

"It's just us, boss."

"Manny? About time! The party's done started already. Get on out here!"

The sounds of hurried stomping and the shifting of loose debris came from deeper inside the ruined house. Then the knob to the other door began to rattle.

"It's stuck!"

"Give it a good push!"

There was a loud bang as the door smashed open against the cabinet.

Irritation flickered across Adrian's face.

A short, shabbily dressed man shuffled in, his face thick with an unkempt beard. Except for two clean circles around his eyes, the rest of his skin was covered with as much filth as he tracked in on the bottoms of his boots. He was followed by another man, not quite as short, but just as dirty. A thick stench of horse sweat and cigarettes clung to them.

"What the hell are y'all doin back there?" Adrian demanded. "Y'all were supposed to come find me first thing."

"We sent Gage looking for you, boss. Think he went to the barn."

"Well, I ain't there. And what're y'all doin in my kitchen?"

"We was hungry. Ain't had nothing to eat or drink all day, so we figured we'd check the old pantry. You know, in case something got missed during the cleanup.

"Idiots. Ain't nothin in there. It's all been gone through already."

"What about—"

"Just stand there and be quiet." He turned to Seth. "Forgive me. These are two of my associates, Manny and Carlos. Well, it's Manuel, but he prefers Manny."

"And I prefer Charlie," the second man interjected. He had a thick Latino accent.

"It's true, he does," Manny confirmed, bobbing his head like a crane and grinning toothily.

"Already got a Charlie on the payroll," Adrian said. "Gets too confusin with more'n one." He turned back to Seth. "Y'all recognize them?"

"Should I?"

"No? Good. Now, you was about to tell me how that little brat kid ended up dead. Listen carefully, boys, because he's goin to describe exactly what happened today and where it transpired."

It took Seth only a moment to realize what Adrian was doing. He intended to send the men out to find Bix's body, perhaps as soon as he finished relaying the details.

"I-I can't promise it'll still be there," he stammered. "Wolves might have—"

"Wolves? Vultures? What next?" Adrian demanded, his face burning with impatience. "Just get on with it!"

In a halting voice, Seth described what had happened that afternoon, how the boys had ambushed the truck, just as Adrian had expected they would. "Mile marker 167, on the east side of a small rise right at the edge of a long flat desert pan."

Adrian nodded, narrowing his eyes. He cast a quick glance at the two men, now leaning against the wall with their arms crossed. Their faces were unreadable. "Yep," he said, "I think I know the place."

"They were waiting for us. Finn on one side of the highway behind a road sign. Bix was at the top of the ridge hiding in some rocks. Your boys on the horses sent our man, Vince Caprio, on the motorbike to scout ahead. When he came back with the all-clear, two of the horse riders went over. That's when they ambushed us."

"How?"

"Explosives. Finn said your man at the footbridge had them. They killed him and took them."

Surprise flickered across Adrian's face. "Ramsay?"

"Look, you assured me they would not be armed. You said this guy would handle them. But not only did he let them get away, they managed to kill him and take his weapons."

"What did they do with him? Did they say?"

"No, and I didn't ask."

Adrian's face hardened. A muscle began to throb on his temple. "And this guy on the motorbike," he said through gritted teeth. "What happened to him?"

"Your man, Luke, put a bullet in his leg soon after all the shooting started. The driver panicked and tried to back up. Everything went completely off the rails after that. The two horsemen never returned — blown to bits — and the boys shot and killed the driver."

Adrian's face turned even redder.

"You assured me your men would be able to contain them. You said we'd be safe as long as I followed your instructions. But the boys outsmarted this Ramsay guy and used his weapons to attack us. We could've been shot! Then Luke decided to yank my daughter out of the back of the truck by her hair and—"

"Is he dead, too?"

"Luke? Yes."

"Which one of them shot him? Which boy was it?"

"I-I couldn't see."

Adrian glanced again at the pair of men. One nodded, the other shrugged. Seth wondered why Adrian kept checking in with them.

"Tell me what happened to the other brat," Adrian said, his voice quiet but shaking with emotion. He was asking the two men, not Seth.

"Oh, that one shot him all right," Charlie answered, casually waving a finger at Seth. "Saw it all. Kid just dropped dead right there in the middle of the road and never moved again after that."

"You saw that?" Seth cried. "You were there?"

Manny nodded. "We was watching. He did it all right."

Only then did Adrian turn back. "I explicitly said I wanted the boys alive, both of them." He sounded more resigned than angry.

"If possible, you said. I had to improvise! They'd beaten your men, shot them all. And when I told Finn you'd taken his brother, he went ballistic. I had to act."

Adrian's eyes narrowed. "By shooting one of them?"

"The way they were going, I knew I could only handle one. I figured, if given a choice, you'd want Finn. The rest got away. I presume to return to the army base."

"And what's to stop them from returning here?"

"They don't know where this place is."

"But them folks at the base do!"

"That's not my problem."

Adrian stared at Seth for several long moments, anger crimping his forehead. Finally, he turned one last time to the two men. The throbbing in his temple was still visible, but it wasn't as prominent as before. "Y'all have anythin else to add?"

Manny pushed himself away from the wall. "Not much," he said. The binoculars around his neck bounced as he shifted his weight to his other foot. One of the eyepiece covers was missing. "Just that after he shot the kid, he goes right over and cold cocks the other one while everyone else is running around trying not to get killed. They all drove away real quick, back up the way they came. We stayed until this guy got the kid into the truck, and I seen the two women get in the back, and they drive off, so me and Gage and Charlie — sorry, Carlos — we left to come here straightaway."

"Then how did he manage to beat y'all here?"

"We ran into trouble coming through Colby Canyon. That last storm dumped a shitpile of rubble into the bottom of it and blocked the way. Had to backtrack, then circle up and around."

Adrian sucked in a deep breath, then shook his head. "The deal was the brother in exchange for both boys. I don't really care that y'all killed one of them— no, that ain't exactly true, because I do, but I can live with not doin it myself. But the deal was y'all bring them both back."

Seth glared at him. "What do you want me to do?"

"Well, by my accountin, that means y'all are in breach of contract. So, the way I figure it, I am owed one warm body."

"I don't understand."

"I'm sayin y'all have an important decision to make regardin the three of y'all before we're done."

Seth's eyes widened. He shook his head. "Not my wife, please. Not my little girl."

"Then it's settled. Y'all better start prayin for yerself."

"For what?"

"For salvation, of course."

CHAPTER

JONAH WAITED FOR HARRISON BLAKELEY TO FINISH getting dressed. He had delayed, hoping to dry off, but the heavy mist wouldn't cooperate. Jonah was impressed that the cold didn't seem to bother him as much, and he wondered idly if it was because of all the drugs Bix said he had taken during his younger and wilder years.

Now was probably not an appropriate time to ask.

The drifting fog provided adequate cover as long as they remained on the dock, but once away from the water, it quickly dissipated, so they did as much as they could under its cover.

Behind him, Kari swiped at the water on her arms, then wrung more from her hair. She had emerged from the lake last, coming from behind with the third rowboat. She explained that it had sprung a leak, which required bailing out halfway here.

Jonah flashed back to the memory of her on the bus, three years ago, a woman alone in her mid-fifties and just as scared as the rest of them. Her face and arms had been deeply freckled then, leathery, weathered, and lined. Later, he would learn the blemishes were from her many years spent outdoors as a nature photojournalist. But inside the sunless environment of the bunker, the marks faded away. Now her skin was a uniform shade of cream, the palest thing about her in the dim light, save for the threadbare bra covering her breasts.

She looks nowhere close to sixty anymore, he thought absently. In fact, if he didn't know any better, he would've pegged her at forty-five.

Of all of the adults who had entered the bunker, she seemed to have benefitted the most, coming out so much more younger looking than when she'd gone in. Nearly all of the adults had. Of them, only Harrison had noticeably aged.

Even the Fujimuras looked younger at the end.

He winced at the decision the elderly couple had made for themselves, after the other deaths, and the knowledge that their choice had been due, in part, to his own father's actions deeply grieved him.

When he finished lacing his shoes, Harrison went over and snatched a heavy pack off the dock and shouldered it, then tossed a black sweater into Kari's arms. They exchanged a word or two under their breath.

Jonah noticed how closely they stood, and wondered at their familiarity. But then again, sounds did carry, and the last thing they wanted at this point was for the rescue mission to be discovered.

She stepped back into the boat, helped by his steadying hand. He handed over the bag, then she pushed away from the dock toward the middle of the lake. Within seconds, she was gone.

"Everything set?" Harrison asked.

"Yeah. Eddie just reported back that the road is clear up past the house. He said the guards are either inside or off a bit. We should be good as long as we stick to the plan."

"Not that I don't trust him, but did you notice anything, you know . . . odd about Eddie? Physically, I mean. He seemed a bit off."

"He's just sore from the horse."

"Tell me about it. My legs are stiff, and they're going to be even more stiff in the morning. And that cold water didn't help."

"We were lucky to have them and the motorbikes."

Harrison nodded.

"He's probably just hungry," Jonah said, returning to Eddie. "I mean we all are, but with those nanites inside him, I'll bet his metabolism is cranked a lot higher than ours."

"I suppose." He raised his hand instinctively to comb the hair out of his face before remembering he didn't have any. "Forget I mentioned it."

Jonah frowned to himself. It troubled him that Harrison had also noticed the odd way Eddie was acting, and he remembered the man's latest worries regarding losing his abilities.

"The fog clears once we get away from the water," he said. "As long as we keep open sky above us, we shouldn't have any problem sticking to the road."

Harrison nodded. "This is when I wish I had Eddie's eyesight."

"He said it's not far to the house. After that, it should be clear till we get close to the gate."

They faced each other, their eyes glistening darkly in the wan moonlight. Harrison didn't have to say anything for Jonah to know what he was thinking. They'd be damn lucky if their plan didn't completely unravel. There were so many ways it could.

Suddenly, Jonah wished he were anywhere else but here. He wished Seth weren't such an asshole. And he wished Finn weren't so damned bullheaded about going after his brother.

But at least with Finn, he could understand it.

They walked on, slower than they wanted because of the darkness and their fear of straying off the road and into the forest with its buried mines. The key to the operation was the element of surprise and the chaos they would wreak. If all went to plan, they would catch Adrian completely off guard, drawing his security force away from the house. Then, while they were distracted, the others would find and rescue the Abramsons, Finn, and Harper.

But the armed men weren't the only dangers. Finn had warned them about the Wraiths set loose in the woods. And while Eddie reported he'd seen none while scouting ahead, it was hard to simply accept his assessment. The consequences of being wrong were dire. And though he might possess superhuman abilities, he wasn't infallible.

They passed the house, which was set back from the road. Light spilled out onto the clearing from a pair of windows, one in front and another on the side. It barely illuminated the burnt trees at the edge of the wood, twisting them into unsettling grotesqueries that Jonah could too-easily envision coming to life. They slipped quickly past, keenly aware of the tight schedule and their tiny margin for error.

At last they came to the trigger device Eddie had left for them a couple hundred feet beyond, and they let out sighs of relief.

"Everyone should be in place," Harrison whispered, connecting the wires to the detonator.

Jonah peered uneasily into the pitch darkness of the woods around him. "I hope Eddie made it back to the—"

A loud bang shattered the night about a hundred yards up the road and off to their left. There was a muted flash of light, but it was quickly doused. The darkness returned, seemingly even deeper than before. Debris rained down through the trees.

Then came the unmistakable thump of a body hitting the ground.

CHAPTER

09

"Okay, I counted at least eight guards this side of where I set the charges," Eddie whispered, "all men. Two are with Father Adrian in the main house. He's making Seth rehash every little detail of the attack, apparently waiting to catch him up on some inconsistency, so I'm guessing those guys must be the watchers on the hill. Can't know for sure, though, since I couldn't get close enough to pick up their scent over the stink of the burnt wood."

"You think he's buying it?" Kari asked. "You know, about us heading back to the base?"

Eddie nodded. "Seth's sticking to the script, so, yeah, I think so. The two men with him essentially corroborated everything he said. Once it starts, figure on Adrian to immediately shift men toward the gate while he hunkers down at this end of the compound."

"And Finn?"

"He wasn't in the room with Seth. Nor were Bren and Kaleagh. But I saw two men standing watch outside of a small shack behind the house."

He turned toward the third person in their huddle, who had, until then, remained silent.

"That'll be the underground cell," Bix said. "If they're guarding it, then he's got people inside, just as we suspected. He'll be hiding Harper in there. Maybe Finn, too."

Eddie studied the boy's face for a moment. He knew the others couldn't see like he could in the darkness and so they wouldn't be able to discern facial expressions as well. Bix had paled at the mention of the shack. Would it be a problem for the boy? Would he freeze up?

"You sure you don't want to switch with Kari?" he asked.

"Naw, I got this," Bix replied with forced composure. "I know the layout. Let's stick to the plan."

Eddie waited a moment, studying the boy's face. "And you're okay with leaving Adrian to us?"

"Let's just get Finn and Harper back."

"Okay, good. Now, as for the other guards, two were asleep in a van by the house. Two more were sitting inside the cab of our truck drinking and playing cards. They're parked at a clearing between the dock and the house."

"That'll be the barn we helped Father Adrian build," Bix said. His throat made a dry click when he swallowed. "Where he had us cage fight the Wraiths."

There was an uncomfortable silence before Eddie resumed speaking again. "I set charges underneath the truck. We'll trigger them on our way out."

"We should drive it into the lake, use it to destroy the dock so they can't follow us very easily."

Eddie shook his head. "That's too complicated. Stick with the plan. All of the guards have night vision goggles and firearms— both rifles and pistols. I couldn't get close enough to see if they had stun guns."

"Assume they do," Bix said.

"Let's just not get shot by anything," Kari said.

"Agreed."

"What about the animal barn?"

"To be honest, I didn't make it that far," Eddie replied.

"Why not?"

"Where I set the charges should provide us all the cover and time we need to get out."

"But the plan was—"

"There wasn't enough time, Bix," he hissed, perhaps a bit harsher than he intended.

The truth was actually much more disconcerting, which is why he chose not to say anything. A few times while scouting he'd felt close to passing out. The sensation came and went. At the moment, he felt perfectly fine, but what if his body decided to betray him at a crucial moment?

Since waking up after his horrible accident in the bunker and discovering his newfound abilities, he'd worried they would betray him. But what if there were even worse long term consequences of having the activated nanites in his body than them simply failing? What if they were killing him?

Just make it through the next hour or so.

"Would be nice to have our own night vision," Bix said. "I mean, Eddie already does, but I'd feel better with a pair of those goggles."

"You'll be fine," Eddie replied. "There's light where we need it. Now, are we straight on everyone's roles?"

Bix nodded. "I got the underground cell. Kari and you have the house. Easy peasy, lemon squeezy."

"Good," Eddie said. "Once we've retrieved our people, you and Kari head straight back to the dock, make sure it's clear. I'll extract Jonah and Harrison and we'll bring up the rear, triggering the other charges."

"Okay," Kari said. "Now, what about Wraiths?"

Eddie exhaled slowly. This was actually the biggest unknown for them and the one variable that could louse up their carefully orchestrated plan.

"I didn't see any. I'm guessing those that weren't killed before were driven away by the blaze."

Bix chuffed. "I don't think fire scares them."

"Every living animal has an instinctive fear of fire, Bix."

"Not Wraiths. I don't think anything scares them. And to call them living—"

"They breathe. They bleed. Just like us."

"Maybe, but the last time I checked, normal animals don't hunt and eat other people like those things do. So, yeah, *not* really like us."

"I just meant that they're flesh and blood. They can be killed." He sighed. "But Bix is right, don't assume the woods are empty. Everyone needs to be on their toes. Shoot *anything* that moves that isn't one of us and isn't where we're supposed to be."

"Which means we need to stick exactly to the plan," Kari said. "Absolutely no deviations from—"

The night was shattered by a sudden distant bang.

"This is it," Eddie hissed. "Wait for the second one."

"Are you sure that was it? It sounded very close."

"It's farther than you think."

The second explosion came, sounding even louder and closer than the first. The crackle of the blast rippled over the lake, then was shortly followed by two more smaller blasts in rapid succession.

"I thought you only set two charges."

"I did! I don't know what the other ones were."

They heard men shouting in the distance, their voices sounding strangely hollow coming through the trees. Then a gunshot, followed by more cries. One of the voices clearly belonged to Harrison. He was shouting for the men not to shoot.

"Christ," Bix whispered. He looked terrified.

"Focus. Your father'll be fine. We expected this. Remember?"

There was one more gunshot, and Harrison's voice cut out. Bix flinched, but didn't say anything. Eddie placed a hand on each of their shoulders and squeezed. "All right," he said. "Let's go."

CHAPTER

10

SOMEONE SHOUTED IN SURPRISE OFF IN THE MIDDLE OF the trees, but whether they were close or far away was difficult to tell. This was followed by a low guttural hiss and the sound of running. Jonah instinctively dropped his duffle and started to edge back up the road toward the lake.

Harrison grabbed his arm and swung him back around. *"Stick to the plan!"*

The boy's eyes were filled with fear. He flailed his arms, forcing Harrison to tackle him, and the two went down in a heap on the road.

"We're too close!" Jonah cried. "We have to get away! The second explo—"

"Quiet!" Harrison whispered. He leaned his entire weight on Jonah's shoulders and pressed his face into the leaves on the road. "Jonah, listen to me! We're safe right here. One of us is dead if we split up now!"

"Get off!"

"I can hear them coming already from both sides, Jonah. They've got guns. There's nowhere to go."

"But—"

Another loud blast sounded, this one further up the road.

"There it is. Now, stay down!"

Keeping his weight on Jonah's back, Harrison cautiously raised himself up to peer out into the darkness. The night was suddenly alive with sounds— shouts of surprise and anger, and of things hurrying about, both on the road and off it. Some did not sound human.

There was a third explosion, near the second but off to the right, followed by a fourth, again right in front of them. Jonah thought he saw a person outlined in the flash. It was tumbling through the air. But the image was gone in a blink, leaving only the sound of the body crashing to the ground.

"Eddie!" Jonah screamed. "He was only supposed to set off two of the mines here! The other charges are for the truck and the dock!"

"*Quiet!*"

The shouts sounded again, closer and more urgent, coming from every direction at once. Light beams pierced through the forest. One lit upon them, followed by a gunshot.

Harrison hesitated, then he was on his feet and waving his arms and shouting.

A second shot soon rang out, followed by the *thunk* of the slug burying itself in the ground somewhere nearby. More light fell on them, passed over, then returned to stay.

"Don't move!"

"Don't shoot!" Harrison shouted back. "Don't shoot! We're not infected!"

More beams of light stabbed through the trees, most coming from the bend in the road toward the house. Sounds of running feet, crackling branches, shouts. And finally, again, a low growling noise, decidedly inhuman and most certainly threatening.

"Stay down!" Harrison growled.

There was a high scream, and one of the beams of light suddenly arced into the air, then went dark. The screams rose, but weren't enough to mask the sound of the tearing flesh and fabric and the last gurgling breaths of the dying man.

"I said don't move, Jonah!"

The sounds of the attack continued. The man who had ordered them to freeze was sweeping his light into the trees in the direction of the sounds, firing at random. The light was taped to the barrel of a rifle, so Jonah was glad it was no longer trained on them.

Despite the horror playing out in the trees, two men ran up the road toward them, both from the direction of the house. They were armed with pistols. "Wilkins!" one of them shouted.

The dying man in the woods let out a final bloodcurdling scream.

"Wilkins!"

"He's gone!" someone else yelled. "Don't go out there!"

"What about them two on the road?"

"We're friendly!" Harrison shouted. He pushed himself back to his knees, fingers twined on top of his head. "Don't shoot. We're here to see Father Adrian."

"Who the hell are—" The man stopped when the sound of feeding abruptly ceased. *"Quiet!"*

Silence. Then came the soft crunch of leaves, drawing nearer. Jonah's skin crawled.

"Shit," one of the two other men said under his breath. "Screw this! It's coming!" He and his partner started edging their way back up the road.

"Stay put!" the first man ordered. "Stand your ground!"

"Fuck you, Jackson! I ain't waiting to get infected!"

"It's only one of them out there!"

"It got Wilkins! How did it get in?"

"That explosion, idiot! Took out the perimeter. Stay on the road out in the open!"

"But it got Wilkins! There's gonna be two of them coming for us now!"

"I said stand—"

A ghostly shape appeared on the road about twenty feet away, between the two groups of men. The guards bunched together, raising their weapons at the deadly creature and momentarily forgetting Harrison and Jonah. The Wraith hissed, spraying droplets of blood from its tattered lips.

"Oh, shit! It's Old Man Hank!"

"Shoot it!"

One of them fired, and just as suddenly the Wraith disappeared back into the trees.

"I missed! He's coming! He's going around! Where is he?"

"Stand your ground!"

The Wraith reappeared on the edge of the road about fifty feet past them. It acted as if it did not like being out in the open. Jonah thought he could smell the blood on it, and for the first time in his life he was terrified enough to lose his bowels.

"Trust Finn," Harrison whispered into his ear. *"It won't get us."*

"I'd have an easier time believing him if he were here."

"Quiet, you two," the man with the rifle said, stepping past them, his eyes glued to the Wraith. "Come on, Hank, you big piece of shit. Come to papa so I can put some lead into that rotten skull of yours." He lifted the gun until the beam of light fell squarely on the Wraith's blood-splattered face. "Come and get me, Old Man." He lowered his cheek to the stock and took aim.

The Wraith stepped forward, then broke into a run, heading straight for them.

"There you go. Just a little closer . . . ."

The man waited, adjusting his aim as it came. But before he could shoot, the monster stumbled and crashed to the road not thirty feet away. It didn't rise.

"What the hell?" one of the other men muttered, after several seconds had elapsed. "Jackson? It's out. I thought you said the mine took out the perim—"

"Quiet!" Jackson ordered. He didn't move. He kept the rifle trained on the spot where the Wraith had fallen. It was still very much alive. Its back rose and fell with its labored respirations, but it made no attempt to come after them.

Still, nobody moved for several seconds.

"Told you," Harrison whispered to Jonah, and pulled the duffle closer to them.

"Hey! I said don't move!" someone shouted at them. "Get away from that bag!"

The man with the rifle slowly edged his way toward the immobilized Wraith, shuffling forward two steps at a time and pausing in between. "Keep an eye on these clowns," he growled at the other men. He leaned down and picked up the duffle and tossed it to the side of the road with his free hand. His eyes never left the Wraith. "Shoot 'em if you have to, but make sure they stay put."

"We came to talk with Father Adri—" Harrison tried to say. He twisted around to address the other man, but he received a blow to the head.

"Told you not to move," the guard growled. "Don't. Fucking. Move."

"Take our weapons," Jonah said, gesturing carefully to the gun and knife in his belt. "Just don't shoot us!"

At last, Jackson turned his attention away from the Wraith, apparently convinced it really was out of commission.

"You just going to leave it there?" one of the two men standing over Jonah asked.

"Old Man Hank's fried. Not sure why, don't really care. The boss'll be here in a few minutes, so let him deal with the filthy thing. I ain't touching nothing without gloves and a cattle prod."

"But he got Wilkins!"

"Maybe Wilkins shouldn't have picked right then to take a dump in the woods."

"Is he dead? We should make sure Wilkins is dead."

"He is if he's lucky."

He shone the light into the trees where the attack had taken place, but nothing moved. Satisfied, he flicked the flashlight on the rifle off and slung the unit over his shoulder. Then he pulled the firearm off his hip and stepped over to Jonah, raised his arm, and took aim.

"Don't—" was all Jonah could get out before he felt the explosion in his chest. He tasted blood as his body was flung backward onto the road, and he hit hard enough to see stars.

A faint wheeze exited his mouth.

Then came the darkness.

CHAPTER

"STAY WITH HIM!" ADRIAN BELLOWED AT MANNY AND Carlos. "He ain't to leave that chair for any reason, understood? In fact, tie his feet together so he can't go nowhere!"

The two men nodded as Adrian swept across the room toward the front door.

"But—" Seth cried, and tried to rise.

Carlos immediately stepped forward and shoved him in the chest. "Stay there and keep quiet!"

"But my wife and daughter!" He tried to get up again and was wrestled back. "Where are they? What's happening out there?"

"You sit your ass down in that chair and don't move a muscle!" Manny growled. He pulled a pistol out of his waistband and cocked it.

"For chrissakes, put that away," Adrian yelled. "If he moves, stun him. He's no good to me with a hole in his head! Especially if we don't find—"

"We had a deal!" Seth shouted. "You promised!"

The second explosion came just as Adrian was pulling the front door open. He stared out into the night, trying to ascertain the exact location of the detonations and fathom their significance.

"Is that ferals tripping mines?" Manny asked. "Because we tested all the perimeter devices. There's no gaps."

"Shut up!"

In the days since the fire, the men of the lake community — Adrian considered them his flock — had combed the woods, capturing the creatures if possible, killing them if necessary. But he was no fool. He knew it was possible the interference devices could fail, though he'd never had one do that before, not unless they were physically damaged first. But with so many ruined by the fire, he'd had to relocate the rest to the fence line to act as a sort of force field.

So how was it possible that a pair of ferals, perhaps attracted by the recent demolition and rebuilding, got inside the compound?

He reminded himself that they did have a tendency to travel in packs. Were these the vanguard of a new mass influx? It was the *last* thing he needed right now.

From the distance, the sound of men shouting came to his ears, followed by a gunshot.

"Jackson!" he shouted out the door for his guard. The man was supposed to be watching over the women. But there was no response. "Frasier? Answer me!"

He stepped into the darkness on the porch, fully aware of how exposed he was from the light inside, and he anxiously fingered the leather holster on his hip without realizing it was empty. He'd set his gun down on the cabinet inside.

"Where is it coming from, boss?"

"Toward the front gate." Once more he turned to the man sitting in the ratty armchair inside. Manny had his hands on Seth's shoulders, holding him in place, while Carlos bound his ankles. "What do you know about this?" he demanded.

"Nothing!" Seth cried. He shook his head and looked just as genuinely surprised as the rest of them. Surprised and scared. "I just want my wife and daughter! Please, let me leave with them. You can keep the boys!"

Adrian flinched as two more gunshots tore through the night. The man certainly didn't appear to have expected this, but what if he was lying?

It didn't matter. There wasn't time to question him at the moment. Adrian spun around and flew across the porch and down the steps, cursing when he nearly crashed into a new stack of debris the men had created in the yard. They kept making piles right smack in the middle of pathways. Anyone with a pair of functioning brain cells to rub together knew not to do such things. Everything needed to be kept clear. Debris piles like this made maneuvering about all the more difficult, more dangerous, and possibly deadly.

He jogged across the clearing, conserving his breath in case he needed it later, and confirmed that Jackson and Frasier had abandoned their guard post, just as he'd guessed. He confirmed the door was secure, then went over to the van where they and the other men took turns sleeping between shifts.

"Wilkins? Roy?" He banged on the side. But as soon as he circled around and saw the back doors flung open, he knew they were gone. And in a hurry, too, by the looks of things.

Dammit to hell!

Two more explosions shattered the night, followed by screams a few hundred yards up the road. Then more shouts. Someone was pleading not to be shot, an unfamiliar voice.

He started to run, but before he could reach them, the sound of tearing flesh reached his ears, and he froze. He knew exactly what it was and what it meant, he just didn't know who the victim was.

"Don't shoot!" the unfamiliar voice shouted again. Adrian remained still and turned only his head. Farther up the road, through the trees around the bend, he could see a cluster of figures in the circle of light. But he couldn't tell who they were or whether any of them were infected.

Beside him, somewhere off in the thicker part of the woods, the rending noises stopped. He felt more than saw the creature move— the woody crick of a foot pressing down on a soggy twig, the faintest impression of a branch displacing air as it swung back into place. He reached for his gun and this time realized it wasn't there.

Shitfire, he thought as the hair on his neck began to prickle. He wondered if he could make it safely back to the house or if he should try and run toward the men ahead.

But the creature emerged out of the trees between them, some fifteen or so yards in front of him. It turned and its dead black eyes locked onto his, and his heart nearly stopped when he recognized the creature as one of the men infected the night of the fire. He waited for it to attack him, but it didn't. Slowly and silently, it turned and disappeared into the darkness back into the woods.

He knew he should yell and warn the others, but if he did, Old Hank — or the wretched, corrupt creature he had become — might decide to turn its attention back on him.

He waited, silently, frozen to the spot. He could hear the men talking up ahead.

He saw Hank step out of the trees among them. A gunshot rang out. A moment later, the feral was gone.

CHAPTER 12

"WE'RE CLEAR!" EDDIE SAID, KEEPING HIS VOICE LOW as he half-ran, half-jogged ahead of the others toward the house. "Looks like most of the guards have gone ahead as planned. Just the two inside with Seth. I'll handle them."

Bix split off and made his way through the yard, but the closer he came to the small, unassuming shack that had once been his underground prison, the stronger the terror inside of him became.

He sucked in a deep breath and reminded himself that Finn was relying on him. He couldn't let him down now. After all, that's what best friends did for each other, right?

Except they hadn't had much time to be friends lately, not since the day the stranger from Bunker Two showed up outside their front door weeks ago and basically turned their nice quiet life upside down.

There had been a few moments, like those few days they'd spent walking, just the two of them on the road like a pair of intrepid explorers. Lewis and Clark making their way across the New World. The camaraderie between them had been so easy then, and they had never been closer.

He wished he could get that back.

It'll be over soon.

He stepped over to the door, now faintly lit by stray light from the house, and this time he nearly did choke when the panic wrapped its icy fist around his throat and squeezed.

You think it's bad standing out here? It's got to be much worse for Finn inside.

He grabbed a shovel leaning against the wall and pulled the door open, cringing at the soft creak it made. Light flooded out from the bare bulb inside, blinding him for a moment. He instinctively raised an arm, to ward off any attack. But the men had deserted their post to investigate the distraction up the road, just as they were supposed to do.

He gripped the shovel near the head and stepped in, ready to smash it against the lock before remembering it had already been broken off. A simple bar lock had since been rigged into place, and it was an easy matter to shift it out of its socket.

"Finn?" he called down into the darkness. The fetid stench of the place, of rotting flesh, of sweat and vomit and human excrement, flooded into his nose and made him gag. "Finn! Harper Bolles! It's time to go!"

Bren's face appeared out of the darkness at the bottom of the stairs. "Finn's not here, Bix! It's just us."

"What? Where is he? Is he in the house? Quick, Bren! We need to hurry!"

He pulled her the rest of the way up the steps and reached down to assist her mother.

"They took Finn, Bix," Missus Abramson said. "They separated us right after we arrived and—" Her voice cracked. "It's all gone wrong. The whole plan has gone wrong."

Bix turned to her, clasping her arms above the elbows to make her stop babbling. "Your husband wasn't supposed to let them separate you!"

"I-I think he tried, but—"

"Where are they? Where's Finn and Harper? Tell me!"

She flinched as he shook her. There was a new scrape on her forehead, and her shirt was torn open at the collar. She held it closed with one filthy hand, her knuckles bruised and bloody. "Harper's not here, Bix," she whimpered. "And Finn's already de—"

"No, don't you dare say it! This can't be happening!"

"He said they already did it," Bren sobbed, clutching at him. "He's gone."

Rage filled Bix. "No! *NO!* It's not supposed to happen like that! Finn was supposed to—"

"We have to go, Bix. *Now!*"

"Not until we find them!"

"Where's Seth? Where's my husband?"

"Eddie and Kari are getting him," Bix said, hesitating. His head was spinning. How could Adrian have already dealt with Finn? Seth was supposed to negotiate with him, to delay any action until the rest of them got here. He'd tricked them all again!

Bix grabbed Bren's wrist and raced toward the front door of the house with her in tow. Missus Abramson let out a strangled cry and tried to pull her back. "I need to find him!" he yelled back at her. "I'm not leaving without Finn!"

He charged up the steps, letting go of Bren's hand when she refused to go inside. The front door stood partially open, but he crashed through it without regard to what he was running into. Finn's name died on his lips when he saw the splash of fresh blood on the wall and the bodies slumped along the baseboards.

"Eddie went after Finn!" Seth shouted from his chair. Kari was kneeling in front of him, hacking away at the bindings around his ankles. He pointed up the road.

"The animal barn? No! It's not supposed to happen like this!"

"He chained Finn to a post! He had a Wraith and was going to—"

"Eddie said to stick with the plan," Kari said, glancing up at Bix. "He said to take everyone to the dock and leave."

"Harper's not here."

"Damn."

Bix rolled the two dead men over. One had his face caved in; the other's neck was clearly broken. He pulled a pistol from the limp hand of the second and checked to see that it was loaded. "Collect their weapons," he instructed Bren and her mother. "Go with Kari. I'm going to find Finn and Harper."

"No!" Kari shouted. "That's not the plan. Bren, stop him!"

But Bix was already pushing his way past the two women, heading for the door. Bren reached out, but missed his arm.

"Bix! You'll get yourself killed! Remember the plan!"

"Eddie's already gone off it! It's all gone to hell, Kari!" he shouted back. He whirled around and pointed at Seth. "Because of him! He was supposed to keep everyone together! You screwed this all up on purpose! We should never have trusted you! This was your plan all along!"

"Bix! Finn agreed to it."

"No, take them, Kari. We'll meet up across the lake. Don't wait!"

"Eddie will—"

"I'm not leaving here without them!"

"You won't find Harper here," Missus Abramson shouted after him.

Bix spun around again. "What? What do you mean? Where is he?"

"The men who were guarding us," she said. "We overheard them talking outside the door. They said it was all a trick to get Finn here, but they never intended to give Harper up. They were looking for something and thought he had it."

"What?"

"I don't know. They didn't say. They tried to search us and—" Her voice cracked, and she spun around to her husband. "Bix is right, you were supposed to keep us together!"

"I tried!"

"They were going to torture us all, Bix!" Bren stammered.

"What? Who?"

"Those men," Kaleagh Abramson said. "The way they were leering at us. And their hands!" She gathered her shirt again. "Do you know what they did to me? I blame you, Seth!"

"I couldn't—"

"They were talking about the things they wanted to do to your daughter!"

Kari stepped between the two adult Abramsons. "There's no time for this. We need to get back to the lake." She turned to tell Bix the same, but he was already gone.

CHAPTER 13

"WHAT THE HELL IS GOING ON HERE?" ADRIAN demanded, swinging around the rifle he'd taken from Jackson. Everyone flinched each time it pointed at them. "Who the hell are these two?"

They were all still jumpy from the encounter. In fact, the close call had so rattled Adrian that he hadn't hesitated in putting a bullet into Old Hank's whiskey-rotted and feral-infected brain the moment he had the gun in his hands, despite his policy of non-lethal force. He was angry at himself for leaving the house without a portable interference unit or a weapon for protection. It was a terribly careless thing to do. Carelessness was how people died. Or became feral. Or made a fool of.

Like them damn boys did the last time they was here.

And on the heels of that thought, another, more troubling one: *Wouldn't have happened if yer sister had just followed instructions.*

He quickly dismissed it.

The men stood around and gawped stupidly at each other, not knowing how to respond to him taking out Hank. They had been banned from any unnecessary killing on Adrian's property and had to account for every dead feral and provide a reason why they'd had to kill it. He claimed it was because all ferals deserved a chance at redemption. But they all knew his real reason was much more . . . practical, though they would never admit it out loud. Every captured feral was a valuable commodity, and every one of them he put into the cage added to his profit, power, fear, and respect.

"Y'all know the old drunkard never woulda earned salvation anyway," Adrian said, by way of explanation.

He tossed the gun back to Jackson and ordered the two strangers on the road be taken to the old barn so that he could question them properly.

"Looks like your sister's going to be eating good tonight," Jackson nervously joked.

Adrian grabbed him by the collar and shook him violently. "No, I just want to keep them away from the house. We don't know who these men are."

He shoved him away, scowling. Maybe it was coincidence, but the timing of their arrival was too suspicious.

* * *

Back at the barn he had vacated less than an hour before, Adrian stepped over to the younger of the two men. Despite being dragged bodily over the rough road, he was still out cold from the shock of the stun gun. Jackson quickly bound his wrists and ankles, but chained the older one to the post where the boy had been earlier in the evening.

"Tell me yer names," Adrian demanded.

But the conscious one wouldn't speak.

"Cat got yer tongue, eh?"

He told Jackson to get the bucket from the middle of the floor inside the holding pen. The water it held, collected from a leak in the roof Jennifer had asked him to fix months ago — *always the damn humanitarian*, he thought bitterly — had turned into a murky green-black soup since the fire, a fetid sludge of ash and algae, rife with mosquito larvae, hatched since the last rain, and stinking to high heaven.

"But, boss, your sister's in there."

Adrian scowled. "She ain't goin to bother no one! Not unless I switch her on." He tossed him the key to the lock.

Jackson gave it a worried glance, then hurried away. A moment later, he reappeared with the bucket.

The water caught the man right in the middle of an inhale, and he jerked back against the splintered post with a strangled gasp. Coughing and sputtering, he fell forward against the chains again and begged for him to stop.

"What's yer name?" Adrian demanded again. He bent down and grabbed the man's chin and squeezed it without mercy, puckering his lips so hard that any words would have been unintelligible anyway. "Who's with you? How many more are there?" He released him, letting the man's head flop back down.

"T-two," the man finally said, slurring his speech. "Just the two of us."

"How did you get past the men at the gate?"

He didn't answer.

Adrian slapped him hard with the back of his fist.

Still no response.

"Fine. Then what about you?" he said, turning around to the young man splayed out in the dirt. He didn't look much older than eighteen or nineteen, though he was muscular.

Adrian assessed his face, his clothes. He was too clean, his skin too lacking of any scars. He certainly didn't look like someone who'd spent the last three years fighting for survival.

"Y'all are from the army base, are ya? I mean, y'all got them military haircuts, but somethin ain't quite right. Y'all work for Colonel Wainwright?"

The older man sniffed and spit, but didn't say anything.

"Wake this one up, Jackson."

"How?"

"I don't care! Just do it." He swung back toward the other guard. "And where inna hell is Gage?"

"He just left to check on the guy up at the house."

"I already got Manny and Carlos up there. Get Gage back here now. I wanna ask him if he recognizes these two."

"You thinking they're together with the other guy?"

"Ain't sure, but we'll soon find out."

Roy shrugged, then grabbed his rifle and stepped out into the clearing.

Once again, Adrian bent over the older man. With his arms pulled up high behind him, he was having trouble breathing. A thin dribble of blood fell from his lips where Gage had hit him. "I ain't gonna ask again. What the hell is yer name?"

"H-harry," the man said. He coughed and spat again, this time ejecting a thick clot of blood into the dirt at Adrian's feet.

"Why're y'all here? How did y'all get in? What do y'all want?"

The man didn't answer.

Adrian grabbed a fistful of his shirt and wrenched his head back.

"Y'all know who I am?"

Still nothing.

The sound of footsteps hurrying toward him drew Adrian's attention. It was Frasier, who'd been dispatched to look for Wilkin's body. He was carrying a heavy duffle bag in his hands.

"Found this on the side of the road." He dropped it at Adrian's feet, spilling out some of the contents.

Adrian reached down and shuffled through it. At the bottom was a large cube-shaped object attached to a power inverter with duct tape. The entire contraption was wired to a twelve-volt battery. "Son of a bitch!" he growled, recognizing it as one of his own devices.

"I figure they used it to come over the wall," Frasier muttered. "They must've set off the mines on purpose. That's how the feral got in."

Adrian shook his head. "Old Hank was already inside. Probably missed him during the sweep."

"But where did they get the device? It looks like one of yours."

"It is. Best I can figure is the boy stole it when he escaped. Took it back to the army base with him."

"You think these two came to rescue him?"

"Maybe. We better add more men to the gate, just in case."

"I'm here," Gage said, stepping into the clearing from the road with Jackson in tow. "You wanted to see me?"

Adrian grabbed the bound man's chin again, forcing his face up into the light. "Y'all were with Manny and Carlos today. Recognize this man?"

Gage leaned forward, squinting, and shook his head. "Never seen him before in my life."

"Take a good look."

Another shake.

"How about this one?" Adrian asked, rolling the second figure onto his back. He was starting to come to, though he was still groggy enough that he hadn't yet figured out he was tied up. "Were they with the group on the road today?"

Gage shook his head again. "Nope. Ain't but the one bald guy there, and he was a lot bigger than either of these two. These look like they're from the army base with those haircuts."

The kid on the ground stirred. "Dad?" he said, jolting awake.

The older man looked over, then up at Adrian. "We're trying to help you. We're not here to cause you any harm."

"If'n y'all had good intentions, why'd y'all sneak in? The polite thing to do would be to show up at the front gate and ask for an invitation."

"Cheever told us your men are trained to shoot first, then ask questions."

"Cheever? As in *Captain* Cheever?" Adrian eyes narrowed suspiciously. "Are you from the base?"

The man nodded and coughed.

"When was the last time y'all spoke with him?"

"Couple days ago. He staged a coup, tried to take power away from the colonel. Me and Joe got away."

"This here Joe, yer son? Why would y'all want to get away from Wainwright?"

"Because he's lost control, letting the camp fall apart. No water, no fuel. It's getting too risky to stay. But my wife was too scared to leave."

"So, y'all left her behind?"

"She's dead," the boy said, and spat bitterly. "You should have tried harder, Dad!"

"She got caught in the crossfire," the man explained.

Adrian was silent for several seconds, studying them. "Well, what Cheever told y'all about my guards," he finally said, "tain't true about them shootin first. Now, what's this business about helpin me?"

"We came to warn you."

Adrian crouched down again, except this time to address the younger of the two men. "What's yer father talkin about? Warn me about what?"

"They're coming," the kid said, wheezing. He pressed his hands to his chest where the stun gun had hit him and winced.

"Who? Are y'all talkin about them people from the bunker?"

The boy shook his head. "I don't know anything about that."

"Then who?"

"The soldiers from the army base. Wainwright's people. They blame you for setting Cheever against him."

Adrian barked out a laugh, and the boy flinched. "Yer lyin. I happen to know Wainwright's dead. Cheever told me himself, said he took out half them soldiers on his way out, plus the munitions storage. So, who exactly am I supposed to be worried about? Bunch of civilians and soldiers who ain't set foot outside the wire in three years?"

"Wainwright's alive," the boy said. He drew himself up to a sitting position and wiped the snot from his nose onto his shoulder. "Everything Cheever told you was a lie, and you fell for it."

"Joe, watch your mouth! Have some respect."

"Naw, let the boy speak."

"I'm sorry. I didn't mean any disrespect, but they are coming. The colonel wants to finish you and wipe this place off the map once and for all."

Adrian frowned. "And why should y'all even care about me?"

"I don't," the boy said, sneering. "I just want the colonel."

"Why?"

"Because," the older man quietly said, "Wainwright was the one who shot his mother."

CHAPTER

"TAKE THEM UP TO THE HOUSE," ADRIAN INSTRUCTED
Jackson. "You and Red. Take the duffle, too. Tie their hands
until I get up there. No, wait. I changed my mind. Stick them
in the hold with the women. Keep them away from our
guest."

"So, you believe their story?"

Adrian shrugged. He didn't want to admit so readily that
he did. But he was convinced. If anyone could recognize
revenge, it was him, and the boy definitely had it in his eyes.
It wasn't easy to mask that kind of emotion. But it was better
if he let the others believe he was simply being cautious. To
the weak minded, decisiveness in others came across as
impulsive and did not instill confidence. They preferred their
leaders to mull things overlong, even if the end result
emerged no different than what it had started off as.

"Lemme have yer sidearm before y'all go," Adrian said
to Roy. "I left mine behind with Manny. Keep the rifle."

"You want me to stay with you, boss?"

"No, y'all go on, now. I'll be there in a bit. Got somethin
I need to do first. Hang tight up there until I get back. I ain't
done with any of them just yet."

He watched them leave back up the road with the two
strangers. Then he pulled the pistol Roy had given him and

inspected it, verifying that it was fully loaded and the safety was off. The metal around the bore was worn smooth, and the grip had lost most of its texture. But it was otherwise well maintained, something many of the other men weren't so careful about, which is why he'd requested Roy's sidearm and not one of the others.

He fingered the trigger and wondered when the day would come that the world ran out of bullets. They were getting harder to find, though he didn't fear that day would arrive anytime soon. One simply had to look harder and farther afield. Or know who to trade with and what they needed in exchange.

He hoped it wouldn't be during his lifetime.

He walked over to the splintered door at the back of the barn, flipped the switch he'd installed on the jamb, then pulled it open. Inside, he could hear his Jenny's grunts and growls as she emerged from her stupor. He shut his eyes and listened to them, imagining that she was speaking in some kind of language only siblings could understand, and he let his rage fill him up again. She deserved better than this, despite her actions. She deserved to have her revenge.

And so did he.

"Be patient," he whispered, as much to himself as to her, and shut and locked the door again before triggering the device that would sedate her once more.

Then, instead of returning to the house, he headed toward the front gate.

He didn't quite know what to make of the new arrivals. Their story made sense— Cheever had lied to him many times before, so it hadn't surprised him that he'd done it again.

"You were too hasty to kill him," he muttered to himself.

Too hasty to get rid of the brother, too.

It angered him, because if he hadn't been under such stress, he wouldn't have made so many misjudgments, and everything would have transpired differently, making none of this necessary.

He was halfway to the old generator shack when he heard the first distant gunshot. It reverberated through the night, bouncing between the earth and sky before tumbling through the forest like an acorn bouncing through the branches of a tree. The sound was so confused by the time it reached his ears, he wasn't sure exactly where it had come from. Had it been from the gate or behind him? Was it the people from the base?

He stopped and listened. Silence reigned and refused to share its secrets.

Then came the distinct sound of automatic gunfire, and this time he knew it was back in the direction of the house.

The series was quickly answered by a succession of five more gunshots from smaller caliber firearms, setting off another volley from the automatic. Finally, two more pistol shots, each one separated by an ominous pause, like exclamation points.

Adrian didn't hesitate. He set off running in the same direction he'd already been heading. He knew the road by heart, knew every bend and every bump, so that he could have navigated it with his eyes shut. Even so, in his haste, his toe caught a root hidden beneath the carpet of leaves, and he sprawled to the ground.

He didn't let it deter him. He jumped back to his feet and ran even harder, this time with his heart in his throat, for in that half second, when he was sprawled out on the ground, he thought he'd heard shuffling footsteps behind him and the whisper of a breath.

He knew exactly where the break was, and he swiveled and entered into it without slowing. The shack was just ahead, a single shining light in the pitch black of the wood.

And inside it, the promise of redemption at last.

CHAPTER

Bix didn't see the figure slip out of the darkness until it was right on top of him, and by then, it was too late to react. It swooped over him, wrapping its arms around his face and smothering any cry he might utter.

"Quiet, Bix!" Eddie whispered into his ear.

He immediately stopped struggling.

"Why aren't you with the women? What's happening back there at the house? Who's shooting?"

"I don't know. Maybe it's Jonah and Dad."

"You need to go back."

"No, I need to find Finn and Harper."

"Harper wasn't in the hold?" Eddie whispered.

"No. But Bren and Missus Abramson were." He pushed Eddie away. "Seth said Adrian had Finn tied up at the animal barn."

"Well, not anymore."

The gunfire erupted again.

"Who is that?"

"I don't know. The plan's messed up. Did Kari get the others out?"

"I left her at the house with the Abramsons." He tried to push past Eddie, but the big man had a hold of his arm, and his grip was like steel.

"They might need your help, Bix."

"That's not the plan!"

There was a distant shout, followed by the sound of an angry voice.

"That was Father Adrian! He's up near the gate."

Bix broke away from Eddie and started to sprint up the road. He ran as hard and as fast as he could, but Eddie easily passed him. Four more strides, and the night swallowed him up again.

The arguing up ahead grew louder, more intense, even as the gun battle behind them ratcheted up several notches. Bix prayed his father was all right. A terrifying image of his father lying in a pool of blood came to mind, yet he kept running. He hoped Bren and Kari were okay, too. He even hoped the Abramsons were safe, all of them, including Seth, despite Bren's father betraying them all.

He nearly passed the opening for the narrow trail to the generator shack, but he heard voices, one of them Eddie's, and he skidded to a stop.

"I will shoot him, if y'all come any closer."

Father Adrian!

Eddie's reply was a low, angry growl. "Let's talk this over. Nobody needs to hurt anybody else." There was a pause. Then he asked: "You okay?"

"No worse for the wear," came a low reply.

Harper?

"Shut up," Adrian snapped. "Y'all don't get to speak!"

Bix stepped silently onto the path. The tree branches diced the light from the bulb on the side of the shack up ahead, disorienting him. He stepped gingerly around a bend and saw Eddie up ahead, his body a large black silhouette filling the pathway.

He couldn't see Father Adrian, but he could hear him.

"I told y'all to back away," Adrian growled. "Step back or I'll shoot the boy!"

"And I'll shoot you," Eddie replied.

The ongoing barrage of distant gunfire made Bix all the more jumpy. He knew his friends and father were in trouble, but there was nothing he could do about it now. He just had to have faith that the extra weapons they had brought with them, taken off the men they had killed on the road that day, would be sufficient to fend off the guards.

What if they're fighting off Wraiths instead?

He hoped it wasn't that.

He took another step. Eddie extended his arm slightly to the side and swept it back, twitching his fingers both to signal that he knew Bix was there and to ward him off. But Bix wasn't about to leave, not now. Not when they'd found Harper.

As if sensing Bix's decision, Eddie stepped forward, further blocking his way.

Then something strange happened. Eddie's body seemed to tremble. He stumbled, like he'd stepped unexpectedly into a hole, and lurched upright to recover his balance.

"Hand the boy over, and we'll leave," he told Adrian. His voice sounded weak, the words tumbling over one another.

Adrian didn't answer.

Eddie took another step forward. This time his knee gave out on him, and he stumbled before catching himself on the tree.

"Something the matter?" Adrian asked. He sounded almost gleeful.

"H-hand him over," Eddie whispered.

"Y'all want him, yer gonna have to come and get him. Come on now, come closer. That's right. Count of three before I blow his brains out. One . . . ."

Bix heard the telltale click of a pistol being cocked.

"Wait," Eddie said, grunting with effort as he stepped forward once more.

"Two."

Another step, and this time he collapsed completely to the ground.

"Three."

CHAPTER

"GET DOWN!" KARI WHISPERED. SHE COULD SEE THE men, dark shapes looming within the luminescent mist hovering at the edge of the lake. As she stood there, crouched along the side of the road just outside the clearing, more of the figures emerged from its depths. She could hear them talking, their voices low and gravelly. She could hear the new rowboats they had arrived in knocking against the piers.

They were big men, armed with pistols. Most definitely not friendly.

And they were blocking any chance of escape.

"How are we going to get past them?" Seth quietly asked.

"Father Adrian?" one of them called out. "That you out there? It's Pierce. Permission to come ashore."

Kari didn't move. She didn't think the new arrivals could see them where they hid. If they could, they wouldn't be asking if Adrian was with them. She turned to Seth and pulled him forward to join her.

"We heard a couple loud bangs earlier," the man continued to shout. "Sounded like some of your mines was tripped. Thought we'd come see if you needed any help."

"How many do you think there are?" Kari whispered.

"I count at least eight," Seth said, his voice rasping through the silence. There was a loud report, a gunshot, though it didn't seem to be targeting them in particular.

"Father Adrian?"

Another gunshot, this one pinging off the road to their left.

"Move back," Kari told the women behind her. *"Back toward the house."*

"But—"

"Do it! Seth and I will be right behind you!"

"Father Adrian?" the man called. "You having feral problems?"

She watched as the man in the lead gestured at the others behind him. They exchanged a few muttered words, too low for her to make out. Moving silently, the half dozen or so men fanned out to either side, blending into the shadows of the taller reeds alongside the dock.

They had to know Father Adrian wasn't here, or else they wouldn't be shooting. They were just trying to get her to respond so they could pinpoint her location.

"Ready?" she whispered to Seth. *"Soon as I start shooting, you take out the guy on the dock."* But when she turned around to confirm he'd understood, he was gone. *"Stupid dipshit!"*

She pulled the butt of the assault rifle up to her shoulder and aimed carefully for the lone figure she could still see, then let loose a short burst. She swung the barrel to her left where she'd seen at least four of the other men go.

The man on the dock fell hard, and several shots rang out from the other side, accompanied by flashes of light from the barrels of the guns that birthed them. A slug planted itself into the trunk of the tree beside her head, and she ducked.

"Oh, holy Jesus!" someone called out. "They got Pierce! Jesus Christ, Sims, I think he's dead! Sumbitch killed Pierce!"

"Shut up, Barry! Shut the hell up!"

"They got Pierce! They got him!"

"I said shut the hell up!"

Kari fired another burst as she backed her way up the road. Several more shots rang out from the direction of the lake, but they were wild. Her shoe scraped gravel, and three more guns fired nearly simultaneously.

One of the men shouted to save their ammunition. "Can't see shit! What the fuck are you shooting at?"

"They killed Pierce!"

"Save yer goddamn ammunition, assholes! They got semi-autos; we got handguns!"

Someone fired.

"We shoulda brought the A-1s, Sims."

"Yeah, well, we didn't, so shut yer trap less'n you want it shot off for you."

He fired again.

Their uncertainty spurred Kari on. She called out for the Abramsons, trying to be as quiet as possible, but they weren't within earshot and didn't answer.

Moving quickly now, she made her way up the road, keeping the rifle cradled in her arms and her finger on the trigger guard. She could hear the men alongside the lake discussing amongst themselves what to do next. She didn't plan to stick around to find out what they'd decide.

The Abramsons were waiting for her around the next bend, calling out to her in an urgent whisper as she passed. "What the hell is wrong with you?" she spat at Seth. "How could you leave me alone back there?"

"I'm not leaving my family."

"Christ. And why aren't you two back at the house? Those men are going to be marching up the road any moment now. We need to take up a defensive position."

New shouts reached her ears then, this time from somewhere ahead. She pushed them all off the road and as deep into the brush as she dared, where they crouched down in the darkness. The cover would be adequate as long as the men didn't have powerful lights or night vision goggles.

Rolling her eyes at herself, she remembered the pair she'd liberated from the back of the van parked outside. She set the rifle to the ground between her feet and swung the backpack off her shoulders. It took her a moment to figure out how the stupid things worked.

The men coming from the direction of the house were getting louder. They were arguing, one shouting at the other to hurry, and the other complaining that he couldn't see anything because someone snatched his equipment from out of the van.

"I'm telling you, it's more of them men we caught up there!" the first man said. "Fucking liars, they are, saying they came alone. You saw what they did to Manny and Carlos at the house."

"Then who're they shooting at? All our guys are behind us."

"Hell should I know?"

"Jackson should be here with us. That chickenshit—"

"Someone had to stay behind with them assholes we caught."

"Shoulda just thrown them in the hold like Father Adrian said. He's gonna be pissed when he finds out about Manny and—"

"He ain't gonna care, Roy. Don't you see? We got bigger problems on our hands. Now hurry yer ass up and shut yer mouth!"

They passed the hiding spot and were thirty feet down the road before Kari felt like she could breathe again.

"Jonah and Harrison are at the house," she whispered to the women. "Sounds like there's only one guard. We can handle that."

"What about Bix and Eddie?" Bren asked.

"I don't know, but that's why we need Jonah and Harrison."

She turned to Seth and shoved the pistol he'd been dangling by his side flat against his chest. "Don't you *ever* leave me like that, you hear me? You either use this like a man, or I'll use it on you."

"Don't tell me what to do."

"No? Well, it's because of you that we're even in this mess! It was *your* brilliant plan to hand over Harper. We're trying to save everyone, and you fucked it all up!"

"I didn't—"

"Just shut up and put that thing to good use instead of thinking only about yourself for once. Everything's gone to shit!"

Another shot rang out from the direction of the lake, followed immediately by several more bangs, then shouts to stop. The idiots were shooting at each other. It was all the confusion Kari needed. She pulled Seth up and pushed him back onto the road.

They stepped out, then stopped when the distinct click of a safety reached their ears.

"Down on your knees," someone growled at them. "Or I'll kill you all right now."

CHAPTER 17

ADRIAN FROZE AT THE SIGHT OF THE BOY. HE HADN'T expected to see anyone else there, much less the little brat he'd believed was vulture pickings some fifty-odd miles southeast of the compound. But the moment the large, bald man collapsed, the truth hit him like a wall of cold water. It had all been an elaborate ruse to throw him off his guard.

And it had worked. Again.

Shoot them both! Kill Finn and—

But Finn reacted first, spinning around and ducking away from the gun. He slapped it away, then wrenched it out of Adrian's grip. Before Adrian knew what was happening, the boy kicked at his knee, collapsing his leg beneath him and driving him to the ground.

"Don't you move," Finn growled as he placed a foot on his neck.

"Finn?"

"Snap out of it, Bix! Check Eddie. Something's wrong with him."

From where he lay, Adrian could see Bix blink in surprise. The boy obviously had no idea why Eddie had fainted.

But he did. He'd seen this before.

Bix bent down and shook him. Eddie's eyes were still open and he was breathing, but he was completely unresponsive.

"I don't know what's wrong with him, Finn."

More gunfire tattooed the night, sounding even farther away.

"Get up!" Finn ordered Adrian. He grabbed him by the back of the collar and yanked him to his knees. "I said get up!"

Adrian slowly rose to his feet. Finn shoved him in the direction of the road. The cold steel of Roy's pistol pressed painfully against the back of his head.

"Bix, move back."

"But Eddie isn't—"

"Move!" Finn snapped at Adrian. "I want you to lift him up."

"I can't! He's too big."

"Do it!"

"But, Finn," Bix said, "we don't know what's wrong!"

Finn didn't answer. He pushed Adrian again, slapping him hard enough on the back to make him cough.

"Now!"

He reached down and grabbed a handful of shirt and started to pull, but the man was too large a mass of dead weight.

"Lift him up under the arms."

It took him several more tries before he could get enough purchase to begin dragging him.

"He's coming to."

"Back off," Finn growled. He pressed the pistol to Adrian's spine. "Give him some room."

The man's recovery was quick. Within seconds, he was back on his feet, though not yet fully himself. He swayed uncertainly for a moment.

"What happened?" Bix exclaimed.

"I-I don't know," Eddie said.

"Can you walk?" Finn asked.

Eddie frowned. "Yeah, I'm fine now. Just a little shaky."

"Bix, stay with Eddie." He ordered Adrian back down on the ground. "Lie flat on your stomach."

"Y'all want to see yer brother, doncha?"

"Shut up."

"He's right, Finn," Bix said. "You can't kill him. He's still got Harper."

"I don't plan on killing him. I'm going to put him in with his sister."

"Jennifer?" Bix asked.

Adrian snorted. "Go ahead."

Finn pressed his knee against Adrian's spine until he elicited a grunt of pain. "Tell me where my brother is."

Another round of distant gunfire ripped through the night.

"Finn, I think we need to go! Kari and the others might need our help."

"Not until I get Harper."

"That's what I'm trying to tell you, Finn," Bix said. "Bren says he's not here! They took him somewhere else."

"What do you mean somewhere else? Did you check inside the hold?"

"Of course I did! That's where we found Bren and her mom."

"You were supposed to get—"

"Boys!" Eddie interrupted. "We need to get back, now!"

The gunfire stopped, a change that seemed even more ominous. He could tell the others felt the same way. Whatever was happening closer to the lake, it sounded like it had come to some sort of resolution. But what that resolution was, he couldn't say.

"He's right. Yer brother ain't here," Adrian said, coughing against the pressure on his ribs. "Y'all ain't never gonna find him."

"Get up! You're taking me to him!"

"That's not poss—"

The nascent silence from the other end of the compound was disrupted one last time by a growing rumble. It seemed to build forever into a roar. The ground shook. Then the sky brightened noticeably above them.

Eddie brushed past Bix and hurried up the path. He returned a moment later and plucked Adrian up off the ground as if he weighed no more than a sack of potatoes.

"We need to go, boys," he shouted. "Now!"

CHAPTER

EDDIE PULLED AWAY FROM THE GROUP AS THEY approached the clearing surrounding the house and circled around to the right. The interior lights had been extinguished, but now the flood lights outside blazed brightly, as if the occupants expected an ambush.

He made his way around the edge of the clearing, keeping to the shadows. The same weakening sensation he'd felt before seemed to play at the edges of his nerves, threatening to sap his energy. Something was definitely wrong with him.

He returned to Bix and Finn after less than a minute.

"Jonah and Harrison are inside. They're both alive but tied up. There's one guard."

"Kari? The Abramsons? Did you see them?"

He shook his head. "If they left like they were supposed to, they're long gone."

"Then what was that shooting? The explosion?"

Eddie hesitated. "It's at the lake. I don't know. We need to focus on this situation right here right now, okay?"

"It's just one guy. We can take him."

"Except he's probably expecting us," Eddie replied. He nodded at Father Adrian, who was now gagged. "We can try to negotiate a trade, though."

Adrian let out a muffled protest, but none of them was interested in what he had to say.

"I say one of us draws the man to the front door," Bix said. "We can use Adrian as a shield, in case the guard gets trigger-happy. It'll have to be Finn."

"Why me?"

"Because I'm a better shot than you. I'll wait behind a tree and shoot him. Meanwhile, Eddie slips around back, in case I don't have a clear shot. We'll have him surrounded."

Eddie shook his head. "The back of the house is a mess. I might be able to get in through the wreckage, but not without making some noise and alerting him. It's too risky. Are you willing to risk him shooting your father? Or Jonah?"

"Well, I'm not giving Adrian up anyway," Finn said. "We still don't know what he did with Harper."

A shot rang out, coming from the direction of the house. Finn and Bix ran out into the road to see, while Eddie kept a hand on Adrian's neck.

"I got your people!" the man inside the house shouted into the darkness. He was wearing night vision goggles. "I can see you out there! I could shoot you right now, if I wanted to. Come out right now or I will shoot them all!"

Finn hesitated, then stepped forward.

"What are you doing?" Bix whispered.

"Buying us some ti—"

"*Wait,*" Eddie whispered, yanking him back with his free hand. He gestured down the road. "We got more people coming."

After a minute or so, Kari and the Abramson's marched into the circle of light, their hands on their heads.

"What are they doing?" Finn asked. "Why would they—"

But the answer quickly became apparent. Several men followed, rifles pointed at their friends' backs.

"Jackson, that you up there?" one of the strangers yelled. "It's me and the boys."

"Red? Look out! There's more on the other side of the clearing!"

"Who? That you, Father Adrian?"

"Answer him," Eddie murmured to Adrian, pulling the gag away. "Tell him not to shoot."

He did as instructed.

"You okay, boss?" the man at the door called over.

"Not really."

"You need help?"

"Everyone just needs to stay where they are," Finn yelled.

"Finn?" Bren cried. "Oh my god, you're okay!"

"Don't move, Bren. If anyone moves, I'll shoot Adrian. If anyone hurts any of our people, I'll will make sure the bullet takes out his knees. Then I'll leave him for the Wraiths. And then I'll do the same to you."

Someone laughed.

"Sure you will," the man on the porch said. "What are you, fourteen? You sound fourteen. Maybe twelve. And scared shitless, too. Why don't you let the adults handle this?"

Finn aimed his pistol toward the house and squeezed the trigger. He was surprised when the porch light exploded.

"Jesus Christ!"

"Next time I take out your left eye."

"Where the hell did you learn how to shoot like that?" Bix whispered.

"I was aiming for the window," he mumbled back.

"Jackson? They shot Pierce," Red said. "And Jase is messed up pretty bad. He dropped a live grenade. Place just exploded like crazy. Fire everywhere. We got him in the water right away, but he's burnt up pretty bad and needs help. Lost his foot. Might not survive. They're bringing him up now."

Further down the road came the sound of a man in terrible pain. Finn couldn't see him, but he could hear the scuffing of several feet as he was carried along.

"Jackson, what should we do?"

The light inside the house came on, and Jackson reappeared for a moment in the doorway before merging with the shadows on the porch. "Bring Jase up."

Finn turned to Eddie, uncertain what to do now. With Jonah and Mister Blakeley trapped inside, the Abramsons and Kari under guard on the other side of the clearing, and a whole cadre of men soon to arrive, the tide was quickly turning against them.

Eddie raised a hand and placed it on Finn's arm. "Wait." He was staring off down the road, listening.

"What is it?"

But he didn't answer.

"Eddie?"

"*Quiet!*"

Adrian stiffened. Finn saw his eyes widen, and he suddenly became very animated. Eddie stepped back in surprise, then bellowed at the top of his lungs, "Get inside! Everyone, get inside the house now!"

With one hand on Finn's arm and the other on Adrian's neck, he shoved them into the clearing. Finn saw the glint of steel as Jackson raised his rifle and aimed it at them, but

Adrian shouted not to shoot. He repeated Eddie's order for everyone to get inside the house.

Finn saw Bren break away from her parents and try to run across the clearing toward him. He wanted to yell at her to stop, but a hand reached out and grabbed her by the hair, arresting her flight. She spun around, arms flailing, a shriek of fury and pain torn from her lips. The man threw her roughly to the ground and ordered her not to move. Missus Abramson shrieked and went to her, but when Seth tried to as well, he was slammed in the back with the stock of a rifle. He fell, coughing and writhing in the dirt.

Finn started to run over to help but checked himself when he heard the first hiss.

"Get inside!" Eddie roared again. He handed Adrian over to Bix and told him not to let him go. "They're coming! They're coming! Get in—"

A scream of sheer terror rose from the far end of the road, followed by a second scream a moment later. Then the entire woods came alive with shadows zipping through the brush, surrounding them, and forcing them all to seek shelter inside the ravaged house.

CHAPTER

"GET OUT OF THE WAY!" FINN SHOUTED.

He grabbed Adrian and shoved him up the steps past Jackson, who seemed frozen with indecision.

"If you're uncertain whether to shoot us or the Wraiths," Bix told him, "may I recommend the Wraiths? They'll eat you. We won't!"

"But—" he said, still not moving.

"Now!" Finn roared.

The man stumbled backward, obviously still unable to reconcile the fact that Adrian was now under the charge of his former captive, or the fact that the boy was giving the orders.

Kari took the opportunity to snatch one of the confiscated guns from the men behind her and joined Eddie and Bix as they ran to fight off the infected creatures.

Seth Abramson pulled Kaleagh and Bren up the steps, knocking Finn into the railing coming back down. Finn caught his arm. "Keep an eye on Adrian!" he shouted, then pulled Jackson toward the yard and ordered him to start shooting into the trees.

"Where the hell did they come from?" the man croaked. "How the hell did they get in? The devices are supposed to keep them out!"

More screams rose from the road ahead, screams and growls and the sounds of flesh tearing and bones being crushed and ground between teeth.

Bix and Kari stopped at the edge of the clearing, just inside the bubble of light, and fired at the ghostly shapes flitting about through the trees. Two of the men from the other group stood beside them doing the same. Kari grabbed Finn as he headed toward the lake. "It's too late to save them," she said, her voice thin and reedy, bled of strength by her terror. Her face had lost all of its color.

The hissing sounds grew in urgency and filled the woods. The guards held their positions, but when a vile shriek pierced the night, their resolve evaporated. They broke rank and fled toward the house.

"We need to get back, too!" Bix said, his eyes flicking madly left and right, as if he were trying to see everything at once.

"Where's Eddie?"

"I saw him run past," Kari said. "But I don't know where he went." She edged backward, shaking her head, her body jolting each time she fired another round.

As a unit, the three turned and began to sprint for the house. Ahead, two of the men were nearly to the porch, another pair thirty feet behind. There was a flash of color and something burst out of the trees and launched itself at them. One of the running men went down in a tangle of arms and legs and gnashing teeth. The other man never even slowed down. He vaulted up the steps, and only when he reached the top did he turn to fire. Puffs of dust rose from the ground around the wrestling pair.

The fight was over in seconds. The man's body went slack. The Wraith paused its brutal attack, as if made uncertain by the sudden lack of resistance.

"He's turning," Kari gasped. *"Jesus, how can he already be turning?"*

The air beside Finn's head exploded. He ducked away to find Bix aiming the pistol back toward the road. The body of another Wraith tumbled to a stop in the dust a couple yards away.

"There's nowhere to go!" Kari shouted. "We're surrounded!"

The man on the porch emptied his magazine, yet despite standing only a few dozen feet away from the horrific scene at the base of the steps, he somehow kept missing. At last, a chunk of flesh on the Wraith's flank exploded in a spray of blood. It turned and let out a shriek so inhuman the blood froze in Finn's veins. He watched as it leapt with supernatural strength and speed toward the porch. Another shot rang out, and the creature fell lifeless to the ground.

The man spun around to duck inside, but he'd dawdled too long. Another Wraith swung down from the porch roof and grabbed him by the hair and dragged him kicking and screaming away.

"We're trapped!" Kari said.

Finn spun to his left in a crouch. He could see the shack off to the side of the house, but there were shapes crawling all around it. Another Wraith appeared further off, a gaping black hole in its chest, the flesh drawn and puckered away from its exposed ribs. It was missing an arm, a foot, and half its face. Deep brown gore streamed down the charred remains of its shirt. The thing that had once been a man named Jase took a lumbering step toward them, clacked its teeth and growled. But then it flopped to the ground, wisps of steam from its wounds drifting into the chilly air.

"Finn!" Bren screamed from the door. "Get in here!"

"Shut the door!" he screamed back. "They're on the porch roof!"

A man ran past her from inside the house and began to fire his assault rifle straight up. Splinters rained down, and the body of a dead Wraith tumbled off. Others fled up into the darkness, away from the fusillade. Both the shooter and Bren disappeared back into the house.

Finn reached the door first, but the knob was wrenched from his sweaty fist as he snatched at it. He slammed against the side of the house.

Bix was right behind. He grabbed for the door, as Kari yanked Finn back to his feet.

Movement below the steps caught his eye. The man who'd been attacked on the yard a moment earlier was starting to rise. The color had fully drained from his skin, leaving a gray husk that concentrated in his eyes. Finn aimed and fired. The man flew backward, then rose again, a thin finger of smoke rising from a hole in his shoulder. Finn squeezed the trigger again, but it only clicked. He was out of ammunition.

"There's too many out here!" Bix shouted and banged on the door. "Open up! Let us in!"

They heard Adrian shout for the people inside not to. He heard Bren scream to let her out.

"Behind you, Finn!" Bix screamed. "Look out!"

Finn ducked and swung the empty pistol wildly about, desperate not to be touched.

The sound of Kari's slug punching through flesh and bone focused Finn's gaze. He caught a glimpse of the Wraith just as it drew back onto the roof.

Something pawed at the toes of Finn's boot, inching toward his ankle, searching for bare skin. He wrenched his foot away and hurled the useless pistol at the Wraith's head. The weapon hit the railing and bounced back toward the house. Kari shoved another pistol into his hands.

"Get that door open, Bix!"

The same Wraith reappeared from above. He fired once at it, not bothering to aim, then once more at the two Wraiths racing across the yard. All three fell.

"Christ, nice shooting," Kari said.

He stood for a split second, stunned that he'd actually hit them at all. And with only two shots.

But he had no time to think about it, as he was yanked inside by the arm. The door slammed shut behind him, and he had to dive out of the way as someone slid a cabinet over to block the door.

Someone else pulled him to his feet. He was surprised to see who it was.

"Thank god you're safe," Seth Abramson started to say. But he didn't get a chance to finish before Finn slammed his fist into the man's face.

CHAPTER
20

"Quick! What do we have for weapons?" Kari demanded.

She plucked a spare rifle from one of the surprised guards and shoved it into Finn's hands. Then she snatched a second one off the floor where someone had dropped it and handed it to Seth with a furious glare.

He looked none too happy that Finn had sucker punched him. He wrapped his fingers around the gun, but she didn't relinquish it to him right away. "Do something useful for once," she told him. "Go untie Jonah and Harrison."

"Eddie's still out there," Finn said. "We need to—"

The sound of the Wraiths climbing around the outside of the house cut him off.

"Can't do anything about that right now, Finn," Kari said. "He's on his own for now. But if anyone has a good chance of surviving those things, it's him."

Not necessarily, he thought, but didn't say it out loud. They already had too much to deal with at the moment to add Eddie's health and well-being to the mix.

"I count a half a dozen rifles and as many pistols," Bix said, stepping over.

"Now hold on there," Jackson said. He pointed his rifle at Seth to stop him from releasing Jonah and Mister Blakeley from their ties. Finn and Kari immediately raised their own weapons and pointed them at Jackson's head. This triggered a similar response from the other two men who had made it into the house.

"Everyone, just calm down," Harrison said. He stood up and rubbed his wrists. "I think a truce is in order. We're going to have to work together if we're getting out of this intact."

"Lower it," Kari growled at Jackson.

"You first, bitch."

She swiveled her aim around and redirected it at Adrian, who was standing in the corner behind the front door, as if he hoped they'd all forgotten he was there. He'd already managed to get free of his bindings. Kari stepped over to him and yanked him away from the wall. "Lower them or your boss gets a bullet in the head."

The other three men actually looked like they were weighing their options. They exchanged glances but otherwise didn't move. Anger flashed over Adrian's face, but he didn't say anything.

"We're on the same team," Harrison said. "At least for the moment."

"Sorta like that enemy of my enemy thing?" one of the other men asked.

"Something like that."

"Do not drop your guard, Red," Jackson warned.

But Red slowly lowered his gun, shrugging.

As if to emphasize their predicament, a thump came from overhead just outside the front door. Then came the crackle of weakened wood starting to give way.

Something scraped at the wall beneath the side window, and Bren, who had been standing closest to it, leapt away.

"What's on the other side of that?" Harrison quietly asked, pointing at the interior door.

"Hallway," Finn said. "Kitchen's off to the left, mudroom at the other end, and—"

"Fire took everything out," Red said. "Most of it's burnt down."

"They can still get in that way," Jackson said. He sighed and dropped his arm, cueing the last man, Roy, to follow suit.

Kari let Adrian go, who returned to his corner and slumped to the floor.

"Back of the house is mostly destroyed," Jackson continued. "Half the walls are gone. So's much of the second floor. We'll need to barricade it."

"No," Harrison said.

"Are you nuts?"

"Shh! The louder we are, the angrier they get."

"But they'll get in anyway!"

"Exactly," Harrison quietly replied. He circled the room, eying the furniture. "We need to barricade the two windows and the front door as much as we can. Leave the back clear, force them to use it. Limit their access."

"Create a bottleneck," Kari said, catching on. "Where we can pick them off. Good idea."

"Exactly. We need to position ourselves on the opposite side of the room with a clear line of sight, give ourselves plenty of opportunity to shoot them as they come through."

"Most of our packs are outside, so I'm not sure we have enough ammunition," Kari said. She reached down and helped Jonah to his feet. "Certainly not enough to hold them off for long. I couldn't tell how many there were, but it looked like dozens."

"And we're only twelve," Seth noted. He clutched the rifle tighter to his chest, as if he regretted drawing attention to himself.

"I've got a few boxes," Bix said. "Couple more pistols, too."

He yanked off his backpack and tossed it over to Jonah, who plucked a pair of handguns out and slipped one into his belt. He gave the other to Harrison. Next, he tossed a box of ammunition each to Bix and Finn, though they wouldn't work for the rifle Finn now held. He kept the third box and thumbed it open.

"What I wanna know is how the damn ferals got in," Red said. He flinched every time there was another knock or scrape or hiss from outside. "You said the boundaries were secure," he said, glaring at Adrian. "You said they couldn't get past the fence."

Adrian shrugged. "Y'all said Jase dropped a live grenade by the dock, ain't that right?"

Red nodded. "Tried to find it and got blown up. Lit him up like a candle. The whole dang place went up in flames—*boom boom boom boom!* Ain't never seen nothing like it before."

"That's because it took out the diesel line runnin along the shore. Water keeps it from freezing in the wintertime. What do you think feeds the back generator?"

Red shrugged.

Adrian stood up and walked over to the front door and pointed. "The jenny powers half them devices along that side of the property. Weren't nothin to stop the ferals from walkin right in after that."

"You said the woods around here were cleared," Finn said.

"They were, until someone let them out of the barn where I kept them." He glared back. "We had them all corralled in the back quadrant again, up against the lagoon. There's a clearing there, water on three sides. They don't like water. And now, because of y'all, they're right back out again."

"But there weren't that many in the barn last time."

"Oh, there were plenty. You'd be surprised how many bodies you can put into a small space. Sorta like stacking logs."

"You're insane."

He shrugged and back leaned against the wall.

Something heavy crashed around the back of the house, followed by a sound of a struggle and more hissing. Everyone raised their weapons and trained them on the back door.

"There's a dozen of us and thirteen weapons," Kari said. "We need to be smart, maybe designate two shooters at a time so we don't waste a hundred rounds on the first Wraith that comes through that door and have nothing left for the rest."

"And then what?" Seth complained. "We can keep shooting them, one by one or by twos, as long as we have ammunition, but we're eventually going to run out. They'll just keep right on coming."

"Then we keep on—"

He stopped when the lights flickered. Everyone tensed up, but the power soon stabilized again.

"We just need to stay calm," Kari said. "If we do as Harrison says, we can survive this. He and I will be the front line shooters. Jonah and Bix can take secondary. That means if we miss, it's up to you. The next pair will be—"

The lights flickered off again. This time they didn't come back on.

CHAPTER

21

"I CAN'T STAND IT," RED MOANED. "IT'S JUST TOO dang quiet out there."

"Not nearly quiet enough in here, though," Seth grumbled.

"I can't help it. I'm a nervous talker sometimes."

"Ever consider going for a walk?"

"Dad," Bren whispered. "He's scared. We're all scared."

"Well, he doesn't have to keep talking about it. It's not helping. We all need to be quiet."

Finn knew Seth was right, but he had to grin anyway when Bren ignored her father and changed the subject to ask, "Do they call you Red because of your hair?"

"No, my daddy misspelt Reid on the birth certificate."

"Well, Red is still a nice name," Bren said. "I mean, so is Reid. My uncle's name is Reid."

"It's on account of where my ma and pa made me."

"Excuse me?"

"Inna reeds along the Waubanaugh Creek in So'kota where I grew up," Red blurted out.

Nobody said anything for several seconds.

"You know those words aren't even spelled the same way, right?" Bix said. "One is E-I and the other is—"

"That's enough, son," Mister Blakeley said.

"Well, my pa never were book smart. He knew a lot about growing things. And killing and eating them, too."

Silence met this confession as well.

"Anyway, that's why they call me Red."

"How about we all just be quiet now?" Seth said.

The quiet lasted no more than twenty seconds before Red broke it again. "I like the name Bren. Is it because you're smart?"

"I beg your pardon? You mean brain?"

"Yeah."

"Jesus, Red, would you just shut up?" Jackson said. "We got bigger problems right now."

"Why did they cut the power, that's what I wanna know."

"We don't know what happened to the power," Kari said.

"You think they cut the wires?"

"Yeah," growled Roy from another corner. "One of them must have figured out how to use wire snips. Sheesh, Red. Or maybe they learned how to shut off the jennies. How many times we gotta tell you to zip it?"

Finn rolled his eyes in the darkness, though he knew no one else could see it. Listening to them speak, he had never been more convinced the world would have been better off if mankind simply died out that day three years ago. All of them, including everyone from the bunkers. It was a cruel irony that the greatest culling in human history not only failed to eradicate stupidity and pettiness, but seemed to enrich for them instead.

He thought about Billy and Luke, the two man-boys Adrian and Jennifer had adopted as their own. They hadn't exactly been the sharpest tools in the shed. And he winced as he remembered the sound of Luke's body hitting the ground after he put a bullet in the man's skull.

Was it just that afternoon that it happened? It hardly seemed possible.

So much for natural selection and survival of the fittest, he thought. *More like survival of the shittiest.*

"Yep, I think they might be planning someth—"

"Dammit, Red! Shut yer damn mouth!"

Idiots and despots, Finn thought. *The only two types of people left in the world.*

And suckers, he amended. *Like the rest of us.*

"I mean, they gotta be hungry, right?" Red wondered.

"Just, everyone, shut up."

Red grumbled a bit before growing silent. They all knew it wouldn't last long.

Between the twelve of them, they had two working flashlights, which they used only sparingly. They also had two pairs of night vision goggles, which the primary shooters shared so they could watch the door. Currently, they belonged to Bix and Jackson. In the event the room was breached, they would shoot the Wraiths as they entered. If they felt overwhelmed or ran out of ammunition or weapons, they would shout *"Lights!"* and the flashlight holders — Bren and her mom, at the moment — would flick them on so the next set of shooters — Kari and Roy — could see and fire on the deadly creatures.

And so on, and so forth.

But the minutes passed with agonizing slowness, and nothing happened. No Wraiths made their way in. And everything outside had grown far too quiet for anyone to relax.

Waiting was not one of the creatures' known traits. They were supposed to be mindless, bloodthirsty beasts, driven by a relentless manic hunger for human flesh and contact. Neither injury nor obstacles deterred them for long.

Which is why this behavior was highly incongruent. Patience was not their habit. Nor was planning. But that's what it seemed like they were doing. What else could explain the quiet?

The uneasy truce between the people inside the room was a nagging complication. They all knew it existed only because of a shared mutual interest for self preservation. But what would happen once their common enemy was no longer a threat? They would immediately revert back to being hostile to each other, a situation Finn did not relish thinking about. Nor did the others, if the sniping remarks were any indication.

He could hear Jackson yawning for the hundredth time in his nest a few feet away, as if he were trying to lure the rest of them to sleep. Finn worried the man himself might drop off and leave them unprotected when the moment came. Then again, if he did fall asleep, maybe Bix could snatch the other set of goggles and—

Stop it! You're supposed to be figuring out how to work together. That's how you get out of this alive, Wraiths or no Wraiths.

Work together? Trust one another? He almost laughed out loud.

If Eddie were here, it wouldn't even be an issue.

Eddie gave them an advantage, especially in the dark. But he was gone.

Finn wondered what had become of him. Why had he left when he did, just as the Wraiths attacked? Had he chickened out and run away? It seemed impossible to imagine the man as a coward. As far as Finn knew, he feared only one thing, and that was the loss of his abilities.

The episode near the gate came once more to mind. What had happened to him back there? Did it happen again.

Was he dead?

Had he been turned into one of them?

This last possibility terrified Finn more than the others. The usual Wraiths were scary enough, but what would happen if one came from a person with Eddie's superhuman abilities? Would it be that much faster and stronger and stealthier?

Would it be that much deadlier?

He heard Bix fidgeting in his spot directly across the room from the door, and he wanted to ask if it was time to switch roles. But he knew his friend would be reluctant to give up the goggles currently in his possession. It was better than sitting completely blind in the pitch dark, as the rest of them knew, flinching at every little creak and snap. Besides, Finn didn't need to be putting all his concentration on waiting for the Wraiths to sneak in. He needed to focus on what they were going to do after.

"Maybe they're gone," Red said. Apparently enough time had elapsed since the last admonishment that he'd either forgotten or figured everyone else had.

Someone let out a deep sigh of resignation, which made someone else chuckle. Finn couldn't help but smile, too. If their situation weren't so dire, it would almost seem amusing. The irony alone was like a cosmic joke.

"I vote you go out and have a look-see," Jackson said.

An ominous creaking noise from the rafters above immediately silenced them once more. Was it the house settling? Its structural integrity had been compromised by the fire and neglect. But the noise repeated, seemingly filled with dark intention.

Something was moving around on the roof. A scratch came at the door, soft and hesitant. Then a hiss.

What are they doing? Finn wondered. *What are they waiting for? Do they plan to starve us out?*

It was driving him crazy.

"This waiting is driving me crazy," Red said.

"Shut your damn trap," Roy snapped. "It ain't nothing to worry about!"

"On the contrary," Adrian murmured. He almost sounded like he was enjoying himself.

The hissing grew in volume, as did the sounds of movement from all around.

"It's making me crazy," Red repeated.

"Yeah, we sorta picked up on that a half hour ago," Jonah said.

The sounds came and went, steadily multiplying. Inside the room, they all expected the attack to occur at any moment. But then the movement abruptly stopped and all was silent once more.

In his corner by the door, Adrian chuckled.

"Why are you doing this?" Finn demanded of him.

"Excuse me?"

"What have you done with my brother?"

"Finn, we—" Harrison started, but Adrian interrupted him to answer.

"Y'all know why, boy." He shifted in his seat. "For what y'all did to my sister, took her away from me. Y'all killed her."

She wasn't dead, not technically. But Finn didn't think the distinction made much difference to the man. "Revenge, is that it?"

"It's more than that. I just let everyone believe that's all it were. Everyone understands somethin simple like that. It's primal, uncomplicated. The truth is—"

"You wouldn't recognize the truth if it slapped you in the face," Bix cut in.

"Bix," Finn said. "Let him talk."

"He lied to us, Finn. He lied about who he was and what he was doing here."

"Same way y'all lied to me tonight?"

"You imprisoned us, then tried to kill us. You infected our friend, Nami. You kidnapped Finn's brother and used him for bait. What did you expect us to do?"

"Keep it down, Bix!"

"I offered you our warmest hospitality," Adrian said, his voice growing louder. "I took y'all in, and what did I get in return? Y'all betrayed me."

"We just wanted to leave."

"Y'all killed my sister."

"The Wraiths got her, you know that's the truth," Finn said. "And for the record, she helped me escape. She had me dead to rights that night, out by the generator shack. But she let me go."

"Another lie. She would never defy my wishes," Adrian immediately replied.

Finn sensed his anger and pressed even harder: "She did, because she knew what you were doing here was wrong. She wanted to help them, fix them, but you took what good she was trying to do and twisted it into something evil."

"You got no clue what I was doin here, cleansing the sins of—"

"You don't get to claim the moral high ground! This was nothing but sick and demented—"

"It was about salvation."

"Bullshit!"

"Finn!" Kari whispered. "This isn't the time or the place for that."

"You could have just let us go the first time. Even after we got away. You could have just rebuilt your sick little playground here, and gone on doing what you were doing before. But no. Instead, you had to come chasing after us, because you're obsessive and sick and—"

"An eye deserves an eye."

"Says the man blinded by his own delusions."

"Y'all think I can't see the world clearly, the way it's become?" He exhaled slowly, as if releasing a heavy burden. "Y'all are the blind ones, not me."

"Tell me where my brother is," Finn demanded.

Adrian didn't answer.

"Dammit, Adrian!"

"Finn, please," Kaleagh Abramson whispered, her voice quivering.

"There's eight of us in here, four of you. We outnumber you. So tell me what you've done with Harper. Tell us and when we walk out of here, we let you live. It's as simple as that."

Adrian chuffed. "Tain't ever as simple as that, boy."

"Tell me what you want," Finn said. He was past frustrated and bordering on homicidal now. "It can't just be revenge. You could have had that when you chained me up at the barn and brought your sister out to scare me. But you stopped her. Why? What more do you want from me?"

"Nothin."

"What if I hand myself over to you?"

There were several gasps of dismay. Bix began to protest and was soon joined by Kari and Bren. But Finn shushed them.

"Give me your word you won't harm Harper or the rest of my friends. Tell me you'll let them all go."

"It is . . . uncanny," Adrian said thoughtfully, "how much alike y'all are, you and yer brother. Only difference bein, yer more the skeptic. Y'all got this wall built up around yerself and ain't no one gettin close."

"That's not true," both Bix and Bren said at once.

"Ain't it?"

"You're wrong," Finn said. "That's not the only difference between me and my brother. We may be twins, but we're nothing alike at all. Harper was always smarter than I was."

"And he said pretty much the same about you, that he wished he could be like you, except he didn't actually use the word smart. He said you were— What was the word? Ah, I remember: *deep*."

"Harper said that?"

Adrian snorted. "First time I saw him inside that dam complex, thought it were you. Couldn't believe my luck, not even when Mister Seth Abramson here told me otherwise. But we got to talkin, and yer brother told me how y'all were the strong one and he was weak. You was always okay on yer own, but never him. He needed other people. That was his downfallin, bein so needy. I let him think I were his friend."

"What did you do to him?"

"I saved him. He just needed a little shove in the right direction is all."

"What did you do? Tell me!"

"Why, I sent him off to find his fabled secret bunker."

CHAPTER 22

FINN KNEW ADRIAN WAS PLAYING GAMES WITH HIM, manipulating his emotions, but he couldn't help himself. "What do you know about that?"

"Oh, more'n y'all realize. For example, I knew about them maps Colonel Wainwright had in his office for all the bunkers."

Finn knew about the maps, too. He also knew they were no longer there. In fact, they were stowed in a cardboard tube beneath the driver's seat of the truck they had arrived in.

"I don't know anything about them."

"Still lyin?"

Finn didn't answer.

"Cheever told me about them months ago, though he were always careful never to let me see more'n a little peek. He thought he could lord them over me, use them as leverage."

"Leverage for what?" Finn asked. "Taking over your operation?"

"That man could never settle on what he wanted. Never happy with what he had— power, women, pain. Other people's pain. Name it, nothin satisfied him for long.

Whatever caught his fancy at any given moment, he wanted more of it. Until he lost interest and wanted somethin else."

"And what does this have to do with my brother?"

"Who else do y'all think told him about the cure but Cheever?"

"That's a lie! Harper already knew about the twelfth bunker."

"Twelve?"

Finn realized his mistake too late. Adrian was aware of only ten, because that's how many maps there were.

"It were Wainwright who told Cheever about them," Adrian went on, not challenging the discrepancy. "Said that they was tryin to make an antidote in one of them. Cheever wanted to search for it, but Wainwright told him never to go anywhere near any of them."

"Why would Wainwright do that? If it was so dangerous surviving out in the real world, why didn't he just take all those people from the base where they could be safe? I mean, we had room for more people inside the dam. We kept watch every day, waiting for survivors. We could have taken in almost forty more people."

"Forty? What good is that when there were hundreds? Who gets to choose?"

"Forty in ours, but who knows how much room in the others."

"Not nearly enough. Besides, Wainwright believed it was more important to protect the people inside them bunkers than out, no matter the cost. He believed the future of the species depended on it. But Cheever disagreed, and he resented Wainwright for it. After all, y'all were livin the good life, growin fat and lazy inside yer walls, where the feral couldn't get to you. Meanwhile, everyone else outside was strugglin just to find their next meal, much less survive each other and the ferals. Cheever decided he was finished with it."

"What do you mean?"

"He were the reason yer brother's bunker up north went bad."

"You knew about that?" Bix exclaimed. "Did you know it when we first met?"

"Not all the details. It weren't until t'other day when I met up at the dam with yer brother that I found out about how it all happened."

"It was Cheever's fault?" Finn whispered, incredulously. His throat constricted at the truth. For the first time in a long time he thought he might have one of his asthma attacks. "He tried to break in!"

"Actually, no. They invited him in after he showed up. But after he told them about the people on the army base, they decided they couldn't let him leave. Food and water was too limitin and the risk too great."

"So, he let the Wraiths in on purpose."

"Men like Cheever are spiteful, but that ain't what happened. He showed them the maps — copies, anyway — and tried to convince some of them to help him find the right bunker for this so-called cure. Yer brother volunteered, but the rest denied him. They took the maps away and tried to lock Cheever up. So he escaped. When they went after him, a feral got inside. All it took was one to spread the infection. It didn't take long."

"That explains why Cheever shot at us when we showed up at the base," Finn said. "When Danny was killed. Cheever must've seen me and thought I was Harper. He panicked, thinking I'd tell Wainwright and expose him for what he'd done."

"Could be. I don't know, as I weren't there, and it never occurred to me to ask."

"Then why did you lure me here?" Finn asked. "If Harper's not here, then what do you want from me? You could've had your revenge, yet you held back."

"Cheever believes yer brother had the copies he showed to him, said he thought yer brother stole them to search for the bunker hisself."

"Harper would never steal anything from anyone!"

"I believe that, too. But someone did take the maps from Cheever, and I think it were this same person who made contact with yer bunker. Else, how would y'all have known where to go lookin for yer brother?"

Finn sucked in a sharp breath. Adrian had known all along. He'd probably even searched through his and Bix's belongings while they stayed here. But why would he want the maps?

"Is he talking about the phone, Jonah?" Bren blurted out.

Bix groaned.

"Threw it away," Jonah quickly replied. "It didn't work anyway. The battery couldn't hold a charge."

Finn let out a silent exhale of relief. He didn't know where the phone was now, but he knew Jonah was lying. He just hoped Adrian bought it. If he got a hold of the maps of the bunkers, there was no telling what the madman would do with the knowledge, though he could easily imagine. It explained Wainwright's own caution.

There was a sudden loud *snap*, and the lights came on. Both Bix and Jackson let out pained cries and tore the goggles off their faces.

"Funny thing happens when yer focused on fighting for yer life," Adrian said, grinning cruelly at them in the unexpected glare. "People tend to forget the simplest things like light switches."

He had one arm wrapped around Bren's head, his hand covering her mouth. The other hand dropped from the wall plate, a pistol in it, which he redirected toward her head. "Now, boy, why don't y'all hand over that phone."

Jonah's face pinched. "I told you I threw it away."

"And I don't believe you. Jackson, check him."

"I already did before."

"Do it again. Thoroughly, this time. Roy, Red, take their weapons away, before I have to hurt this pretty little thing."

"You lay a hand on her and—"

"And what, boy?"

Finn stepped back.

Jonah's face turned to stone as Jackson patted him down. He looked like he wanted to punch the guy in the face. He shut his eyes and suffered the indignity.

"Not here, sir."

Adrian's gaze swept the room. "No, he wouldn't have it, would he? Not after bein the sacrificial lamb back there." His eyes alit on Harrison, who had been with Jonah when they were captured on the road, and he slowly smiled as he understood the cleverness of their ruse. "No, but check him." He swung his finger over to Bix.

Jackson found the phone inside the zippered inner pocket of Bix's jacket. He flipped it open and waited for the screen to brighten. "It works, boss."

"And the files?"

"Looks like it's all here. Maps, descriptions, lists. Lots of numbers and stuff. Don't know what any of it means."

"No, but I know someone who does." The smile widened, intensifying the evil look in his eyes. "Roy, put the guns in the bag here. Bring it with us. We're leavin."

"What about the ferals, boss?"

"Oh, they ain't gonna bother us," Adrian confidently replied. "They were never gonna bother us in here, not with this device." He nudged the duffle with his foot toward Roy, who picked it up and slung it over a shoulder.

Without bothering to check that the way was clear, Adrian yanked the back door open. Then, before stepping through it, he shoved Bren back and into her mother's waiting arms.

"Watch yer step," he reminded the three men following along behind him.

Jackson was the last to exit, backing his way out with his rifle trained on the group. He pulled the door shut behind him, wrenching it into place.

Finn immediately tried to follow, but Bix stopped him. He was furious with himself, with the fact that Adrian had so completely fooled them. Furious that the madman had been right about them forgetting even the simplest of things. How could he have been so stupid, so blind?

But there was no time to punish themselves. With Adrian's departure, the Wraiths were coming. Already, the chorus of growls and hisses outside the walls and above their heads was growing to a frightening level. But this time there was nothing to keep them from getting in.

And no weapons to fight them off when they did.

CHAPTER

"BLOCK THE DOOR!" JONAH CRIED, LEAPING OVER THE coffee table. He began shoving the second couch toward the back corner, where he lifted it onto one end and tilted it up against the opening. With a pair of stiff kicks, he wedged it into place.

"Are you crazy?" Seth yelled. "We need to get out of here now! We'll be trapped!"

"We're already trapped," Harrison said, stepping in to intervene.

"You don't know that! We can get out!" He pushed Harrison aside and began tugging at the couch, trying to rock it away from the wall.

Jonah knocked his hands off. "Leave it!"

"I'm not staying!"

"You go out there now, you're dead. Or infected."

"Dad!" Bren screamed. "Please, stop! We can't fight with each other."

Jonah shoved Seth back, repelling a more forceful second attempt to remove the couch. "Listen to me! Those things have been out there the whole time! They were incapacitated before, but now they're not. You hear that? They're all around us!"

"Incapacitated?"

"We had a device," Harrison explained, pulling him away. "Jonah and I had it in the duffle." He turned to Finn. "I'm sorry, I forgot all about it."

"I should have remembered, too."

"Wait! What device?" Seth demanded. "Tell me!"

"Not now, Mister Abramson!" Finn cried.

The Wraiths were pushing at the front door, scratching and making it creak against their weight. They were still hissing and growling, which meant they hadn't yet transitioned into their bloodthirsty mode.

There was a crash overhead as something fell through the damaged roof and landed heavily on the upstairs floor. Then a scratching, scrambling sound and several more thumps.

"They're getting inside the house!"

Several gunshots sounded from outside, followed by a shout, then the roar of an engine. A moment later, a vehicle sped past the house.

Seth was visibly shaking, his eyes wide with panic. Kari grabbed his arm and drew him over to Kaleagh and Bren, both of whom seemed much calmer. Or maybe they were just too paralyzed by fear. "Listen," Kari told them, "we need to defend ourselves. We can do this, same plan as before. We limit the ways they can come in, and we kill them when they do."

"How?"

She peered around herself. Jonah and Harrison were moving the rest of the furniture around to protect their weak spots. Bix had pulled up the rug and was tearing it into pieces. It was old, worn, and thin. He began to wrap bits of it around his arms to protect his exposed skin.

Kari bent down and pulled a pair of knives from their sheathes beneath her pant legs. She also had a tiny handgun with a pearl grip, which she had hidden in a holster under her arm and beneath her shirt. They had luckily remained undiscovered when Red frisked her earlier.

"That's it?" Seth exclaimed. "We can't defend ourselves with a pair of knives and a cap gun!"

"It happens to be a 9mm Ruger, asshole. But don't worry your little head. It's not for you. The kick'd probably knock you on your ass." She reached into her pocket and counted the rounds. "I've only got about a dozen and a half."

"Eighteen? That's not going to help!"

"Shut up, Mister Abramson," Bix snapped.

Harrison gave his son a stern glance.

Jonah took one of the knives and attached it with strips of cloth to the end of one of the coffee table legs he'd broken off. When he was finished, he gave the makeshift spear to Harrison, then cloned it with the second knife and another table leg. This one, he kept.

The Wraiths were crawling all over the porch now, scratching at the window screens and prying away at the siding, searching for a way inside. The scurrying overhead seemed to come and go, as if they became easily distracted when an access point didn't immediately prove itself productive, and went off to find a different way in.

"I hope the door at the top of the inside stairs is shut," Bix murmured to Finn.

Finn frowned and glanced over at the back door. The staircase was just past it inside the hallway. He could sense the creatures up there trying to figure out the knob.

"Mister Abramson's right," he said. "We can't fight them off with what little we've got." He glanced around, then threw cushions from the couches to Bren and her mother. "Shield yourselves with these if they get in. Do not let them touch you!"

The remaining two table legs were snapped off. They'd work as bludgeons for him and Bix. But that still left the women with no weapons to protect themselves.

Finn handed Bren one of the shaped dowels, then bent down to inspect the floor. The boards were old and worn, the wood soft. "Give me your spear," he told Harrison, and he stuck the tip of the knife underneath one end of a board and pried it up. A wet, earthy smell rose up from the crawl-space underneath.

Bix placed a hand on Finn's arm to stop him. "You sure they're not under there?"

Finn cautiously placed his ear near the opening and listened. He didn't hear anything.

"They've made it into the back of the house," Harrison reported. He leaned against the couch. Just as he finished speaking, the first body slammed against the interior door, jolting him backward. The second hit was slighter, experimental. But the third and fourth were considerably heavier than the first, more frantic.

As if on cue, the hissing all around them stopped. There was a momentary lull. Then, as a unit, the creatures began to wail. The sound raised the hairs on Finn's neck.

"That's not good," Bix said.

"Get ready, everyone. Here they come."

Finn wrenched the loose floorboard up and away, then snapped it in half with his foot. "Watch the nails," he told

Bren's mother, handing her one of the pieces. He reached down to remove a second board.

"There's a crawlspace down there," Bren said, peering into the darkness.

"If it comes to it, we may have to retreat under the house. Help me widen this opening."

"You don't know if they can't get under there!" Seth cried. But when they ignored him, he tried to pull Bren away. "Listen to me! You're just giving them more ways to get in!"

"Get back over there and guard the front door!" Finn ordered.

But the Wraiths were focusing their attack on the back, as if they knew it was made of flimsier wood. They battered at the door, scratched the panels, and repeatedly knocked it open a few inches before Harrison and Kari could shut it again. Jonah went over and threw his shoulder into it to help, leaving the other access points unmanned. But the creatures were relentless.

"We can't hold them forever!" Jonah shouted. "We need to figure something out!"

"Working on it! Mister Abramson, mind the front door!"

The glass in one of the windows shattered. The cabinet blocking it started to shake.

"Don't let them in!" Finn yelled. "Bix, take the other window. Bren, switch places with Kari! I need her and Missus Abramson holding the front door! Keep them blocked!"

The other window shattered, and Bren screamed when a bloody arm, withered and pasty in color, reached around the side of the coffee table. Black veins, like alien worms, bulged from the emaciated flesh, seeping blood the consistency of molasses from where the skin had peeled away.

"Don't let it touch you, Bix!"

"I'm immune, remember?" he cried back, but he ducked away anyway as the fingers raked the air before his eyes. He pressed his body against the broken table, pinning the Wraith's arm in place, then swung the table leg at the appendage. With a loud crack, the arm snapped just above the elbow. The Wraith shrieked and drew back, but it didn't give up. It pummeled at the table with renewed vigor, and even extended the mangled limb through the gap a second time.

Finn tore at the next floorboard, straining against the inflexible wood until, with an earsplitting screech, it yielded.

"You're wasting time!" Seth roared from his post by the other window. The cabinet was tilting inward beneath the weight of the Wraiths forcing their way in. They couldn't reach him yet, but they were gaining leverage. "Help me!" he pleaded.

"Finn!" Kari shouted. The tiny window at the top of the front door had broken, and a pair of hands reached in through the opening. The shards of glass still embedded within the frame sliced deep into the creatures' flesh. Blood oozed out in viscous runnels. Finn shouted at the two women to look out, and both leapt away to avoid the serum. No one knew if the blood was as contagious as the skin. Would a single droplet be enough to turn any of them into a killer?

Anyone except Bix, he reminded himself. *And maybe Mister Blakeley.*

He tried not to think about it. He couldn't ask his best friend or his father to engage them in hand-to-hand combat. They wouldn't last long against monsters that bit and clawed and had the strength and stamina of multiple men and an abnormal resistance to pain.

Besides, what if Bix's theory about immunity was wrong? What if they found out Mister Blakeley wasn't immune after it was too late?

They were losing ground fast. Barely ten minutes had passed since Adrian left them. They weren't going to last another five.

"Missus Abramson! Kari!" he yelled. "This way, now!"

"Don't do it!" Seth ordered his wife. "Kaleagh! Don't you go down there!"

Kari leapt across the room and pulled Bren from between Jonah and Harrison. "Go with your mother!" she said. "Now, Bren! It's the only chance we've got. We're too vulnerable up here."

"Hurry!" Finn shouted.

Bren slipped her legs into the opening. She gave Finn one last look before sliding off the boards and disappearing into the darkness beneath the house. Her mother soon followed.

"Bix!" Finn yelled. "Go!"

But before anyone else could move, there came a bloodcurdling scream from deep beneath the floor.

CHAPTER

FINN HAD NO TIME TO REACT BEFORE HE WAS THROWN backward by something bursting through the opening. It moved so quickly and so forcefully that several additional boards were dislodged and thrown into the air, showering them with dust and splinters.

The figure spun around and grabbed Finn, yanking him to his feet. "Hurry! Get down there now!"

"Eddie?" Finn sputtered, as he fell backward.

The man pulled Kari away from the door and directed her toward the hole in the floor. "Follow Bren and Kaleagh! You, too, Bix! Go!"

"But—"

"Now!" He grabbed two of the longer floorboard pieces and began to wedge them against the coffee table. "Hold these in place, Finn!"

Finn leapt to his feet, but Bix was already there to help him. Eddie scowled in annoyance, but didn't press the issue. He used the table leg and his foot to pound a small piece of the wood with several nails still embedded in it to the floor as an anchor to keep the wedges from moving.

"Now go, both of you! The rest of us will be right behind!"

"Where did you—"

"Stop talking and go! Follow the women!"

Bix practically dove into the opening head first. Finn followed, spinning around as soon as he hit the dirt. The drop was less than six feet, and he had to duck to see beneath the rafters.

"Over here," Bren called from the distance. "There's light!"

He saw a trio of silhouettes hurrying down what appeared to be a stone-lined tunnel extending beyond the walls of the house.

"Where does it lead?" Bix asked.

"I don't know, but go, follow Bren. She seems to know."

Finn waited near the floor opening, listening to all the shouting and running above him. Another pair of feet appeared beside his head, then Seth Abramson was through the hole. He stumbled on the uneven surface, but Finn steadied him. "That way."

Something heavy was dragged across the floor above, heading toward the back door. The only piece of furniture left was an entertainment console made of rough-hewn logs. The thing had to weigh a thousand pounds.

Harrison dropped into the hole, and Finn grabbed him by the shoulders and directed him toward the others.

"Where's Jonah?"

"He's coming."

"Don't wait, Finn!" Eddie roared from overhead. "Just go!"

There was more hammering, then the screech of wooden planks straining.

Jonah fell to the ground beside Finn and rolled nimbly to his feet. "Go! Eddie can't hold them off for long, Finn!"

"But—"

There was a crash, and several objects fell heavily to the floor.

Jonah shoved Finn forward, forcing him to run. They went as fast as they could, weaving between the support beams with their heads down until they reached the tunnel. Eddie's roars quickly faded. "Keep going," Jonah said.

Finn wanted to make sure Eddie would make it, but Jonah grabbed his sleeve and pulled him around. A final massive crash shook the house, sending dust fluttering down over them. The light coming through the hole in the floor was gone.

"What happened?"

They couldn't see anything behind them. It was pitch dark. Then, something started shuffling in their direction.

"Go!"

They reached the end of the tunnel a moment later, roughly eighty feet from where they'd entered it, and exited through a ragged hole torn through another wood-lined wall. Boards lay scattered on the floor.

The moment Finn staggered out, the smell hit him, and he was once more inside the underground room where Adrian had kept them locked up. The tunnel had been hidden beneath the stairs. Finn remembered trying to pry the wooden wall loose during his imprisonment, but he'd been too weak and lacked proper tools. Light spilled down from above.

A moan from a darkened corner drew their attention. Then a cough. The blaze of color on the stranger's head told them it was Red.

"Everyone be quiet," Eddie whispered, emerging from the tunnel. He went to the person on the floor and lifted him to his shoulder, then stepped nimbly across the room to the

wooden steps, despite the low ceiling and the bundle he carried. The stairs creaked beneath their combined weights.

"Absolute quiet," he whispered. Then he carefully pushed through, letting in a welcome rush of fresh air.

He kept the group in a tight huddle as they surfaced into the night. Around the corner of the shack, they could hear the Wraiths tearing at the walls of the house and making their way inside.

"We don't have much time," he whispered. "Those things are going to figure out where we are and how to get to us soon enough. We need to be gone."

"Why are we taking Red?" Seth asked. "We should just leave him behind. Let those things have him."

Eddie ignored him, except to tell him to keep quiet.

"The truck is in the clearing where the new barn burnt down. I disconnected the explosives. Finn and Bix should be able to show you where to go. There's also a portable tank of diesel and a pump, but it's manual. Harrison and Jonah, see what you can do about getting some of that fuel transferred over."

He turned and thrust Red's slumped form into Seth's arms. "You carry him. Keep him quiet. And don't let him out of his bindings."

He checked the gag to make sure it was snug, then nodded in satisfaction.

"Now, whatever happens, you need to be on that truck and heading out of here in less than ten minutes. Be as quiet as possible. And keep out of sight of the house until you do. If even one of those things sees you, it's over."

"Where are you going?" Seth asked. He turned to Harrison. "Where's he going?"

No one answered.

"Come on," Bix whispered. "The clearing's near the lake. It's a two-minute jog, which leaves us less than eight to gas up."

"Why don't we just take the rowboats? That was the original plan, wasn't it?"

"Dock's blown up," Kari reminded him. "Boats are gone. Now shut up and follow orders for once, Seth."

"I followed orders!"

"Keep it down," Finn whispered.

They made their way to the road, each of them pausing to glance over to the house. They could still hear the growls and moans of the deadly creatures crawling around inside, interspersed with the sounds of tearing fabric and breaking wood and glass.

Once at the truck, Seth dropped the still unconscious Red onto the ground, and it was up to Finn and Bix to help lift his dead weight in back. Bren and her mother pulled him toward the front of the bed by his boots.

"I'll drive," Bix told them. "I've already crashed the gate once." No one argued.

Jonah and Harrison struggled to figure out how to draw the diesel out of the tank. There was no hose, and the pump leaked like a sieve. "Get a bucket," he told Finn, when he asked if they needed help. "Or something to hold the fuel. Buckets, bottles, whatever. And a funnel, if you can find one."

A few minutes later, they had the valve open. The bucket quickly filled. Jonah snatched it away and Finn slipped another in its place.

"We need to go!" Seth said, appearing beside them after the third bucket. They had only managed to get a dozen or so gallons into the tank. Most of it had spilled onto the ground. "It's already been fifteen minutes."

"Just a few more buckets," Finn said.

"No, Seth's right," Eddie said, once more appearing out of the darkness with the stealth of a Wraith. His forehead glistened with sweat, and he seemed out of breath. "I told you ten. They're coming. They're almost here."

He grabbed the half-filled bucket and handed it to Seth. Then he reached into his pocket. "Leave the valve open, Harrison. Let it drain onto the ground. You ride up front with Bix. The rest of us will be in back."

The engine roared to life as Finn climbed in. Eddie slapped the side to let them know to go, then followed as the truck began to circle around for the road. He tossed a lit match onto the grass, and the puddle lit up. The flames crawled over the ground, then leapt high into the sky, spreading and scorching what little combustible fuel remained in the woods. The fire drew the Wraiths away from them, though it wouldn't hold their attention for long.

"Faster!" they heard Harrison shout to his son. The tires hit the road, spraying gravel. A moment later, an explosion lit up the night, raining splinters and metal and body parts all around.

The truck bounced over the uneven surface. In the dim red glow of the lone working taillight, Finn saw the crushed body of a Wraith, its abdomen broken open by the truck and its guts splattered about in a wide swath. It struggled to get back up, but was hindered by a broken spine.

Eddie reached over and smashed the other taillight, extinguishing the view.

They saw more of the creatures, some chasing after them, some lying motionless in the road, their bodies flattened beneath the tires of the truck.

Then, the moment they reached the long straightaway at the end of the drive, Bix shouted to hold onto something. But there was no crash. The gate zipped past, its temporary barriers already flung aside by Adrian and his men in their hurry to escape.

One final figure stepped into the roadway behind them, its face a bloody mask of horror and the front of its shirt stained crimson.

It was Jackson, and he gripped Roy's head in his hand by the hair. Roy's severed gullet glistened underneath, dripping gore. The thing that was once Jackson dropped the gory object and gave chase, but it soon fell behind, vanishing in the cloud of smoke and dust.

Apparently, Adrian had no more use for the men.

"Once you get to the main road, head south," Eddie shouted up to Bix, who tooted the horn in reply.

They finally emerged from the trees and the sky opened up overhead. Finn turned to Eddie to thank him. "But why are we bringing Red along?" he asked, repeating Seth's earlier query.

"Because he knows where Adrian's going. We find him, we find your brother."

CHAPTER

"I DEMAND THAT YOU TELL ME ABOUT THIS DEVICE that incapacitates the Wraiths!" Seth said. "Where did you get it? What does it look like? How does it work?"

Eddie looked over. He had been leaning against the tailgate, watching the dark road behind them to make sure no one, or nothing, was following.

As soon as they were out of the trees, a cold wind buffeted the truck, slipping in beneath the bottom of the canvas and around the sides, so they'd switched places with the women, giving them the heater in the cab and taking it upon themselves to guard Red in the back.

Eddie got up and went over to where the others were huddled together for warmth near the front.

"I think what happened to me back there," he began, "when I lost conscious—"

"I asked a question! Tell me about this device!"

"That's what I'm trying to tell you, Seth," Eddie said. "Ever since we arrived at the compound, I'd been experiencing these odd symptoms— periods of weakness, inability to see or hear as well as usual."

"I don't think usual is how I'd describe your abilities," Bix mumbled.

"It started when we first arrived. I thought it was the nanites in my body beginning to fail."

"They don't fail!"

"Wait," Finn told Seth, pushing him back. "Are you talking about back there near the generator shack?"

Eddie nodded. "I think these devices affect me like they do the Wraiths."

"You're sure? It might be your abilities fading."

"No. It's the device."

"Dammit! What device? What does it look like?" Seth asked again.

Jonah held up a hand. "How do you know, Eddie?"

"I was in the woods when you all made it inside the house. I knew I couldn't get in the front, so I circled around back and managed to get onto the roof. I was worried about possible weak spots. But then it hit me again, just like before. I was paralyzed. Thankfully, so were the Wraiths."

"That must've been when Adrian turned it on the first time. I think we heard you up there."

"Felt like every cell in my body was trying to separate from every other cell. I was totally incapacitated. I don't know how much time passed, but all of a sudden it was gone again and I could move."

"The battery?" Bix asked.

"Wouldn't have died that abruptly. No, this was instantaneous, like it had been disconnected. Snapped me right out of the paralysis. I got out of there, and was lucky I did, as it must've been rectivated somehow."

"Adrian was sitting on the duffle. He was messing with our heads," Harrison said, "turning the device on and off, ratcheting up our fear."

"To what end?" Eddie asked.

"Turns out he was fishing for information. He wanted to know how much we knew about the other bunkers and the cure. And he was searching for the phone."

"He didn't get it, did he?"

"Yeah."

"That's another thing you need to tell me," Seth interjected. "Where did this phone come from?"

"The man who showed up at our bunker, Mister Williams," Finn replied impatiently. He turned back to Eddie. "But how—"

"No. Answer my questions!"

Finn sighed. "Williams showed up again after we got out. The Wraiths were after us. He was infected, but before he turned, he gave me the phone. He thought I was Harper."

"And this incapacitating device?"

"Adrian had them— *has* them. They mess up the Wraiths, turns them off or something. He's been using them to protect the compound. I stole one when I escaped the last time. Jonah and Mister Blakeley had it with them when they were drawing the guards away from the house, for protection in case of Wraiths."

"Adrian confiscated it, then remembered and used it to his advantage," Jonah growled. "Stupid of me to forget about it."

"And there's more?" Seth asked.

Finn nodded. "Adrian had them all over the compound."

"Except I overheard the guards say the fire destroyed about half of them," Harrison said. "They relocated the working ones to the perimeter of the compound."

"That would explain why I was able to move about on the road," Eddie noted. "There must be some sort of threshold signal strength that triggers the effect. I just happened to cross the barrier back there."

"It's a very sharp boundary," Harrison acknowledged. "The Wraith on the road charged us, but once it got within about twenty feet, it just collapsed."

"These devices," Finn said, finally turning to Seth to explain, "Adrian never said where he got them. And he didn't know how they work."

Seth stared at him for a moment, then looked at Eddie. "And it affects you the same way it does the Wraiths?"

"I don't know if it's exactly the same mechanism. All I can say is it completely saps all my strength."

"But no one else?"

"Not as far as we know," Finn said. "Certainly no one else in the house was affected."

Seth sat back, scratching his temple and muttering to himself. At last, he shook his head. "It's called resonance uncoupling."

"Raisinets what?" Bix asked. "What do dried grapes and chocolate have to do with this?"

"Resonance uncoupling," Seth repeated. "It's something I was told was discovered in the early design and pro-gramming of the nanites, a flaw. A specific high frequency radio signal that interferes with the function of the nanites inside the body. They tried to exploit the phenomenon — as anesthesia, for motor control, behavior modification, etcetera — but I heard rumors it was too big of a vulnerability, so engineers were brought in to patch later iterations, ones which were intended to be distributed to the general population."

"Well, then somebody dropped the ball, then."

"What the hell is he saying," Bix said. "Sounds like gibber jabberwocky to me."

"I'm saying it shouldn't happen to Eddie or anyone else, even the Wraiths." He turned to Eddie. "I was assured the uncoupling flaw was repaired."

"If it affects Eddie like the Wraiths, does it mean he's infectious, too?" Bix asked.

Mister Abramson didn't answer.

"What exactly does this mean, Seth?" Eddie asked.

"I don't exactly know yet. I need to think about this. I came onto the project afterward, and it's been years since I've even given RU a second thought."

Finn shook his head. He was still trying to wrap his head around it, too. "We know that the nanites in Eddie's blood are responsible for saving his life after the accident in the bunker. Is it possible that activating them also triggered some kind of change in their programming that made them vulnerable to this resonating thing?"

"Raisinets," Bix corrected.

"I'm telling you, it's not supposed to happen!"

"And yet it is," Eddie said. "Okay, here's another question for you: Can we use this to our advantage?"

"Yeah," said Finn. "Like, can we make more of the in-capacitating devices?"

Seth shook his head. "I don't know anything about RU from a technical standpoint. The frequency was a closely held secret. But if I'm correct, then what Eddie is alluding to goes much farther than just stopping the Wraiths."

"And what's that?"

Seth glanced around at them. They could barely see each other in the darkness, but there was an unmistakable note of excitement in his voice: "It might be the key to reprogramming the nanites."

"Is you saying what I think you're saying?" Bix asked.

Seth nodded. "Yeah, it makes the possibility of a cure that much more likely."

CHAPTER

RED FINALLY REGAINED CONSCIOUSNESS, GROANING and rubbing his neck and giving them all resentful looks. At least until he learned what had befallen his comrades after Adrian ditched them to fend for themselves. But even then he didn't seem very grateful.

"I may have hit him a bit too hard," Eddie admitted.

"Why south?" Finn asked him. "How do we know you're telling the truth and not sending us on some wild goose chase?"

"He better be telling the truth," Bix said, "or we'll take him back to his friends."

Red's face visibly blanched.

They had stopped at the top of a gentle rise that afforded them clear views all around and were trying to decide what to do next. The sun was coming up, turning the sky behind them a pale black-blue, but the horizon ahead was still cloaked in darkness. They were all hungry and tired. And they had no proof they were even on Adrian's trail anymore, although Kari noticed that the weeds growing out of the cracks in the middle of the road showed signs of tire damage.

"All Red gave me before I conked him was south," Eddie said, turning solemnly to Finn. " 'Due south.' That's what he said."

Finn wandered over to Red, who was sitting against one of the truck tires, still tied up, and grabbed his shirt. "You better start talking! Where's Adrian going? Where's my brother? South doesn't mean anything! You need to be more specific!"

"South," Red repeated, coughing. "All I know is what I heard him telling the others before that monst— Before he grabbed me." He pointed at Eddie.

Bix stepped forward, raising his fist to strike the man, but Finn stopped him.

"And what else did he say?"

"Something about a church, some place of worship or something. Said it was where he growed up."

A church? Finn frowned. That could mean anything, especially when it came to Father Adrian. He threw religious terms around carelessly, using them to couch his demented ideas with a sense of legitimacy. And south wasn't very helpful.

"You remember what Jennifer told us," Bix said. "After they left the Wal-Mart they'd been trapped in, they headed due north by car for a couple weeks before finding the compound."

"So, we're talking about anywhere from a couple hundred miles to the southern tip of South America," Finn said. "We don't know how fast they were driving or how often they stopped. Doesn't narrow it down much."

"Let's start with what we know," Harrison said. "Due south of us is Idaho. Below that are Nevada and Utah."

Finn growled in frustration. "And south of them is . . . ."

"Oklahoma, Texas, Mexico," Bix rattled off. He frowned at Jonah's eye roll. "What's your problem?"

"You never said you were a geography bee champion. You've been holding out on us!"

"It was in third grade! And what of it? Besides, I happened to spend a lot of time navigating for Dad when he was playing gigs."

"You're just full of surprises, Blackeye," Jonah teased.

"Focus, you two," Finn said. He turned back to Red and nodded for him to continue.

"Adrian said they'd need enough goods to trade for fuel, since they'd have to stop twice."

"Well, that's a start," Jonah said. "Given the typical range for a van, maybe four hundred miles on a full tank, we've now got a better idea how far he's going."

"Still a lot of uncertainty," Harrison noted. "We could be looking at anywhere between five hundred miles and well over a thousand, depending on if they started off with a full tank or not."

"Where's he going to refuel?"

"There's a storage depot in Utah."

"Utah's out of range. Where in Utah?"

"Missoula. It's underground, so the diesel won't freeze. Most people around these parts know about it."

"Missoula's in Montana, not Utah," Jonah pointed out. "And that's in range."

"You should know," Red continued, "Missoula is run by a rough group of people. They mostly won't mess with you bad if'n you can pay their price, but it can get pretty steep, depending on their mood."

"How steep? What do they take in exchange?"

"Anything useful— food, ammo, guns." His eyes went to the front of the truck. "Women."

"No way," Seth said. "We're not going there."

"Then we'll need to bring something else they want," Finn said.

"Where the hell are we going to get anything here? No matter where we go, it's all been picked over."

Bix nodded. "We had a hard time finding anything after we escaped the last time. That is, unless they want pink Hello Kitty pajamas, then I know where we can get a ton of those." He winked at Finn, who ignored him.

"We'll find something along the way."

"Or we could go back to the bunker. There's still a lot of food stores there," Jonah said.

"No, that'll take too long." Finn turned back to Red. "Where's the second fuel stop south of Missoula?"

"That would be in Pocatello." He paused and glanced at Jonah. "Montana, right?"

"Idaho," Bix offered.

"Due south of that is Salt Lake City," muttered Harrison. "There's a church there. You may have heard of it."

"Big ass one," Bix agreed.

"Language, son."

"Really, Dad?"

Finn growled impatiently. "You mean the Mormon Temple?"

Harrison nodded.

Finn turned to Red. "Could that be it? Is he talking about the Mormon Temple?"

Red shrugged. "He said it was a big place, big enough to hold hundreds of people in it. Said it was where he was inspired to preach."

"At the Mormon Temple?" Bix said, dubiously. "I'm not so sure that's the place then."

Finn shushed him. "Red, have you been to Salt Lake City since the Flense? Do you think that's where Adrian is going?"

Despite the dim predawn light, Finn clearly saw Red's face pale.

"I been there," he said, haltingly. "Never wanna go back."

"Why?"

"It's the same with any big city. You wanna stay out of them. They're full of ferals. Going to one of them is like walking naked into one of Father Adrian's cages. Ain't no way to protect yourself."

"Then that's where he's taken Harper," Finn said. "He knows the risks. He also knows he'll be safe as long as he's got one of those devices with him."

"He might have one, but we don't," Jonah pointed out. "We should've grabbed one while we had the chance."

"We can go back," Seth said.

"I said we're not!" Finn snapped. "Forward only. We can catch him before he gets there."

"You're guessing that's where he went, Finn," Jonah said. "We could be driving all the way there, only to find out we totally guessed wrong. And you heard what Red said—any densely populated area before the Flense is now going to be crawling with Wraiths."

"Harper's there. I can feel it. That's where Adrian is going, so that's where we're going, too."

Eddie shook his head. "Assuming you're right—"

"I am."

"Assuming that's Adrian's destination, we still have a big problem. We're not going to reach the fuel stop in Missoula before we run out of diesel. Tank's down to about an eighth. We might have another hundred miles at the most. Maybe one-twenty. And we're talking really mountainous terrain with questionable roads. That's going to eat up time and diesel. And the truck's in questionable shape."

"Then we need to keep our eyes out for another vehicle."

"The truck's the best thing for a drive like this," Jonah said. "Roads through the mountains are going to be in terrible condition. There'll be blockages, washouts, that sort of thing. The truck's high carriage will be an asset."

"And Adrian's in a cargo van," Finn noted. "As long as we're on his trail, we may not even need to reach Missoula. We could catch up to him long before then. Once we do, we'll have a better chance of getting to Harper. Besides, we can siphon fuel out of other vehicles along the way, can't we?"

Jonah pursed his lips. "Don't count on it."

"Why?"

"Well, for one, we'll be lucky to even find other diesel burners."

"Well, it's probably a two-day drive to Salt Lake City," Bix said, and headed for the back of the truck. "Adrian's going to need to sleep at some point. I suggest we do the same while we can."

CHAPTER

"WELCOME TO THE UNITED STATES OF THE FLENSE," Finn muttered gloomily at Mister Blakeley as they passed the NOW LEAVING CANADA, COME BACK SOON sign shortly after switching drivers again and approached a shallow rise.

The road they were on funneled them toward a now-defunct inspection station with both sides bordered by vertical walls of rough hewn rock.

"Land of the infected and home of the insane. Where killers and cannibals roam . . . ."

"I think you're mixing up two different songs," Harrison said.

Finn let it go. It saddened him that the country he had once known was forever gone, replaced by something that made even less sense than it had before. There were no laws to follow or break anymore, no social norms to abide. It was like the Wild West, except the sheriff had been killed and everyone was a bad guy.

Harrison looked over in sympathy. "Keep your chin up. We'll—"

Finn threw his hands up to the dashboard and screamed, "Stop!"

Harrison slammed on the brakes, sending the truck into a skid. About a quarter mile ahead stood the gates to the inspection station, but the road immediately in front was blocked by an immense pine tree that had fallen over. The tires slipped on years of accumulated leaf debris, sending them skidding sideways toward the obstacle.

"Oh, shit!" Finn yelled, and leaned away. "Get down in back! We're going to hit!"

Several cries of alarm rose from the bed.

Harrison spun the wheel, but the tires locked. The tree rose up toward them, its shattered branches appearing as sharp as spears. The tires jittered over the road, and for a moment it looked like they would stop. But then they hit a slick patch and the next moment were engulfed within the branches of the felled pine. They snapped against the metal sides of the truck. They tore into the canvas in back. One of the limbs entered Finn's half-open window, piercing halfway across the cab. Side branches snapped off against the glass and frame, showering him with pine needles and splinters.

"You okay, Finn?"

He looked over and saw that the side of Harrison's face was covered in blood, but they were only scratches. He wasn't seriously injured. "Yeah, you?"

He nodded, then jumped out of the truck to check those in back.

Finn took in a deep breath and extended a shaky hand to the branch. Six inches closer and the thing would have decapitated him. He brushed himself off, then slid over to the driver's side and tumbled weakly onto the road.

"Everyone okay?" Harrison shouted.

"We're all right," Bren replied. "What happened?"

They piled out, including Red, whose hands were still bound, even though there was nowhere for him to run to and no reason to escape. He was safer with them than on his own.

The canvas had been punctured in several places, but thankfully the truck itself did not appear to have sustained serious damage.

"Can we move?"

"Not until we clear some of these branches out of the way," Harrison said, after a quick survey.

"And how are we going to do that? Can we break them off?"

Harrison shook his head.

"How about pulling the tree trunk away?"

Another shake. He pointed at the top of the wall beside the road where the tree had been uprooted, some twenty or thirty feet up. The ground was torn and several large rocks had tumbled down onto the shoulder. "The trunk is too heavy. And the top is wedged tight against the wall on the other side."

"If we can't get through, then Adrian couldn't either," Seth said.

Jonah rejoined the group. His hands were muddy, and the skin on his arms and face was covered in scratches. "This is a fresh fall, not even an hour old. Maybe as little as ten minutes. There's still worms on the exposed roots and the dirt is wet."

"Meaning?"

"Meaning I think Adrian brought it down," Jonah said. "There's skid marks on the other side of the road and some deep ruts in the softer earth on the shoulder. I think he may have used the van to pull the tree down. Probably didn't take much. The thing was perched right on the edge of the cliff. And that oil slick behind us isn't natural."

"That means he knows we're tracking him."

"Knows or suspects."

"That's good news then!" Finn said. "We need to figure out how to get past this!" He jogged around to the other side of the truck. Several limbs as thick as his upper arms were wedged underneath the carriage between the axles, and the one in the cab was a good three inches in diameter. "We have to cut these branches."

"And then what?" Kari asked. "We still won't be able to get past the trunk."

"I think I saw a utility road," Harrison said. "Maybe a quarter mile back. There was a chain on the ground and a sign that said authorized vehicles only. It might have once been an administrative road servicing the staff here, since it's so remote. Might even have a maintenance garage. At the very least, it might allow us to bypass this mess."

"I'll check it out," Jonah offered.

"Be careful."

Kari handed him the Ruger. "It's ready to go," she said. "You've got six rounds loaded." She handed him the rest, which he pocketed. "If you get into any trouble, whistle and we'll come running."

He nodded and jogged back up the road.

"Dammit," Bix growled unhappily a second and a half later. "Somebody's got to watch his back." And he took off after him.

They used the knives to hack at the branches, cutting notches close to the main trunk until Eddie could snap them off. It was slow going, but a half hour in they were finally able to extract the truck. Harrison moved it away so they could get a better look at the obstacle. With a clearer view, it just became all the more apparent moving it would be impossible with the equipment they had.

"Hey, guys! Up here!" Jonah's whistle echoed through the cut, drawing their attention to the top of the cliff. He pointed back up the road. "There might be a way through ahead. Back the truck up. I'll meet you where it joins up."

He disappeared from sight. The rest of the group loaded up and they drove to where Jonah was already waiting for them.

"Use the truck to break off this DO NOT ENTER sign," he shouted up to Harrison's window. "We'll need it to wedge beneath some rocks in the way."

Finn jumped out of the cab and joined Jonah on the side. "Where's Bix?"

"Went ahead to check for supplies. Mister Blakeley was right, there's a couple of buildings up ahead."

"I thought he was watching your back."

"I don't need anyone watching my back," Jonah snapped. "Certainly not him!"

They walked up the incline ahead of the truck until they reached the first boulder. "If we can't move the tree, how do you expect us to be able to move this thing?" Finn asked.

"With leverage and a little momentum. It's pretty round. And you can see how far it rolled to get here." He pointed about thirty feet up the road.

Using the broken sign post, Eddie and Harrison were able to lever underneath the boulder enough to rock it, but it had sunk into the softer earth. It took them another ten minutes to dig out the downhill side before they were able to move it away.

The remaining boulders from the rock fall were smaller and more easily shifted.

At last they were able to drive the truck past the obstruction and down to a small compound of buildings. Bix emerged to meet them, waving excitedly.

"Looks like Adrian might've done us a favor by knocking that tree down," he said.

"What do you mean?"

He held up a tin can with a faded label. "We've got food — okay, it's not the best stuff in the world. Okay, so it's asparagus, but right now I'm so hungry I'd eat anything. There's also drinking water, and ... check this out." He pulled an orange pistol from behind his back. "Flare guns."

"Great, but we need fuel."

"Then you'll want to check over there." He pointed to a white tank in the far back corner of the lot. "I think it's full."

CHAPTER

"YEAH, IT'S FUEL ALL RIGHT," JONAH SAID, "AND there's a lot of it. It's just not the right kind."

"What do you mean? The label says gasoline."

"And the truck runs on diesel."

"I never really understood the difference," Finn said. "Why can't you run gasoline in a diesel engine?"

"Gas is a lot leaner, much lower in aromatic compounds. Oils," he added, when he saw the blank look on Finn's face. "Gas requires higher temperatures, so it burns less efficiently in a diesel engine. You can put gasoline in, but you'll end up with very little power, *if* it ignites at all. Most of the gas will pass through unburned, then ignite once it comes into contact with the hot surfaces in the exhaust system."

"How do you know that?"

"From hanging out with my brother. He knew just about everything there is about cars and engines. Of course, my dad wasn't too pleased how he chose to apply that knowledge, especially after the shop got raided by the cops. And he wasn't happy about me spending so much time there." He gave Finn a wry grin. "Which is probably why I did."

Finn slowly scanned the compound for other options, but the only other vehicle in sight was a forklift. "There may be some diesel inside the tank there," he said. "Looks like it might hold fifteen gallons. If we're lucky, it'll be full."

Once more, Jonah frowned. But he shrugged and followed Finn over.

The piece of rebar he stuck into the opening hit the bottom with a muffled *thunk*, and when he withdrew it, a thick, brown gelatinous goo dripped off. "No good. It's waxed up from the cold, just as I feared. And the reason it's brown is from rust. Diesel absorbs water."

They checked the sheds and found a portable generator, but this time the fuel tank was bone dry.

Harrison reported that the group was loading food from the kitchen into the truck— packages of rice, canned goods, anything that was still edible that hadn't been eaten by mice. "A good amount of it is ruined," he said, "but there's enough to hold us and perhaps trade for some fuel once we get to Missoula. Did you find any fuel?"

Jonah and Finn exchanged glances. "No diesel. And unless we find a car that can run on gasoline, we're out of luck."

"We haven't seen any cars here, but there are a couple large tanks behind the kitchen you should check out. They look like they might hold fuel."

"With our luck, it'll be something useless like propane or natural gas," Finn moaned.

"We might get lucky."

They headed over, passing the rest of the group who were still sorting through the foodstuffs. Bix handed them each a bag of stale potato chips and bottles of water, which they quickly polished off.

Walking through the empty dining area felt strange. The staff had abandoned the place in a hurry, leaving chairs overturned and meals half eaten. The remains, long since petrified, sat on plates and tables coated with dust. But the fixtures still gleamed in the unlit room.

The kitchen was in a similar state— tidiness teetering perpetually on the edge of chaos. Bix looked up from where he was loading knives into a large cooking pot for easy carrying. Bren was adding other objects into an old wooden fruit crate— boxes of matches, soap, rags, pots and pans and dishes.

They passed a large metal grill, to which a faint rancid smell clung. "Old cooking oil," Harrison said, scrunching his nose. There's a couple drums of it in there, ready for recycling. Don't make the same mistake I did and open one."

He pointed to a side room, which contained several large trash bins, as well as a number of white plastic drums through which a dark brownish liquid could be seen. A stack of empty five-gallon paint buckets occupied one corner.

"We'll grab a few of those," Jonah said. "They'll come in handy."

Down a short hall from the walk-in freezer, which he advised them not to enter unless they wanted to lose whatever food they'd eaten, they came to an exit. It appeared to have been kicked in recently. The wood was freshly splintered. The floor was covered in a thin layer of dust, through which two pairs of tracks could be seen.

"Ours," Harrison explained. "Eddie broke the door."

Once more they were outside, although within a protected enclosure bounded by a high trellis. A tattered umbrella stood over a picnic table, shredded bits of sun-rotted fabric still clinging to the wires. At the far end, near a large wooden gate, were three more tanks, each approximately a hundred gallons in size.

"Vegetable oil," Finn read, swiping away the dirt caked on the surface of the first tank. "Seems they ate a lot of deep fried food here." He rapped on the side with his knuckles. "Sounds empty."

"Propane in this one," Harrison said. "Also empty. Jonah, any luck? Please tell me it's diesel."

Jonah looked up with a quirky grin on his lips. "Not diesel, but that's actually a good thing, since it'd be gelled up and no good anyway."

"Then what is it?"

"Kerosene."

* * *

"You sure this is going to work?" Seth asked. "I know diesel engines are fussy. That's why I never bought one myself. Accidentally put the wrong fuel in and you've got yourself a massive repair bill."

"It'll work," Jonah said sharply.

He pushed the man out of the way as he hefted the two half-filled five-gallon buckets of kerosene and carried them inside. It was obvious the man resented the fact that Jonah had a possible solution to their dilemma, while he could do nothing but stand around and offer insights that were both useless and inaccurate. The man may have been a high-paid engineer in the tech industry at one time and probably had a catalog of degrees and certifications under his belt, but he didn't know crap about alternative fuel engines.

"What are you going to do with that?" Seth asked, trailing him. "Will kerosene work in the truck?"

"No," Jonah said, relishing the man's ignorance.

With the search completed and anything useful loaded up, the rest of the group was now curious to see what Jonah was planning. He hadn't said more than a word or two, and it was driving Seth crazy.

"Okay, pay attention," he told them as he turned into the room with the trashcans and set the buckets onto the floor. He glanced over at the others huddled in the hallway. "Listen up, guys. I need you to follow my instructions to the letter. Do that, and we'll be back on the road in ten minutes with a full fuel tank. We're going to need at least eighty gallons of this mixture. About twenty full buckets."

He went over to the first drum of waste cooking oil and opened it up. A rancid smell immediately swept through the room, bringing tears to their eyes. A few of them buried their noses in the crook of their elbows and gagged.

"Carefully skim off any solid scum layer, then add about one and a half gallons of the waste oil to three gallons of kerosene. Mix it well."

"That'll work?" Bren asked, incredulous.

"Kerosene is also known as diesel number one. It's sometimes added to the fuel in diesel engines to help prevent gelling at low temps because, like gasoline, it's leaner in regards to the amount of aromatics it contains, though not quite as lean as gasoline. It also burns drier and produces less power than diesel, but it'll give us enough to get us where we need to go. Straight kerosene will eventually ruin a diesel engine, since it doesn't provide the necessary amount of lubrication. That's what the vegetable oil is for."

He straightened up and wiped the sweat from his forehead with his sleeve. "Mix it in at a one-to-two or one-to-three ratio with the kerosene. There should be enough here, just be careful not to stir up the solids on the bottom, or else we'll clog the lines. Then bring it out to me so I can filter it."

Twenty minutes later they were back in the truck and heading out through the opposite gate they had come in. Harrison was behind the wheel again, but this time with Jonah in the seat beside him to listen for problems with the engine.

They'd barely gone a hundred feet, when the truck skidded to a stop on the steep downslope.

"What's the matter?" Finn called up to the front. He stuck his head out through one of the holes in the canvas.

"Road's blocked."

They got out to find a weathered forest-green Ford Explorer with government plates some hundred yards before the path rejoined the main road. A thick chain lay in the dirt, plastered into the dried mud. The utility vehicle sat on four flat tires, and its driver's side door was flung open. Grass grew out of the cracks in the faux leather on the front seat. A purse lay on the floor, its contents strewn around it.

"Barrier spikes," Jonah said, pointing to the retractable metal teeth half hidden in the weeds beyond the vehicle. "I noticed a set on the other side, too, but they were buried in mud and gravel. Those things'll shred your tires if you're going the wrong way, just like they did to this guy."

"Good thing we're going the right way then. Can we push this wreck aside?"

"Shouldn't be a problem."

"Well, this explains why the buildings back there weren't ransacked," Harrison noted. "With both ends of the road blocked, who's going to bother checking out what's beyond?"

"That's not the only reason," Bix said. He was standing by the drainage ditch beside the car. He leaned forward and swept the tall grasses aside with his arm, revealing a pair of skeletons, the bones bleached white. One was small enough to be a child; the other had a few golden strands of long hair still clinging to the grinning skull. The surfaces of the bones bore clear signs of having been gnawed by human teeth.

CHAPTER

"MISSOULA."

They topped a long gradual rise and came to a stop, the engine idling noisily and spewing black smoke that smelled like rotten potatoes and fish. The city opened up beneath them, a sprawling, mostly treeless expanse of low houses and squat, colorless buildings in a shallow desert pan, the sky a desolate lid of sooty clouds. It had rained heavily earlier, and puddles still covered the ground. The wind was bitingly cold, and the air stunk of ozone.

Nothing moved. They saw no smoke, no evidence of life. Nothing seemed to grow except for scrub, which was either one shade of brown or another.

"Lovely," Eddie grumbled, and reached around to slap the window at the back of the cab to alert the others.

"Where now?" Finn asked Red on the seat beside him.

The man was still bound, a length of rope between his ankles limiting his freedom. He had made no attempt to escape, but now that they were near any semblance of civilization, the group wanted to make sure he wouldn't disappear on them.

He lifted both hands and gestured through the windshield to a spot along the western edge of town, way off to the right. "See them tanks? There."

"Defenses?"

"Armed guards. But don't act stupid and everything will be fine. With what you got, shouldn't be any problem to trade for fuel."

"You saw what we got back there. What do you think we should offer for a full tank?"

"Start with the food and don't mention the women. They'll probably have enough of the first, but none of the second."

Finn studied the man's face for a long moment to see if he was hiding anything. At last, he nodded to Eddie, who stepped out to talk with the others. When he was finished, he climbed back in, shifted, and began the descent into town.

"How many people should we expect?"

Red shrugged. "Don't know. Been a while since I been down this way. Used to be a couple hundred, maybe. Most of them don't do much. Started off with a fenced-in community, even a little garden like at the army base. Within a year, they cleared the city of ferals, mostly by burning them out. But I heard there was an outbreak since then." He frowned in concentration. "Last year? Or maybe it was this year. I can't remember exactly. It was right after the first thaw, and it took out a lot of men."

Finn wondered what the Wraiths did during the winter. Did they hibernate? Did they travel south? How did they survive the cold weather? How did they manage when there was so little food for them to eat?

Did they prey on each other?

A wolf emerged from between two buildings a couple blocks ahead and turned toward them, making its way down the center of the road at a leisurely jog. It seemed completely unconcerned that a massive, loud, stinky monster was approaching it. The fur around its snout was stained dark red, and more red dripped from the fur on its neck and flank.

"Well, that's certainly something," Eddie said.

Finn shivered at the sight. He raised his pistol, but before they could get any closer, the animal veered off between some houses. It was gone when they passed the spot.

"Engine light just came on," Eddie said.

Finn leaned over to check. "Are we out of fuel already?"

Eddie shook his head. "No, we're actually doing fairly well. Temp's a little high, and oil pressure's good. I don't know what it could be."

"Jonah might."

"We'll have to ask him afterward." He glanced over, but Finn was staring intently out the windshield, as if he expected the wolf to reappear.

They continued down the road, moving at a cautious fifteen miles an hour. The surface was littered with rocks and tumbleweed and trash. The bitter wind they had felt at the top of the rise was tempered somewhat down here amongst the buildings, but every so often a gust would turn the corner ahead and rush at them like a ghost with a grudge. The chill was yet another reminder that winter was coming.

Eddie rolled his window further down and stuck his nose out and sniffed the air.

"What do you smell?"

"Gasoline," he said. "It's pretty strong. Human waste, mostly old. And . . . ."

"And what?"

He shook his head. "We're too far away."

The storage tanks grew ever larger as they erased the last half mile separating them. And still no one had come out to meet them.

"Entrance is up ahead," Red said. He seemed troubled by the silence and lack of welcome. "The road curves right, but the gate'll be on the left. Someone should be there, waiting."

"You said a couple hundred people live here?" Finn said. "Where are they?"

Red's frown deepened.

"Something's not right," Eddie said. He stopped the truck and let it idle.

"Everything okay?" Harrison asked, shouting through the glass at the back of the cab. Propped between his knees, the end of the barrel just visible through the window, was an AR-15, one of two found tucked behind the back seat of the ranger vehicle, along with a pair of 9mm pistols and ammunition for both, all safely secured inside locked black plastic cases. To say it was a lucky find was an understatement. Not only could they now defend themselves, they also could trade the weapons for fuel, if it came down to it.

For now, however, they were locked and loaded and in the hands of capable shooters.

"Eddie?" Harrison called.

Finn turned around. Bix's face appeared in the opening, similarly querulous.

Eddie held up a hand to quiet them, then shut the engine off. After it stuttered reluctantly to a stop, all was quiet save the ticking of the engine.

"You hear something?" Finn asked.

Eddie's face was as still and hard as stone. At last, he shook his head. "Not really."

"Smell?"

"Just gasoline." He shrugged and looked over. "Which I would expect. I just— I don't know. Wouldn't expect it to be so strong."

"Might be one of the tanks has a leak," Red noted.

Finn nodded. "Or a spill. Should we drive closer? Or should we go the rest of the way on foot?"

"No, we stay with the truck. Safer that way, especially with wolves on the prowl."

He stuck his head out the window again and waited. Once more, he shook his head. "Just paranoid, I guess."

He restarted the engine and put it into gear. A cloud of black smoke belched out of the exhaust and swept over the windshield from the top of the cab, momentarily blinding them. But the wind soon shifted and the view cleared.

They came to the curve, and the scene opened up to their left. The storage yard was a massive cement pad. A trio of tanks rose at the far end, streaks of rust bleeding down from the top. The steel staircases spiraling up around the outsides were likewise rusting.

"Not surprised there's leaks," Finn said, gazing up at the top of the nearest tank. "How about we agree that no one lights up a smoke, okay?"

Eddie sniffed.

"There. Gate's open."

Once more, Eddie let the truck roll to a stop. No one came out to greet them.

"This is all wrong."

This time, it was Red who spoke the words. He leaned forward and stared out into the yard, alarm written all over his face. "They shoulda had someone here by now. They wouldn't just leave it open like that."

"You said there was an outbreak," Finn said, curling his fingers around the grip of Kari's Ruger. He scanned for signs of Wraiths. "Maybe they're all dead."

Eddie slowly edged the vehicle into the compound, all the while sniffing the air himself and listening intently for any sound he could hear over the rumble of the engine.

They approached the first tank without incident and passed it, their tires making sticky sounds on the wet surface. A flurry of movement off to the right in the shadows caught Finn's eye and he jerked his head around. But he was too slow. Whatever had been there, was gone.

"More wolves," Eddie said. He nodded toward the mirror on Finn's side. The pack was running away from them, a half dozen animals the color of shadows and concrete.

"If they're in here, it's probably safe to say the place is abandoned," Finn said. The hairs on the back of his neck prickled. "Which means we need to keep an eye out for Wraiths."

Eddie drew the truck into the shadow of the second tank and asked Red where the access point was for the underground diesel storage. Red gestured for him to keep going.

As they cleared the second tank, the view opened up again, and they all saw it at once. Eddie stomped on the brakes in surprise. A deep red sheen covered the wet tarmac at the base of the third tank, spreading outward from a writhing amorphous black mass.

"What the hell is that?"

As they watched, several pieces of the object broke away and lifted into the air before flapping away.

"Crows. But what are they eating?"

"I think it might be Adrian," Eddie said. "There's the van."

No one said anything for a moment. Then Eddie shouted for the people in back to be on the lookout for Wraiths. Slowly, he inched forward, toward the murder of feasting crows. They were unwilling to abandon their bounty. Such treats were increasingly rare in a world of diminishing rewards.

But then, one took flight, crying out in alarm, and the rest followed all at once. Their calls echoed eerily through the artificial canyon.

"Something startled them."

The truck brakes squealed in protest as Eddie brought them to another stop.

They could tell that the corpse was thoroughly eaten, the flesh shredded from the bones. It was a sure sign of Wraiths. Not even the crows could do that much damage.

"Not Wraiths," Eddie whispered. "Wolves." He reached across the cab and pointed out Finn's window to a small trailer on the edge of the field.

"Is that . . . ?"

"More bodies. Half a dozen, at least."

They stared at the mound for a moment, still under siege by the pack animals and surrounded by even more crows waiting for a chance at the fresh meat. Beyond them, nearly out of sight, gasoline gushed from an open valve. It emptied into a sluice of some sort, which directed the flow onto the concrete.

"Jesus Christ! Hold on!" Eddie screamed. He jerked the gear shift forward and wrenched the steering wheel to the left, gunning the engine. The tires spun on the slick surface, sending a rooster tail of gasoline and rainwater mixture into the air.

But even as the vehicle bucked and stuttered against the sudden stress, he caught out of the corner of his eye a flash of orange light. It arced upward toward them from the far back end of the compound, and he knew it was already too late to escape it.

The flare slammed onto the concrete and skipped to a stop a hundred feet away, casting off angry sparks and white smoke. A curtain of fire rose before their eyes and swept toward them like a tidal wave.

A moment later, the truck was fully engulfed.

CHAPTER
30

"SHUT YOUR WINDOW!" EDDIE SCREAMED, AS HE rolled his up.

They tore through the ocean of flames, blind to any obstacles in their path. Eddie shifted, pushing the truck to a breakneck speed. But they soon began to lose power at an alarming rate.

"What's happening?" Finn cried. He wasn't sure Eddie could hear him over the roar of the engine and the flames, as well as Red's screams of terror. "Eddie, why are we slowing down?"

"No oxygen!"

They hit something and the truck careened onto two wheels for a moment before crashing back down again. They skidded, jerking from side to side as Eddie tried to regain control of the vehicle. Cries rose from the back.

At last they broke through the wall into a veil of thick black smoke, then out into open air. Fuel that had splashed onto the surface of the truck was still burning.

"Stop!" Finn shouted. "We've got fire extinguishers behind the seats."

"No way!" Eddie replied. "Those storage tanks are going to blow!"

So they kept going, regaining speed as the engine sucked hungrily at the undepleted air.

"Canvas is on fire!" Bix shouted behind them. But there was nothing they could do in front. They had to get as far away as possible.

"There's the gate!" Red yelled. "Go go go!"

A rumble filled the air, followed by a sort of whooshing vacuum of sound, which was followed by a massive explosion. The back of the truck lifted up from the blast's concussion. The first pieces of shrapnel began to rain down on them as they rocketed out of the compound and onto the street. Liquid balls of fire exploded all around them. The heat was incredible.

The truck crossed the empty road at a sharp angle, but Eddie couldn't make the turn fast enough. They jumped the opposite curb, plowing through a street sign and light post and narrowly avoiding clipping the corner of a building before swerving back onto a side street.

"You guys okay back there?" Finn shouted, twisting around in his seat. He could see the canvas disintegrating on the metal framing, orange flames eating the material away. Bix and Jonah were busily trying to untie the ropes holding it into place. He couldn't see Bix's father anywhere.

They careened down the road, moving as quickly as possible away from the fuel depot. A second fireball rose into the sky, accompanied by a roar and the *whump* of the blast hitting them. The ground shook. Both Bix and Jonah fell to the floor of the bed, but immediately scrambled to get back up again to resume their untying. The truck rocked and swayed along the potholed road. At last, the burning canvas billowed free and fluttered to a flaming heap onto the ground behind them.

"Mister Blakeley's gone," Finn said, spinning back around to the front.

Eddie gave him a grim look, then turned back to the road. His face was as white as his knuckles, but he didn't stop or even slow down.

The flames on the hood went out, leaving the paint puckered and streaked black.

They didn't speak again until they started the climb back up the rise where they had first seen the city below. As they reached the top, the third and final tank exploded, filling the late afternoon sky with a mushroom cloud of black, oily soot.

"That asshole knew we were coming," Finn said, his voice shaking with fury. "He was waiting for us."

Eddie drove on, downshifting to make the grade. The check engine light on the dash glowed a bright orange, silently entreating them to stop before it was too late. The rattle beneath the truck had returned. And now there was an alarming hesitation to the engine.

Finn turned to Red and grabbed a handful of the man's shirt and shook him. "He knew we were coming because he told you to make sure we were, didn't he!"

"Finn! It's not Red's fault."

The man shook with fright. "I-I didn't know! He left me behind, too! I almost died! Please, I didn't know anything about this!"

Eddie pulled off the road and honked to alert Kari and the Abramsons. A moment later, they emerged from their hiding place and ran toward the vehicle. Finn was out before the truck came to a complete stop. He ran to the back, where he was shocked to see Harrison Blakeley squatting on the floor and holding his head. His fingers and shirt were covered in blood, and his dirty blond hair was slicked to the side of his face with it.

Seeing the surprise on Finn's face, Bix nodded an assurance that he would be okay. "He hit his head on that first explosion. Laid him right out."

Bren stepped to Finn's side and touched his fingers with hers. As he turned to her, she leaned in and began to sob. "We thought we'd lost you. We saw the explosion and—"

"I'm fine," he replied, pushing her away. "We're all okay."

They reloaded the supplies, which they had removed for safekeeping from the men they'd expected to bargain with down below, each of them trying to come to terms with how lucky they had been to survive the attack. If Eddie hadn't realized the trap when he did, if he hadn't managed to navigate the truck through the blinding wall of flames, they would all have been burned to a crisp.

But Finn had no time to dwell on their fortune. Adrian was now well ahead of them and in a fresh vehicle the women had seen driving away.

And their own truck was quickly dying.

CHAPTER 31

THE FIRE HAD BEEN ABSOLUTELY TERRIFYING, A living, breathing, vibrant thing that grew and grew until he thought it would consume him where he stood a quarter mile away. And for just the briefest of moments he remembered thinking that it might not be such a bad thing if that were to actually happen. Fire was cleansing. It burned away one's sins as thoroughly as water could. It left the soul pure. It tempered the alloy of one's resolve.

Even from a distance, he felt its heat. The flames rose like a waterfall in reverse, rising and spreading before falling again in a vortex of destruction. And in the center of the swirling maelstrom were the boys.

Cleansed, once and for all of their trespasses.

He stayed only long enough to see the shrapnel of the first tank begin to pelt the landscape. The blast was like a glorious exhortation, reverberating for miles around. It brought to mind images of a crowd of celebratory parishioners, their voices raised in exaltation. Here was a hallelujah that not even Handel could have imagined.

The fireball rose, a giant hand whose fingers curled continuously inward, black and red like a bloody, scorched fist punching a defiant hole through the sooty sky. It stole his breath away and left him humbled. It almost made him want to shout in joy.

He wanted to stay and watch, but this little diversion had already cost him far more time than he had wanted, more even than the tree back at the border. He had places to go, as the saying went, and people to do.

People to do, he thought amusedly, rolling the words around in his mind until he chuckled out loud.

People to do, like the men who sold their fuel and demanded a man's dignity in exchange. Not even two years could erase his memory of the rape and the torments they had subjected him and his Jenny to the last time they had been down this way.

But now they were dead, and deservedly so.

He supposed it was a shame that the fuel in those tanks had to go. It was a costly sacrifice. Though, he reminded himself, less of one for such men as himself, who made little habit of relying on mechanized contrivances such as automobiles. Horses were far more reliable. In a few years, when the world had finally stripped away the last bit of vitality from the last manmade invention, he would still have his horses, teams of them to do his bidding. He would be like a savior then. He looked forward to this new world and the people he would share it with.

But only if they are worthy.

Those who weren't, well, he would help them find their salvation.

For now, however, he must make do with this truck, a faded but well-maintained silver Chevy, taken from the unworthy men he had released from their mortal bonds. It was, he was forced to admit, a good vehicle, with a jacked-up suspension and oversized tires, as well as air conditioning that actually worked. He'd need the extra clearance to make it through the rougher areas that were to come over the next day or so. And, truth be told, he was glad to be rid of the van. It was clunky and the speaker in the door had an annoying tendency to pop on and off, emitting the most god-awful sounds even though the radio had been removed, leaving only a few loose wires sticking out of the dashboard. He didn't have a clue how to make the noises stop. Even stabbing the speaker with a screwdriver hadn't worked.

Luckily, the handful of men who ran the depot and guarded its stores had been as adept at maintenance as they were at sexual assault. They had kept their vehicles in excellent running order.

But, of course, they no longer needed them, and he only needed the one, so he'd flattened all the tires on the rest.

Just in case.

No need to worry. They're dead this time.

He remembered that Jenny had always been the one to keep the machines running. She would have known how to silence the unholy demons tempting him through the van's speakers.

He looked over at her in the passenger seat and his heart swelled with emotion seeing her there, her face so beautifully unworried. A line of red-tinged drool slipped from the corner of her mouth and down her chin. He felt compelled to wipe it away, but it would mean having to don gloves, and they always made his hands itch.

Was she happy, he wondered, buried so deep inside herself that even he could not reach her? She looked happy. For now, at least, she wasn't hungry.

He nodded at the grim memory, which passed before him like a scene from a movie. There was the old retribution to be made, after all.

He would have rather it played out differently, that she'd have fed first on the boys' flesh instead of those filthy, rough, evil men. After all, it was they who were responsible for condition.

Once more, he was tempted to touch her cheek, to sweep the tangles of hair from her face so he could see her eyes. She had their mother's eyes, while he had his father's. Well, to be honest, hers no longer looked anything like their mother's. And his father's eyes had been nothing more than empty bleeding sockets the last time they had spoken.

He drove on, leaving that burning place behind. His gas tank was as full as his heart, and a smile crept over his face. Eight hours to Pocatello, where the guardians of that depot were much more reasonable to deal with. He would not sacrifice them as he had these; there would be no need for retribution, since the boys were dead and his Jenny's stomach was full. She wouldn't be ready to feed again until they reached the city. Then, after he got what he needed from the twin, she could have him for her next meal.

A ferocious yawn bubbled up through his chest, startling him. He must not sleep, not when he was so close. He had a long night of driving ahead of him, but thankfully the rain had stopped and the clouds were breaking up. Tomorrow was a new day.

He chuckled and realized there was no reason to wait to celebrate. After all, the new day — the new world — had already begun.

CHAPTER

THEY DROVE SOUTH THROUGH THE NIGHT OVER WHAT
had once been Route 93, switching drivers and navigators to
stay fresh while the rest of the group huddled together in the
uncovered bed in back beneath a tarp and several layers of
old army surplus blankets, where they tried to sleep.

After they entered the old Bitterroot National Forest,
their going significantly slowed. The roads grew narrow,
became steep and windy, and were sometimes in such bad
shape as to be nearly impassable. Slides were a frequent
obstacle. But through many of these they saw fresh tire
tracks, and so they knew they were still on Adrian's trail.

The afternoon's storm clouds had cleared just before
evening, turning the sky into a kaleidoscope of colors. And
with the starlit skies came the bitter chill of night. The
temperature dropped into the low forties and remained there
like an unwelcome party guest.

Kari couldn't sleep. The noise of the truck seemed
unnaturally loud in the stillness of the wilderness, and so she
wrapped a couple drop cloths they had scavenged from the
border station around all but her head and snuggled with the
rest of them toward the front of the bed. She hugged one of
the AR-15s between her knees and regarded the passing
world through the green screen of the night vision goggles,

watching for Wraiths while realizing their chances of seeing one should it attack them were slim. The creatures were too fast, too stealthy, and too unpredictable.

She imagined them hiding in the trees overhanging the road, ready to drop down on them like the ticks she and her past lover would often have to tweeze off their pant legs while hiking the trails of the White Mountains years back. The merest contact with the brush would trigger the insects' release, and they would latch onto whoever might be passing by. The tiny bloodsuckers had always made her skin crawl, but they now seemed quaint in a world infested by human flesh eaters.

At last, they reached a flat stretch of road at a place called North Fork, and drove for a while along a twisting river with steel and rust-colored stones that glimmered like clotted blood in the moonlight. Theirs was the only light in the otherwise coal black night, and it made them feel exposed and vulnerable enough that Jonah decided to continue on without the headlights. Kari handed over the goggles, but remained too anxious to sleep.

The river thinned to a stream, and the stream became barely more than a ditch. The road straightened, no longer bent by the will of the landscape. They made up time then and hoped the gap between them and Adrian was growing smaller. Indeed, as they entered the ghost town of Salmon and the road began once more to aspire toward the tops of the next set of mountains, they caught a glimpse of a light far off in the distance, so high up and winking tantalizingly as it passed around curves and through trees, that it might have been a passing satellite low on the horizon. Adrian was perhaps a half hour ahead of them. They were close, and getting closer.

But their excessive caution on the winding, uncertain road cost them, and they lost sight of the other car. It wasn't until an hour before dawn that the road flattened once more and the vista opened up enough to see any distance.

The concrete unrolled before them like a thin silver ribbon. They saw no lights for the next twenty minutes, not until the route met up with Highway 15 at Blackfoot. Then, in the gray pre-dawn gloom, they were startled to see a smattering of lights in the distance, the first signs of a settlement they had seen in many days.

Pocatello slept like a glimmering jewel nestled in the shallow bosom of a woman in repose.

And on her throat, like a solitary ruby threading its way along that delicate silver necklace, twinkled a single red bauble.

" 'THIS IS A SAFE HAVEN COMMUNITY,' " BIX READ OFF the hand-painted sign along the side of the road. The underlying billboard could still be seen through the whitewash, a public service announcement encouraging people to get their flu shots. " 'To ensure that it remains that way, please respect our rules. Failure to do so will result in swift judgment.' "

"Wonder what they mean by that," Finn said, glancing at Red.

They'd finally untied him, after he promised not to run. He claimed he no longer felt any loyalty to Adrian and was grateful to them for saving his life. In fact, he wanted to see the man dead just as much as the rest of them. "Roy was my friend," he told them. "None of us deserved what Adrian did, but least of all Roy."

Neither Finn nor Bix wanted to let him go. They had seen how he and other men like him had acted back there at the compound, before their escape. They were animals with the taste of blood on their tongues.

But Bren felt sorry for Red. Surprisingly, Harrison agreed with her. He even declared he'd take responsibility for him. Finn heard Bix grumble unhappily that his father might have hit his head harder than they realized back there in Missoula. But he didn't argue.

They had stopped at an old rest area populated by several picnic grills thick with rust and protected by an overhang constructed of rough-hewn logs. The site afforded them a clear panoramic view for at least a quarter mile around. Some of the grills appeared to have been used recently, and all were stuffed full of garbage— spent wood, shards of foil, charred animal bones. Several fire rings, and more than a few ratty sleeping bags, also littered the area.

While there, they prepared a hasty breakfast of canned dog food over boiled rice, and washed it down with coffee they had found at the station, which they had to strain between their teeth for lack of filters. It was the first coffee most of them had had since leaving the bunker, and their first decent meal in more than two days.

They debated whether to leave the bulk of their supplies and half their crew behind, but in the end, after listening to Red's assertion that the settlement was a pocket of civilized behavior run by strong but fair people, they decided to risk it. Their best chance of catching up with Adrian was here, but if they missed him, they didn't want to have to backtrack too much to retrieve anything. They were getting too close to Salt Lake City, and if they failed to stop him before he reached it, their task became monumentally harder, if not impossible.

"No guns," Bix remarked, as he went on to read the list of rules. " 'Weapons must be surrendered upon arrival and will be returned upon departure.' "

At the very bottom was one final ominous admonition: *Treat our Haven with respect and civility, and Haven will return the favor. Don't, and punishment will be meted out without prejudice.*

"They're not fooling around."

"It's a decent place," Red said. But when they asked him why, if it was as decent and safe as he said it was, didn't more people take up permanent residence there instead of passing through, his only response was, "You'll see."

Like Missoula, the outskirts of Pocatello, as well as the vast majority of the city center, were abandoned. Signs were posted everywhere warning visitors to be aware, to not leave their vehicles, and to not dawdle. Another sign declared there were no emergency services, reminding them if they met with any trouble, they were on their own.

The main road in had been lined over the years with fencing material, plywood, and other objects. Where they could see past it, the city was a shambles, a bleak junkyard stretching on for block after block. Windows were broken, buildings burned. They saw no animals— no dogs or birds, anyway. But in the shadows, things moved and hissed and growled.

"Christ," Kari whispered, as they drove along, moving swiftly through the cleared streets. "Why don't they kill them? There must be hundreds of them still in there."

"Thousands," Red said. "Maybe tens of thousands. Now you see why most people don't stay?"

"How on earth did they manage to set up a stable community in the middle of all this, then?"

"The army came through when the feral first came, and they shot anything that moved. When the survivors returned, it was nearly empty. They built a safe zone near the fuel depot and started trading. The ferals came in the years after. They're kept back by the fences and armed guards."

"Safe zone or not, I don't think I'd ever be able to sleep knowing they were out here like this. What's to stop them from overrunning the defenses? These barricades don't look like they'd cut it."

"Lack of any ability to mount a coordinated attack," Jonah mused.

"Heads up!" Finn shouted. "We got someone coming up on us from behind! They're moving fast!"

He stood up and braced himself against the cab as he watched the rapidly approaching vehicle. It appeared to be a sports car of some sort. He raised his pistol, but Kari placed a hand on his arm and told him to wait.

It honked once, then raced past them in the narrow space to their right, traveling at least fifty miles an hour. The window was open and the driver whooped as he passed. He skidded to a stop ahead of them, then shouted that they'd better speed it up or else they were going to be toast. Then he tore out again, leaving a patch of black on the road and a cloud of white hanging lazily in the air.

The car disappeared around the bend, the sound of its engine fading. Some ten or twelve seconds later, a series of honks echoed through the canyon of buildings.

"Better pick it up," Kari told Harrison. "With all the noise that jackass just made, every Wraith here is probably making its way to us right now."

Indeed, the shadows beyond the fences were much more animated than they had been before.

Harrison gave the truck more gas. They soon passed a series of signs that told them to honk three times, then to keep going as long as the light was green.

"What light?" Harrison asked.

"You'll see it when you reach the last straightaway," Red shouted back. "Green means it's clear and you can enter the opening. You just keep going, don't stop or slow down until we're inside. Then you hit the brakes."

"And what if it's red?"

"Then you're on your own. There's an escape route just past."

They made the last sweeping turn and saw the outer fence a quarter mile ahead, a twenty-foot high sheer wall of solid wood in a patchwork of colors. An opening in the wall directly ahead, blocked by a gate and looking much too small to accommodate the truck, was topped by a blazing globe of green. Coils of barbed wire covered the entire surface of the wall.

"Honk!" Red shouted. "Three times. And keep going unless it turns red. If it does, veer to the right for the escape ramp."

"What will they do if we try to crash the gate?"

"They have anti-tank missiles and flamethrowers."

"Shit," Bix murmured. "Don't crash the gate, Dad!"

Harrison let out three quick blasts from the horn and maintained his speed. The buildings beside them were a blur, but their focus was on that green light. A quarter mile became a tenth, then two hundred feet.

"Why aren't they opening up?" Finn cried.

"Don't stop!" Red shouted.

Eighty feet.

Sixty.

Thirty.

Suddenly, the bottom of the wall swept up and in. Everyone but Red ducked as the truck zoomed through the opening. A split second after they passed through it, the gate dropped heavily into place with a loud clang.

Red laughed as Harrison braked to avoid hitting the inner fence about sixty feet in. "They got it down to the millisecond."

Armed men approached from either side, appearing out of concealed openings in the wall. "Weapons down!" they shouted gruffly. "Prepare for inspection!"

A third man appeared, really no more than a boy. He had shockingly yellow curly hair and freckles. And his eyeglasses were held together at the bridge with tape. He looked like he belonged in a laboratory, but while he appeared to be the polar opposite of the armed men, they clearly took their orders from him.

"Welcome to Haven," he said, his voice cracking on the last word. "You can put away your guns. You've nothing to worry about here. You're safe."

CHAPTER 34

"YES, WE HAVE DIESEL," SHAW CONFIRMED, AS HE walked them across the enclosure. "But are y'all sure you want to just top off and not have us drain and replace what's in your tank?"

He spoke with a relaxed southern drawl, yet assured them he was actually a local boy. His folks had been born and raised in the Oklahoma panhandle and moved to Idaho right before he was born. "They had such thick accents that I couldn't help picking it up myself. But other than a wasted year of college in Utah to study international relations, I've lived here in this very town purty much my whole entire life."

"And Caspar?" Eddie asked, referring to the man with the broken glasses.

"Head of security. Decent fella, from Colorado. Used to be a real estate agent. Y'all don't wanna mess with him."

The man had directed the inspection, which, while polite, was as thorough as a military operation. Their weapons were tagged and secured away and they were provided an accurate receipt, along with instructions on how and where to retrieve them upon departure. The paper also listed the possible repercussions of breaking any rules. Most of the "judgments" were vague enough to warrant erring well on the side of caution.

After the search was completed, the truck was escorted through the inner wall and into the compound, which buzzed with activity. It was there that they were introduced to Shaw, the man responsible for dispensing the fuel. He was another study in contrasts, a short, chubby, jolly Asian fellow with a shiny face, graying hair, and stained green coveralls, but the slow drawl and gait of a Texas cowboy.

He handed them a printed list of items suitable for trade and how much fuel would be provided for each one— items such as rechargeable batteries, ammunition, medicine, and, of course, food. For the group, it seemed almost surreal to be discussing trading goods with such clearly defined parameters and no surprises. It was disorienting to encounter such civilized behavior after the utter absence of structure that had dominated the past couple weeks.

But if Shaw noticed their unease or their relative naïveté on the subject, he did not acknowledge it. And it was a relief to them to see that they would be treated in exactly the same way as anyone else.

Shaw glanced dubiously at the thick black smoke pouring from the truck's exhaust. "I mean, not to stick my nose in where it don't belong, but that concoction you're burning in there is gonna give your engine a coronary sooner rather than later. You might want to stick around a couple days, see what our mechanics can do for you. They'll flush the system and clean her out."

"We only need to get it to Salt Lake," Harrison said.

The man's forehead wrinkled, and he shook his head. "I assume you mean the city. You don't want to go there. It's lost to the ferals. Place is full of them. No one goes there."

"To be honest, we're trying to catch up with someone. If possible, before he reaches the city. So, as you can guess, we're sort of in a hurry."

Shaw nodded thoughtfully and shrugged. There was a flash of curiosity in his eyes. "A full tank will get you there and back, assuming you ain't totally crapped out the engine before then. I can only imagine what that used oil has done to your lines. But I got some additive I can give you to help open them up a bit."

"Thanks, we appreciate it."

"Ain't nothing free of course."

"Of course."

Shaw nodded. "Malcolm'll get you straightened out." He handed a second man a sheet of paper with a few scribbles on it. After studying it for a few seconds, Malcolm grunted and walked off without a word.

"This person you're going after," Shaw said, "he wouldn't happen to be driving a gray pickup truck?"

"Oversized wheels?" Kari asked.

Shaw nodded. "Dualies in back. Came in maybe an hour before you showed up."

"That's the one."

Shaw stuck his pencil behind his ear and scratched an itch on his neck. The pencil was well chewed. "We may be a little isolated here in Haven," he said, "but that doesn't mean we ain't fully aware how it is out there. It's rough, lawless. That's why we do things the way we do in here. We consider ourselves a last stand against the complete end of civilization."

They nodded in appreciation, but waited for Shaw to get to his point.

"I won't ask what you want with this man. I can only assume he must have crossed you in some way, maybe robbed you. Maybe it has something to do with the woman he had with him, I don't know."

"Woman?" Finn cut in. "What woman?" He glanced at the others, suddenly unsure they were even pursuing the right vehicle anymore. "You sure he wasn't alone?"

"He came in for gasoline alone, but there was something strange about his behavior, so one of our guys followed him out to see what he was up to."

"The red sports car?"

Shaw raised an eyebrow but didn't respond to this.

"Your man stopped at one of them abandoned buildings just outside of town and went inside. When he came out again, he was carrying a body all trussed up inside a thick blanket. Looked like a woman by the hair, and she was really putting up a fight."

Finn's eyes found Bix's and he knew by the look that his friend was thinking the same thing he was.

"What is it?" Kari asked.

"I think it might be Jennifer, his sister."

"I thought she was infected."

"She is."

"Infected?" Shaw asked, his curiosity ratcheted up several notches.

Finn didn't explain. "Was it just the one woman?"

Shaw nodded. "Like I said, I don't know what your beef with this man is. Ain't none of my business. Lots of stuff happens out there, bad things. We can only control what happens in here."

"He's not a good man," Bix affirmed. "He's definitely not our friend."

"How so?"

Finn gave Bix a wary look.

"He firebombed the fuel depot up north," Red told him, speaking up for the first time. "Killed the people running it."

"North?" Alarm flashed across Shaw's face. "Which one?"

"Missoula. He killed the people there and destroyed the entire place by opening the valves and lighting it on fire."

Shaw's face pinched. "We here in Haven may not agree with how those brothers run things up there. Operations like theirs encourage violence and force good people to seek alternate routes. Traffic is our lifeblood, if you know what I mean. But that station is a critical stop in our supply chain, so we're forced to accept it. Destroying it, however, not only endangers the lives of anyone needing that fuel, but it jeopardizes this station's livelihood, too."

Harrison glanced over at Eddie. Finn could see the men silently plotting, and he began to worry about any decisions they might make.

Since arriving, he'd begun to feel an affinity for these people. They seemed genuine, and he chalked up any brusqueness in their dealings to experience dealing with people who weren't. The last thing he wanted was any problems that might threaten their budding relationship, especially since he had begun to consider asking the Abramsons to stay behind while the rest dealt with Adrian and found Harper. From here on out, the risks were simply too great.

"Eddie?" he said, frowning slightly. "What are you thinking?"

"This man we're going after," Eddie said, addressing Shaw directly, "is armed and dangerous."

"And completely unhinged," Bix added.

"Would it be possible to trade some more goods for additional weapons?"

"We don't trade in weapons. Anything we acquire is pressed into service in defense of the community."

But Eddie would not be deterred. "We need to stop this man before he reaches Salt Lake City."

"If that's where this man is going, then he's already heading straight into a whole heap of trouble. The city may do any dirty work for you."

"He has the means to protect himself from the Wrai— the ferals. But if we don't stop him, there's no telling what he might do next."

"If you're saying he'll come back, we can defend ourselves."

"Are you sure? You let him in once without knowing what he was capable of doing. Your system is to invite first, ask questions later."

Shaw's temple throbbed. At last he sighed and nodded. "I may have something," he said. "But as we don't have a protocol in place for trading weapons, we'll have to come up with an arrangement for the ammunition you might use. Assuming you survive, which I'm counting on, we'll square up when you return."

Harrison frowned, clearly surprised by his willingness to discuss terms. "What's the catch?"

"You bring him back for us to deal with. Alive. And uninfected. Do that, and the debt will be fully satisfied."

"And if he's dead?"

"Just make sure he ain't."

CHAPTER 35

"CAN I SHOOT IT?" BIX ASKED. "PLEASE, PRETTY please? Just a practice shot or . . . you know, two or three hundred."

It was a clear day, and even though the temperature was only in the mid-fifties, they were speeding down the highway with their windows down. Finn had his head stuck out through the open roof. The chill air froze the skin on his face and brought tears to his eyes, making it nearly impossible to breathe. But the cold energized him. For the first time in a while, he felt optimistic about their chances.

"My uncle used to have a chocolate lab who loved doing that," Bix shouted up at him. "You sort of look like him. Stick your tongue out and drool."

He turned back when Finn ignored him and patted the unmounted M240 machine gun on the floor beside his feet. "Come on, Dad, just a quick go. We need to be sure it works."

"No, for the last time, no practice shots," Jonah snapped. "It's wasteful, and we might need all the ammo."

"We've got six-freaking-thousand rounds!"

"No one is shooting the machine gun," his father shouted back from the front seat of the army Humvee Shaw had loaned them.

"We should practice."

"There's no need to practice. You point, squeeze, and sweep. You can't miss."

"Except we do want to miss. We need Adrian alive," Eddie reminded them.

It was the five of them inside the vehicle. Eddie was driving. The three boys occupied the back. Kari had insisted on accompanying them in the lead vehicle, too, but Eddie had asked her to follow along in the truck. "I'd feel safer with you watching over Bren and Kaleagh. You're probably the only one of us who can shoot the eye out of a crow from forty yards."

"A hundred, actually."

She didn't put up much of a fight, undoubtedly because she knew he was lying to her. If any of them had the visual acuity of a sniper, it was Eddie. What remained unspoken between them, but which Finn suspected, was that Harrison was starting to have feelings for Kari and wanted her as far away from the action as Finn wanted Bren.

They'd left the truck in their dust soon after departing Haven, which was now two hours ago. The plan was to catch up with Adrian and stop him before he reached the city. But with that much of a lead already, it was going to be very difficult. They'd need all the breaks they could catch.

"Can you pick it up?" Finn asked, dropping back inside and leaning forward so Eddie could hear him over the roar of the engine and the wind.

The Humvee hit a pothole and they all bounced in their seats.

"You should put your seatbelt on," Jonah told Finn.

"I'm going as fast as I dare," Eddie called back. "We break an axle and—"

They hit another patch of crumbling road, and the Humvee rattled and fishtailed as they passed over it.

"If we break an axle, we'll never catch him!"

"How far are we now?"

"From the city? Eighty miles, according to the signs. Maybe ninety-five to the temple itself. Another hour and a half or so."

"We need to catch him before that."

"Yeah, we know, Finn."

Shaw had told them that, given the poor condition of the roads, it was usually a solid five or six hour drive from Pocatello, so they'd already cut more than an hour and a half off that pace. Still, would it be enough?

"If we don't see him soon—"

"We will," Eddie said.

"Then can I shoot the gun?" Bix asked. "I want to strafe his ass."

"We need him alive, Bix."

"Seriously? We're actually going to bring him back to Pocatello alive? What are they going to do if we don't? Hell, what's to keep us from returning the Hummer and the gun back at all?"

"We made a deal."

"And what? They'll come after us if we renege?"

No one answered.

"I say we just pump his crazy ass full of lead and put him out of our misery. He deserves nothing better."

"Bix!"

"Dad!"

His father turned in the seat. "Son, if we let this world strip us of what little remains of our civility, what have we got left?"

"You're joking, right? You never used to be so anal about things."

"The day may soon come when we find decency and our word are all the currency we have left."

Bix scowled at his father, but he didn't argue. The relationship the two shared had always been something of a puzzle to Finn. Harrison used to be so hands-off, letting Bix find his own way in the world, allowing him to express himself in his own unique way. Though he'd always emphasized decency, he'd never really called Bix out before on his behavior, even when it got heated between him and Jonah.

Finn looked over at the other boy and caught him shaking his head at the exchange, a flicker of irritation crossing his face. He felt a pang of regret over what had happened to Jonah's parents back there in the bunker. They'd both been taken away from him, his father by Jonah's hand, and his mother by her own. And while Mister Resnick might have deserved his son's hatred, his mother didn't. She certainly didn't deserve her fate.

"We're getting close," Bix said breathlessly. "I can feel it, man. Can't you?" He nudged Finn.

Finn tried to return the smile, but the truth of the matter was, that sense of dread had returned with a vengeance. What if Harper really wasn't there? What if he wasn't even alive anymore? It was like a cruel joke, this mission he was on. He hated how it kept raising his hopes, only to dash them, again and again.

"Can you speed it up?" he prodded Eddie once more.

Bix raised a curious eyebrow at him. They were already barreling down the road at seventy-plus miles an hour, and the tires were getting a thorough work out, not to mention everyone inside the vehicle. Every incremental increase in speed greatly increased their chances of failing.

"Never mind," Finn ceded with a sigh and slumped in his seat, ignoring the way Jonah's eyes kept flicking to his seatbelt.

"Someone's hormonal," Bix softly sang to Jonah, though loud enough for Finn to hear.

Jonah chuckled and leaned back. He shut his eyes, a nervous grin curling the corners of his mouth.

"It's just that I want this all to be over," Finn said. And he did. He was tired, exhausted. He missed the relative monotony of the bunker, its safety and security and knowing that there were walls all around him keeping everything else out. He'd forgotten how big the world was, how exposed it made him feel. He also missed the soothing hum of the turbines to lull him to sleep. He missed not having to worry about anything but whether or not the food inventory was done for another week.

And he missed his father.

"There!" Eddie said, jolting Finn out of his reverie. Both he and Jonah leaned forward at the same time and knocked heads. Stars exploded behind Finn's eyes, and his vision swam, but he ignored the pain. He needed to see for himself.

"Where?"

"Maybe five, six miles ahead."

"I can't see anything."

"It's him," Eddie assured them. "Gray vehicle. Raised carriage."

"Double check the license plate number, Eddie," Bix joked. "Better make sure it's the right one."

Finn sneered at Bix. "Where are we? How far do we have before we reach Salt Lake?"

"About forty miles before we reach the city limits. The junction with Interstate 84 is just ahead."

Excitement rose up inside Finn. They were actually going to catch him! He hadn't wanted to hope, but there he was. They could catch him, and when they did, they'd demand he take them to Harper and—

There was a rapid series of loud bangs, like gunshots, and the Humvee slued suddenly to the right, heading straight for the guard rail. Eddie wrenched the wheel to the left, but the vehicle responded sluggishly. They tilted onto two wheels for a moment before crunching back down on all four, jolting them. Finn grabbed for his seatbelt, noticing too late that both Jonah and Bix already had theirs on.

They careened back toward the right shoulder. Eddie fought it, straining against the vehicle's stubborn determination to leave the roadway. For a moment, it looked like he might succeed. But then the tires bit into the softer material on the shoulder, and it was all over. They skidded over the gravel and shot down the embankment. A moment later, they blasted beneath a chain link fence, hit a shallow erosion dike and went airborne.

Their flight was cut short almost immediately as the front of the vehicle jerked upward and flipped backward. They came to rest upside down thirty feet off the side of the road.

"What happened?" Jonah said, coughing through the cloud of yellow dust. He was the first to react. He tried to exit through the back door, but it was jammed shut. Below them, the opening in the roof was blocked by the ground. Sand and rocks had been swept inside by the force of their slide. The mounting post for the M240 was wrenched backward by the fencing it had hooked.

"Tire blew," Eddie said, waving away the dust. He unhooked his seatbelt and tumbled to the ceiling. "Everyone all right?"

Jonah looked around at the jumble of loose items. The M240 had fallen to the back of the vehicle, where it lay wedged in one corner. It appeared to be okay.

Bix was there, cursing as blood trickled down his face.

But Finn was gone.

CHAPTER

36

"ALMOST THERE, SWEETIE," ADRIAN SAID, STEPPING over to her window. He tossed the emptied cardboard box to the side of the road and wiped the black metal dust off his hands. Some of the sharp pieces had pierced his chapped skin, raising spots of blood, but it was worth it to assuage that last little itch of doubt in the back of his mind. One could not be too careful, especially of late. Some people just didn't seem to understand how to properly die.

She didn't move. Her head lolled to the side, facing away from him, a blessing given the blackness that stole away the blue in her eyes. Her body was completely slack, thanks to the newly operational device at her feet. Even so, he decided to recheck the connections. He didn't want to push his luck again. He'd almost waited too long last time.

He did not understand at all how the device worked, only that it did. And even though it was manmade and relied on other manmade contraptions, such as batteries and electrical inverters, he was perfectly comfortable with the idea that it was God's will working through it. God made man, who made the box. And since the box kept him safe, it meant God was keeping him safe to do His work.

Find the cure, God had spoken to him in his visions, *for it is an abomination to my will. Find it and destroy it, and I will make you a king while you still walk this earthly sphere.*

Lately, however, he had begun to worry that God might not be so happy if He knew of his secret desire to use the cure on his Jennifer. He presumed the scare that morning, when she nearly broke free of her bindings, had been a warning to him not to defy the Lord's will.

He chuckled nervously at the memory and wiggled the battery connections to make sure they were good and secure.

Can't have her waking up again.

He supposed it had also been the hand of God, rousing her to wake him before he could crash. He hadn't even been aware he'd fallen asleep at the wheel.

He caught himself just as the truck was about to leave the road. To the side was a steep ravine. Had it happened, he had no doubt he would have died there alone and forgotten as punishment for his selfish thoughts. Or worse, be found by the ferals for entertaining his own selfish desires.

Thankfully, they were close to Pocatello by then, just a few more miles. He would barter for some jumper cables to recharge the battery so that she could go back to sleep again.

He was well aware that there existed preferential price lists, but in his hurry he hadn't bothered to negotiate a better deal. So the fuel and cables had cost him more than they should have, including both his sidearm and the stun gun, as well as a few other sundry items. Of course, where he was going, he wouldn't need the weapons. He only needed to keep the device powered. It and God's hand would protect him.

As long as he didn't give in to temptation.

It had not been easy getting her safely out of the truck and securely trussed for the duration of the trade, even in her semi-drowsy state. But by the time he returned, the battery was fully depleted and she was completely awake. He decided it would be more expedient to wire the device directly to the truck's battery rather than wait for the spare to recharge. But when he opened the hood, he found the battery terminals caked in the greenish-white moss of corrosion.

Yet even that turned out to be fortuitous, as it forced him to dig through the toolbox behind the seat for a wire brush. There, hidden beneath a false bottom, was another handgun.

He giveth as He taketh away.

And he knew that God had placed scales over the eyes of Caspar's men, for when they did their search, they did not find the weapon.

He giveth and He giveth.

It was a testament of the Lord's generosity, and a reminder that he should not think of his own selfish desires.

The good Lord has a purpose for my Jennifer. I just don't know what it is yet.

He shut her door after checking the connections, then circled around behind the truck, peering down the road behind him. He expected to see the army truck rising over the horizon like a ghost ship. But there was nothing, no glint of sunlight on a windshield or the hum of an engine. And he smiled at himself for what he had done back there in Missoula.

The boys are sure and truly dead.

Even so, it was better to be safe than sorry. He spit onto his hands and rubbed away the last of the metal filings and dried blood, then went in and got behind the wheel and started the engine.

They reached the outskirts of Salt Lake City shortly after, and he was once again surprised at the level of destruction it had incurred. It was hard to believe that this was where he and Jennifer had started out, all those years ago, just two lost souls in a world that had forgotten all about them and couldn't care less.

Where he'd finally found his spiritual calling.

He remembered so little of himself before then, as if the feral had been his baptism, cleansing his mind of all the terrible things he had endured before it. He had been reborn in that place, his sanctuary remade from the heart of all that was wrong with the old world. And now he was returning.

It felt like he was being born anew.

He slowed to navigate through the obstacle course of abandoned vehicles, many the final resting places of their deceased occupants, their bodies now desiccated husks of leathery brown skin and brittle bones. Going forward, most of the roads would be either impassable from debris or perilous with ferals. But he had his faith to guide him through, and God's hand to protect him. Just like it had always done before.

"Almost home, sweetie," he said, and grinned at her slack face. "I suspect yer probably hungry again."

CHAPTER 37

"**THIS ABSOLUTELY CANNOT BE HAPPENING!**" **FINN** screamed in frustration. He pushed Bix's hands away. "We were this close!"

"Sit still!" Bix ordered, as he dabbed at the scrapes on Finn's face and shoulder. "I'm trying to help."

Finn collapsed in the shade against the side of the Humvee and dropped his head into his hands, wincing at the pain wracking his battered body. How was it possible to hurt all over, yet still be able to move?

"Told you to wear your seatbelt," Jonah grumbled, and walked stiffly away.

Finn had been ejected when they flipped, but was fortunately thrown clear of the vehicle, where they'd found him unconscious but without any broken bones. Nevertheless, the tumble had taken its pound of flesh, mostly from his shoulder and thigh. The scrapes looked angry and painful, but Finn was in such a state of agitation that he barely cared, except when the others tried to peel away the tattered remains of his shirt and poured water over the wounds. His jacket had offered some protection, but the material had been reduced to little more than strips and threads.

"We'll still get him," Bix said. "I promise."

"How?" Finn cried. "Huh? Tell me how!"

"We keep going. We don't stop. We don't give up."

Finn caught the look Jonah gave Eddie. They all knew it was useless to keep trying. There was no way they'd catch Adrian now, and entering the city would be certain suicide.

Of course, that was assuming they could even get the Humvee back on its wheels and running again.

"Let's just focus right now on surviving long enough for the others to reach us," Eddie said. He mounted the overturned vehicle and scanned the horizon for movement. There were a lot of places for Wraiths to hide in the desert. They could only hope that the creatures had long ago fled from the unrelenting sun and scarce food to more distant and hospitable environs.

"Think the four of us can lift it?" Jonah asked.

"There's five of us," Finn said.

"Like you'll be any help."

"Lay off him," Bix said.

Harrison shook his head. "It's armored. Thing's got to weigh a good four, five thousand pounds. Maybe more."

"We've got Eddie," Bix said.

Eddie snorted. "I'm not Superman."

"We can at least try."

"Won't make any difference." He hopped nimbly to the ground. "We've got three flats and only one spare."

"How on earth could we get three flats at one time?"

Eddie extended his hand. "Found this embedded in one of the tires, and the road's littered with them. He knew we were coming."

"Maybe he did, maybe not," Harrison argued. "No way he could've seen us before you spotted him."

"Then why litter the road with these?"

"Because he's batshit crazy," Finn said.

Eddie tossed the object away. The thing resembled an oversized metal jack, the kind the kids used to play with in grade school. Except this one had razor sharp points. It was meant to shred tires. "I kicked the rest off the road. The others will be coming along eventually and we can't afford to lose the truck, too."

"Come on, Finn," Bix said, urging him to lean forward. "Let's get that scrape covered up. Last thing you need is more dirt getting in it. Or sunburn."

"No," Finn said. He touched his shoulder and winced. The pain was actually becoming bearable. "Let it air dry."

"You're damn lucky you didn't break anything," Jonah yelled.

"I'm fine."

"You're not fine! You should have worn your seatbelt!"

"Gee, maybe I should have worn my seatbelt! Too bad nobody said anything about that!"

"Boys," Harrison muttered. "Enough."

Finn scowled at Jonah and forced himself to stand up, despite the howls of pain coming from every quarter of his body. He wanted to prove to Jonah he wasn't a little baby to be coddled and reminded to wear seatbelts. Surprisingly, he found it tolerable enough. Maybe it was a second wave of shock setting in, but a sort of numbing sensation was infusing his body.

"We'll get you some medicine once the truck arrives," Harrison quietly said. "For now, we need to conserve our energy and our water. We'll discuss what to do then."

At last the others arrived. Bren leapt from the back of the truck while it was still moving, drawing an angry shout from her father, which she ignored.

"Don't touch," Finn begged her, backing away from her hands. "It's still pretty raw."

In truth, the stinging was now almost completely gone, but so was the numbness. Now he was suffering from a maddening itchiness. Though not nearly as debilitating as the pain, it wasn't any more welcome, and the slightest touch made it flare up.

The two stood awkwardly facing each other, neither of them sure what to do, until Jonah passed by them muttering how he wouldn't have been hurt if he'd been belted in like everyone else.

"You weren't wearing your seatbelt?"

"Can we just drop it already? I've already got one nanny, I don't need two."

"You don't have to be such a jerk about it. I can't help it if I care about you."

Finn apologized, then they found him a spare shirt and began transferring what they could scavenge from the Humvee back into the truck. The M240 was unharmed, but without the mount, the unwieldy weapon could only be hand-fired.

Finn was offered a seat in the cab, which he refused. He climbed determinedly into the bed and positioned himself right behind the cab to stay out of the wind. He tried not to lean against anything, though, as he knew the vibrations would only bring more discomfort. Instead, he sat hunched over with his eyes shut and his thoughts turned inward until he fell into a sort of trance.

The itching sensation took its time receding. It felt like his skin was alive, like something was crawling around underneath it. Envisioning the worst, he pulled the fresh shirt away from his shoulder, expecting to see the flesh writing. But it appeared as normal as it could given the circumstances. The wound was angry and red, the scrapes already turning dark with clotted blood and dirt. There was some seepage, but it was slight, yellow, and clear.

With a relieved sigh, he gingerly pulled the shirt back on.

Only then did he realize where they were headed. It was late afternoon, and the sun was to his left, a red blob producing a blinding glare as it reflected off the eroded salt pan. They were heading south, instead of north, onward to Salt Lake.

But why?

Adrian would have entered the city already and might even have reached the temple. What could they do now?

He struggled to his knees, then pulled himself to his feet so he could see over the cab. Eddie glanced over from where he stood behind Kari, who was driving. He had the machine gun in his hands, resting it on an old pillow so it wouldn't rattle. In the distance, shimmering off to the right, were the brackish waters of the Great Salt Lake, and up ahead rose the tallest of the buildings from the ghost town by the same name.

Jonah and Bix each had a rifle and were sitting at the back corners of the bed, ready to defend them against an attack.

It was just about the only thing they could count on now.

CHAPTER

BIX WAS THE FIRST OF THEM TO FIRE HIS WEAPON. HE let out a string of profanity as the Wraith failed to drop, despite losing a chunk of flesh in its right thigh. If anything, the wound only seemed to make it more determined.

Jonah's follow-up shot put it away, but within seconds two more took its place, appearing simultaneously from opposite sides of the road.

"Blockage ahead!" they heard Seth shout from the passenger seat. "Turn right up here!"

They braced themselves against the sides of the truck bed as Kari braked and made the turn down a side street.

"It's a dead end!" she screamed. "I'm backing up!"

The gears rattled as she tried to shift. The truck lurched and bucked, resisting the change in momentum.

"Hurry!" Seth yelled.

"Stay down," Harrison told Finn, Bren, and her mother. He slid a pistol and a box of ammunition across the floor to Red, then braced his shoulder against the right side of the cab and raised his own rifle. Finn felt helpless, but the injuries he'd sustained in the accident prevented him from fully extending his arms without inviting a wave of nausea. The three of them huddled in the middle of the bed, hidden behind boxes of supplies, while the rest kept the Wraiths at bay.

Another shot rang out. Then two more, all of them coming from the back of the truck. The engine whined as they reversed out of the narrow street and reentered the main road. Kari spun the wheel and they straightened out again, heading back the way they'd come.

"Oh, shit!" Seth screamed. "Oh, shit! There's too many of them!"

Finn tried to stand, but Bren grabbed his shirt and pulled him down. The pressure of the fabric on his shoulder made him cry out, and he dropped.

The M240 roared to life overhead. Between bursts, Eddie shouted for Kari to drive faster. "I saw a side road back a little ways, looked like it had been cleared. It'll be on your right side now. Go! GO!"

Spent shells and metal fragments from the 75-round bandoliers rained down around Finn's head. Kari yelped when a few ricocheted into her open window and scorched her arm and leg. Eddie kicked aside a box of water and sidled toward the middle, shouting at Harrison to move out of the way. The machine gun hammered against the roof of the cab as he swept the barrel from left to right across the road and back again, clearing a path ahead for them to take.

"Need another bando!" he shouted. "Now!"

Harrison reached over to the open 50 caliber ammo can, grabbed one of the olive green packs and tore it open, dumping the bandolier onto the bed of the truck. He found the right end and handed it up. "Bren, keep these coming!" he shouted, showing her what to do. Then he spun around to defend the flank opposite Red.

"Turning!" Kari shouted, and they all tilted as she made the right Eddie had pointed out a moment earlier. She weaved around a series of vehicles that appeared to have been strategically placed to prevent someone from driving directly through at high speed. Shortly after, the road opened up again, and they had a clear path ahead.

The M240 fell silent.

"Well, that was fun," Bix chirped. He tried to smile, but the lack of color on his face told a different story.

"That was nothing," Jonah replied. "It's only going to get worse."

"I say bring it on."

"Don't ask for trouble, Blackeye."

"Why not? My middle name is Trouble."

"I thought it was Loser."

"I know you are, but what am I?"

Finn was about to tell them to stop, when they broke out in nervous laughter. It didn't surprise him that they would fall back into their old routine when things got hairy. They were just diffusing the situation. But there was nothing routine or familiar about any of this anymore. No longer were they the kids they had been inside the bunker. Their petty squabbles, once matters of utmost gravity, had morphed into an outlet for their tension. It helped them reclaim some semblance of sanity and perspective in a world that had gone completely bonkers. They were all adapting to this new reality. Nevertheless, the changes manifested themselves in ways that unsettled him.

They continued on for a short distance until they reached another blockade and were once more surrounded by the deadly creatures spilling out of the alleyways. It was getting darker, the shadows longer and deeper, making it harder to see them. But with every side and corner of the truck defended, as long as they kept moving, the Wraiths could not get close. The only time they ever came into contact with the vehicle was when Kari mowed them down.

They kept the towering spires of the abandoned Mormon temple in view, visible between the buildings and through the trees. Their persistence paid dividends as they slowly but steadily made their way closer.

Finally, the vista opened up before them and the entire front of the building came into view across a broad open area of concrete and overgrown lawn.

"Anyone see the truck?" Finn called out.

No one acknowledged that they could.

"Everything's blocked," Kari shouted. "I can't find a way to get closer!"

"Just drive across the lawn!"

More Wraiths came, drawn by the sound of the truck engine and the gunfire. The fighting grew more intense with each passing moment.

Bren cracked open a second ammo box and fed Eddie a new bandolier, but he dropped the machine gun to the floor with a hiss of pain before he could load it. "Can't hold it any longer," he grunted, and pulled his fists to his chest, wincing. "Too hot."

The barrel smoked where it lay beneath one of the wooden bench seats.

Missus Abramson poured water over his hands. Eventually, he was able to pick up a handgun and fire that. In the interim, the Wraiths had gained ground.

"We're going to run out of small caliber rounds soon!" Jonah announced.

"Hold on! I think I found a way in," Kari shouted. "It's a straight shot, but it's going to get bumpy! And it's uphill, so hold on!"

Finn struggled once more to his feet. Most of the discomfort had left him by then. He knew it was probably the adrenaline and that he'd be paying for it later when it wore off again, but he managed to make his way to the corner behind her window. "Don't stop for anything!" he shouted. "If we're lucky, he's still here and the device will keep the Wraiths from getting too close to us!"

He spun around to the others and shouted for them to spare their ammunition if possible.

Kari gunned the engine, and the truck lurched forward up the hill, crunching the bones of several Wraiths beneath its tires.

They charged through the remains of a ruined concrete and chain barrier and raced up a set of steps toward the front doors.

"They're blocked!" Seth shouted from the passenger seat. "There's a car parked right up against them in front. Go around to the side!"

"They're still coming!" Bren screamed. "They're not stopping!"

"It's clear ahead! Go to the left!"

"There's another chain! I have to circle around it."

Finn spun around and pointed to Red, motioning him to the other side of the truck bed. "Clear a path over that way! We're circling around!"

The truck made a wide loop across the open cement pad a hundred feet below the front of the temple, jumping curbs and knocking over lamp posts. The Wraiths trailed along behind. Finn thought how it was a blessing they were incapable of planning a step ahead, or else they'd take an angle to cut off the truck's escape.

The gunshots continued amid shouts of reloading and more ammo and for Kari to hurry. At last they were heading back toward the temple, angling toward the left side of the massive building. More Wraiths poured from around the corner, moving fast, yet not fast enough to avoid colliding with the truck. If they weren't run over, Bren and her mother used whatever they could to knock them away. And if they managed to grab onto the moving truck, their hands were shattered by the stocks of the rifles Bix and Harrison held. Only Finn was left with little to do but cower in his corner and watch.

Finally, the way became clear again. They sped around the side of the building, revealing for the first time the destruction behind the temple's facade.

"Go back!" Seth screamed.

"No!" Finn roared, despite knowing they wouldn't find anyone here.

"It's no use! We're dead if we stay!"

"I said no! Keep going. I need to see! I need to be sure."

"He's not here, Finn," Kari said and began to brake so she could turn. "The temple's destroyed! He's not inside!"

It had been razed by fire, long enough ago that the charred wood no longer smelled and small trees sprouted from the rubble. All that was left was the intact facade and a massive pile of collapsed wood caked with old ash, large twisted metal girders, and stone.

"I have to check!" Finn cried. He placed his hands on the bedrail and prepared to jump off. "I can't just leave him behind!"

Eddie grabbed him and pulled him away from the edge. "Don't be stupid. You can barely move your arms. And you can't run."

"I need to check! Harper! *HARPER!*"

Leaving his hand on Finn's arm, Eddie shouted over to Kari's window. "Keep driving. Get clear. Don't stop."

"No!" Finn screamed.

"Drive two miles," Eddie continued. "I need you to draw the Wraiths away from here. Then come back for me. Circle the plaza once. No matter what happens after that, whether I'm here or not, you leave."

"You can't do this, Eddie!"

But the big man was already off the truck and sprinting across the front of the temple toward the far corner, heading away from the creatures.

"Eddie!"

"You heard him," Kari shouted. She forced the truck into reverse and backed away, then spun the wheel. The truck's front end skidded around. "Hold on!"

They returned the way they had come, then turned and headed once more into a different section of the city, driving just fast enough to draw the Wraiths away. They fired on the quickest among them, opting instead to save their dwindling ammunition.

"We need to find a path where we can circle around," Kari said. "Keep an eye out. I'd rather not have to stop and backup again."

"There's a parking lot ahead on the right," Harrison announced. "That shopping plaza there! See if you can go around. I think this is far enough."

"No!" Seth yelled. "We're not going back! Eddie's gone! He's dead. We need to leave now! We need to get out of here!"

Kari ignored him. The truck bounced the people in back off the floor as she jumped the curb, jerking the wheels one way, then the other. She threaded her way between abandoned cars and overturned shopping carts, hitting some and sending them careening away. They flew past a store that had been boarded up, its windows covered in holiday wrapping paper, evidence it had once served as a refuge in the early days following the Flense.

The Wraiths trailed them, now numbering several hundred. They surged like a tsunami between the vehicles, over and through the obstacles, swarming ever forward, their numbers growing with each passing second. Kari headed around the side and toward the back of the plaza.

"Better hope it's not blocked," Seth yelled.

"Are they following?" Kari asked.

"Yeah!"

"Good!" Kari gunned the engine as soon as they cleared the next corner and spun the wheel.

"Duck!"

The drooping electrical line caught the top edge of the windshield and snapped with a loud *crack!* It whipped away and wrapped around a dead tree. The shower of dry leaves seemed to confuse the Wraiths for a moment. Several fell to the ground. The wire caught a crimped lamp post and began to pull it the rest of the way down. The weakened metal screamed; bolts popped out of its base. It crashed onto the roof of a vehicle, exploding the windows and showering the lot with glass.

"Gun it!" Harrison yelled. "They've stopped following! Give it everything you've got!"

They exited the lot at full speed and skidded back onto the main road. Except for a few stragglers, which failed to get out of the way, the street ahead was clear.

CHAPTER

IF THERE WAS ONE THING CHARLIE BOLTON HATED more than waiting, it was babysitting. Always had, always would.

Babysitting was pretty much all he had ever done, both growing up and in his adult life, and in no case had it ever been because of any choice he had made for himself. First, there was his mother, who made him watch over his kid brother, Gibson. Then came the Criminal Court of Jackson County, which decreed he was in need of babysitting himself as a soldier in the United States Army. But after boot camp, the army dumped him off at Westerton, not very far from his old stomping grounds. This was back before the damn planet went to shit. Then, instead of babysitting Gibson, he was charged with keeping an eye on trucks and boots and brown underwear and MREs.

He didn't think it could get much worse than that — and he'd seen worse — but after the feral came and Cheever weasled his way into Wainwright's favor, it did. Cheever had Charlie babysitting the stupid civilians, making sure they weren't breaking curfew and doing stupid shit that put them all at risk. It was his job to make sure they attended the daily security briefings and carried out their daily stupid chores.

The civvies were like children; they hadn't a clue about anything. They didn't know how lucky they were, protected by able bodied soldiers such as himself. But if he thought he'd seen the worst of them even then, he hadn't. For example, this entitled brat he was assigned to watch over now was worse than any he had ever met before.

First of all, the kid was too stupid to even know when he was being insulted, and though it had been somewhat amusing at first to make fun of him, it soon got old. Four freaking days of this damned nonsense was just about two days too much.

But what really got under his skin was that he'd been made to pull the duty in what had to be the most mother-fuckingest godforsaken shithole in the middle of what was, without a doubt, the absolute worst feral-infested place he'd ever seen.

Of course, he hadn't really seen too many, but he'd heard about them.

And to top it off, the building where he had to pull it was cold and drafty and full of eerie echoes. It was too damn big, too damn open, and had too damn many places for a feral to hide in. Too many more where they could sneak in, too.

"You either choose to think of them as dangers," Flossie tried to reason, soon after their arrival, "or you can think of them as security, 'cause ain't no one going to sneak up on us in here. Am I right?"

"I ain't scared of them," Charlie's little brother, Gibson, had asked. He was barely twenty, though he acted twelve, and was still the same old dumb shit he had always been when Charlie was growing up. Still as dumb as a lump of coal and just as flaky. He asked the stupidest questions, not because he was curious, but because he didn't know any better. And that was why it burned Charlie up something good that the kid was still alive. If he and his little gang of troublemakers hadn't been trying to siphon gas from one of the base's tanks the day the world went into lockdown, who knows where the kid would be now. And if his damn momma hadn't made him promise to look after him before the phone lines went dead, Charlie would have kicked the jerk outside the fence a long time ago.

Because if babysitting was the thing he hated most in the world, the thing he hated second most — after waiting, of course — was whatever it was he'd been forced to sit.

"Course it's true, Lightning Bolton." Flossie always grinned at Charlie whenever he called his brother that, because he knew it bothered him. "We're safe in here. See? We got the box. The ferals don't like the box. Remember?"

"Flossie says we're safe, Charlie."

And then Flossie flashed that shit eating grin of his, the one with all the gaps where every other tooth had been knocked out during a drunken bar fight before the world went to shit. "Yeah we're safe. Fact, why'nt you go out to the truck and get us another case of stew cans?" He pretended to reconnect the wires to the box Father Adrian had provided for their protection. "I won't turn it off. Promise. It's only just a few feet out the front door."

"I don't care. Them ferals don't scare me," Gibson said, puffing out his chest. "Ain't nothing scares me."

"Yeah, you're a regular badass, Lightning Bolton."

Charlie briefly considered smacking the kid in the mouth like his father used to do. But when he thought about the promise he had made to his momma, he decided a good ear cuffing was the better option instead. His mother preferred the ear cuffing, especially when it was delivered at the end of a wooden spoon.

But he didn't have a wooden spoon, and god dammit if the stupid kid was too quick for him anyway, ducking out of the way before Charlie could land a good one on him.

"M'man," Flossie said, laughing. "My Little Lightning Bolton!"

"You should be afraid of them," Charlie snapped. "Both of you should."

"Well, you can be scared, Charlie, but we ain't. Right, Flossie? We ain't scared of nothing."

But Charlie was, and he freely admitted it. He had a healthy respect for the ferals and a strong survival instinct feeding it.

Thankfully, Flossie was no longer his problem. In fact, Flossie was nobody's problem anymore. Not unless you happened to be outside without a device and you happened to come across a feral with a lot of gaps where most of its teeth should be. And now, Gibson had a good and decent appreciation for the fuckers, too, because he'd finally seen what they could do to a man.

It was unpremeditated. Just that morning Charlie had asked Gibson to ask Flossie for the truck keys to get some more water. But Flossie wasn't about to let the damn fool kid anywhere near his keys, no matter what he may have dared Gibson to do in the past. He got the water himself.

The moment his back was turned, Charlie yanked the wires off the device, then blocked the front door so Flossie couldn't get back in.

The ferals reached him while he was screaming bloody murder at Charlie, saying he was going to gut him and his kid brother unless he opened the damn fucking door right now!

There was blood, a lot of it arterial, and a lot of guts. But not enough of either to actually kill the man.

The creatures fed on his flesh for a couple minutes, tearing into the soft parts of him something good. But then they suddenly departed to hunt elsewhere. Flossie was still breathing. He lay there for a few minutes, not more than a couple feet away from the front door, gawping air and bleeding from a hundred bite wounds and not saying much of anything that made any sense. He was in absolutely no state to gut no one.

By rights, he should have died, but the infection was faster. After a little bit he just got right back up and wandered off, hissing and growling like the things that had attacked him.

So that left just the two of them to babysit— Gibson, and the brat kid.

And the brat wouldn't shut up.

He was like some kind of freaking public service announcement that kept running day and night on the television, telling them that they could save the world if they just put their differences aside and trust one another.

Charlie considered this message for, like, exactly one nanosecond before ordering Gibson to put a gag on the kid so they wouldn't have to listen to his mouth diarrhea anymore. But then, because Gibson was such a stupid shit-for-brains who couldn't tie a knot to save his life, the gag fell off, unleashing another torrent of happy-happy bull crap.

Emboldened by his promotion to group leader brought about by Flossie's "accident," Charlie decided to take a little affirmative action himself. He smacked the brat in the kisser something good, like his daddy used to do.

Except, maybe a little too much like his daddy. The damn fool kid went out like a busted light bulb, a cut on his lip and a big old fat goose egg where he fell and hit his damn fool head.

But at long last he was quiet.

Of course, Charlie had always had the damnedest luck. Who should decide to show up right then but Father Adrian, driving up in a monster gray Silverado and circling the lot twice before parking around the back of the building. Fearful of what the man would do if he found the kid so misused, Charlie splashed the last of his precious drinking water on the kid's head. Thankfully, the brat woke right up, sputtering and shaking his head not seconds before Father Adrian marched in through the double doors in back.

"Where's Flossie?" he demanded by way of greeting.

"Dead. Out front. Well, he was dead, but then he—"

"Never mind." Adrian frowned impatiently at the three of them, as if deep in thought, then nodded once and told them to sit tight. "Got some business to tend to in the back. Don't move." And he disappeared once more, leaving poor Charlie and Gibson with little to do but to sit and wait, which were the two things Charlie hated most to do in the world.

That had been well over two hours ago. Meanwhile, the stupid boy had found his tongue again and, despite Charlie's orders to shut the hell up, he wouldn't.

The waiting was infuriating. Not being able to smack or cuff him was worse.

Charlie heard the first sounds of gunfire in the distance roughly three hours after Father Adrian's sudden arrival.

"Father Adrian?" he shouted. "Are you still here?"

Adrian emerged, his shirt sleeves rolled up and a look of bitter contempt on his face, but his impatience turned to outrage when the gunshots repeated. Charlie thought they were louder now, which meant they were getting closer.

Adrian spun around again and hurried toward the back, shouting that they had better get ready to leave.

In his haste to collect their few belongings, Charlie knocked the device to the floor, where it shattered into a half dozen pieces.

The gunshots were so loud now that Gibson nearly brained himself running into a metal pipe. Charlie peeked out the window in time to see a large truck careen into view, a horde of ferals following close behind.

He tracked it around the corner, then ran into the back, where he found Father Adrian standing at the door peering through the tiny window. There were several loud crashes outside.

"Son of a bitch!" Adrian cried, "My truck!"

"Who the hell is that?" Charlie yelled, even though the sounds were already fading away into the distance.

Adrian turned, his face bright red. "Where'd y'all park? Quick!"

"In front, but—"

From somewhere in the hallway behind them, Gibson let out a high pitched scream. Then a shot rang out and the boy bolted out of one of the rooms and nearly brained himself again against the opposite wall. "They're inside, Charlie! I just shot one! I shot one, Charlie! I got me a feral!"

Adrian shoved Charlie to the side and ran to the room. "What have y'all done?" he screamed. "Y'all shot my sister!"

"Sister? No, Charlie, I swear! It was infected, I saw it. The black was in her eyes. She was standing there."

"Oh no!" Adrian wailed. "Oh, no! Jenny! *Noooo!*"

Charlie turned to his brother. "Ma, I'm sorry," he said. "I tried."

He raised his pistol and cocked it. His last thought before he pulled the trigger was how nice it was going to be not to have to babysit anymore.

CHAPTER

THE TRUCK SKIDDED TO A STOP IN FRONT OF THE temple, tires smoking and the group screaming Eddie's name. Harrison and Bix leveled their guns at the Wraiths making their way up the street and readied to shoot them down. They were still too few and too far away to expend their precious ammunition. But more were following, and coming fast.

"Thirty seconds at the most!" Bix yelled.

Without warning, Jonah vaulted over the side of the truck and began to sprint toward the spot where they had last seen Eddie a few hundred feet away.

"Jonah!" Bren shouted. "Come back!"

"Damn it! Go! Just go!" Seth cried. He reached for the steering wheel, but Kari batted his hands away. "The Wraiths are coming!" he shrieked. "We need to go!"

"Hey!" Finn shouted through the glass. He tapped on it with the butt of the pistol, then pointed the business end at Seth's head. He was tired of the man's behavior. All he could think about was himself. "Keep your hands off the wheel!"

"Finn!" Bren cried. "Don't."

The sound of Jonah's voice shouting Eddie's name reached them from around the corner.

"Go," Finn told Kari. "Follow Jonah. But only as far as the corner."

"They're almost here!" Bix yelled. "Fifteen seconds!" He fired twice. One Wraith stumbled but kept coming. The other fell and remained down.

Kari gunned the engine and drove toward the far corner, purposefully moving slow enough that Eddie could still catch them in case he appeared, but fast enough to keep the Wraiths from gaining ground. They found Jonah standing in the middle of an overgrown field with his hands cupped around his mouth. Far below, near the bottom of the slope where Jonah couldn't see them in the tall grass, slunk a second group of Wraiths.

"Jonah! Behind you!"

"Eddie!" Jonah shouted again at the wreckage, not hearing Bren. "Eddie!"

There was a shout from the far back corner of the building and they all turned to see Eddie running toward them. "Go!" he screamed, his voice echoing off the temple's facade. "Go! Get out of here!"

A third mass of Wraiths appeared behind him, close on his heels.

He was limping as he ran, losing ground. Blood streaked his arm. "Get out of here!" he screamed, then tripped and nearly fell.

"Jonah! Over there!" Finn and the others shouted, but with all the echoes, their cries became confused.

Kari leaned into the horn, blasting it for a solid couple of seconds.

"Behind you!" Bren screamed. "Run!"

Jonah spun around and saw the Wraiths just as they burst into a full run. But they were closer to him than he was to the truck, and he had the steeper part of the hill to climb.

The truck lurched forward, smashing through a line of slender concrete posts before careening down the hill toward Jonah. He waved them to his right, angling his trajectory so they would cut him off, but Kari was going too fast and the tilt of the slope was too steep for her to change direction.

"We can't leave Eddie behind!" Bren screamed.

"We can't save them both!" Harrison shouted back. His face was white with fear as he watched the gap between Eddie and the infected creatures narrow.

The big man stumbled again, and the creatures leapt onto him. He lashed out, kicking at the closest and sending it crashing into the one behind. But they couldn't tell if he escaped the rest, as the ground rose to block their view while the truck careened down the hill.

The once-manicured lawn was heavily rutted by gopher holes and thickets, bouncing them around so violently they could do nothing but hold on for dear life. Kari somehow managed to keep them going straight.

Finn threw himself to the right side of the bed, landing hard on his injured shoulder and wincing in pain. He planned to grab Jonah as they passed by. But the closer they drew, the more it looked like they were going to miss each other altogether. Jonah glanced back, then tried to turn. His feet slipped, and he went down in a cloud of dust and grass pollen. He somersaulted once, then popped back up again.

"Help me grab him!" Finn shouted, but they were going too fast. He leaned over the side as far as he could, extending his arm despite the agony in his shoulder. Their hands slapped each other's wrists, then slipped. Fingers clasped, grabbed, and locked. Jonah's feet flew out from under him.

"I need help!" Finn screamed. He nearly let go after Jonah's weight pulled him painfully against the tailgate.

The truck hit a bump and bounced them all off the surface of the bed. Jonah's head banged into the bumper, yet he somehow managed to keep his grip as his feet skied over the flattened grass. He flailed with his other hand, trying to grab something, anything.

The truck lurched to the right, sending both boys to the other corner. Then Harrison was there, reaching down, grabbing a sleeve. Jonah caught on with his other hand.

"Pull!" Harrison shouted at Finn. "Now!"

Finn locked his other hand on Jonah's wrist and leaned back, screaming in effort. Jonah flew into the bed and landed on top of them. A blast rang out as Bix fired on the Wraiths, but the shot was wild.

"Hold on!" Kari yelled.

They hit the perimeter road at the bottom of the slope at an angle, skidded, then corrected, barely missing the wall on the other side by inches.

"Go back!" Bren yelled. "Eddie got away!"

They saw him coming down the plaza, heading straight for the base of the property where they would be in a few seconds. He was moving incredibly fast, and the other Wraiths were close behind, no longer chasing him, it seemed, so much as following his lead.

"No!" Seth yelled. "He's turned! Don't stop!"

Finn watched in horror as Eddie dropped to all fours, using his incredibly powerful arms to stabilize him as he loped along. The distance between them evaporated.

"Faster, Kari!"

The truck sped past and didn't slow, and for a split second they were certain they had outrun Eddie. But then he launched himself into the air. Bren screamed as he hurtled toward them, arms outstretched, blood streaming away from the dozens of wounds on his body. He landed heavily onto the bumper and began to climb in.

"Get away!"

Beneath the gore and filth, the skin on his face was gray and his eyes were dark pools of ebony.

Bix raised his gun.

"No!" Jonah cried and batted it away. "Don't shoot!"

But Bix pushed him away and aimed.

"Don't shoot, Bix," Eddie said, panting as he held on. "I'm okay."

He lifted his other leg over the tailgate and slumped into the corner, curling himself into a ball.

Finn put a hand on Bix's arm. "Don't shoot," he said. "Not yet."

CHAPTER

"WE HAVE TO GO BACK."

"Haven't you heard a single word that's been said, Finn?" Jonah countered. "Your brother wasn't there. He never was. Nobody was."

"That's not what Eddie said."

"Eddie was delirious, Finn. Those things just about tore him apart."

"He said he didn't see or hear any sign of anyone, but he never mentioned smell! We should have asked him about that."

"I'm pretty sure he would have mentioned it, if he had smelled them," Jonah pointed out. "But he didn't."

"How would he know what Harper smells like?"

"Finn, think about it."

Finn rubbed his shoulder. It felt weird, like someone had painted a layer of rubber over the wound. The pain wasn't as bad as he thought it should be, though it was swollen and stiff and felt a little warm. And . . . itchy. "I just think we should ask him."

"He's still asleep. Let him rest."

Jonah sighed and tossed another piece of wood into the fireplace and watched it catch. He shook his head. "Look, I'm sorry this didn't pan out better for you, Finn, but it's simply too huge of a risk for all of us to go back in there. As it is, we lost half our supplies, and we're lucky everyone got out alive."

"No thanks to you," Finn grumbled. "What the hell were you thinking jumping out of the truck like that?"

"Yeah, how stupid was that?" Bix said.

Finn ignored his buddy's attempt to back him up. Where was he when he needed him a moment ago?

"In my defense, we needed to find Eddie and get the hell out of there," Jonah said.

"Well, he can obviously take care of himself and doesn't need our help!"

"I'll say," Red muttered, speaking out for the first time on the subject.

No one acknowledged his comment. In fact, by the looks on their faces, Finn could tell they resented Red chiming in, too. It didn't matter how invaluable he had been to the group back there — holding off the Wraiths, helping to reload weapons — he still wasn't their friend and probably never would be, so his opinion on Eddie's abilities was definitely not welcome.

Which was not to say the subject was even close to being resolved. Based on everything they knew about the Flense, Eddie should have been infected after coming into direct contact with the Wraiths. Yet here they were, hours later, holed up inside an abandoned farmhouse on the outskirts of the city, and instead of having to put a bullet into the man's head, they were waiting for him to recuperate from his injuries because he was apparently immune to whatever it was that made people turn into bloodthirsty monsters.

And it made no sense whatsoever.

The issue affected Bix the most, as it conflicted with his theory that the Flense required nanites to spread. But if that were true, then why hadn't Eddie caught the disease? There was no question he had the nanites in his body, and that they were still active. They were responsible for his superhuman abilities. And for his current accelerated rate of healing.

Bren had suggested it was because he was covered in ash from digging through the burned temple, but her father immediately dismissed the theory. But as the one person who knew the most about the nanites, he wasn't being very forthcoming. He just kept insisting he didn't know why, only that he was sure it had nothing to do with the ash.

Finn didn't believe him. He suspected the man was hiding something, and he sensed the others did, too.

He wanted to ask Kari what she thought, but she had gone up to the roof with Harrison and the night vision goggles to watch for any dangers. Finn had been instructed, along with everyone else, to try and get a little sleep.

Yet how could they, when there were so many questions left unanswered, and Harper was still somewhere out there?

"I'll take the truck myself then," Finn said. "Alone, if I have to. I'll go first thing in the morning."

"Finn, the temple was totally trashed. You saw it yourself, it was uninhabitable. Harper was never there, and neither was Father Adrian. We've been chasing ghosts. Maybe Adrian was lying, hoping to lure us there."

"Then why set those traps on the road? He's been trying to kill us."

"Maybe this is just one more."

They all turned to Red, who raised his hands in a conciliatory gesture. "All I know is that Adrian was going to get the boy where he had his very first sanctuary."

"You said it was a church before," Finn said, jumping to his feet. "Was it a church or a sanctuary?"

Red frowned. "He said church. I think. Ain't they the same thing?"

"The same?" Finn yelped. "Jesus! Never mind. Bix, do you remember what Jennifer said about their safe place, where they were stuck before they drove north?"

"It was a Wal-Mart. You think that's what he meant?"

"Do you have any idea how many Wal-Marts there must be in Salt Lake City?" Jonah asked.

"Probably as many as there are churches."

"And now you think we're going to search them all? How do we figure out where they are? How do we even get to them? Finn, listen to me. We're nearly out of small arms ammunition, and Eddie's really the only one who can manhandle the machine gun for any length of time."

"He'll be better by morning."

"And what about you? Just a few hours ago, you could barely move."

"I'm fine. I'll manage."

No one said anything. Finally, Bren rose from her seat and crossed over to Finn. "We search them one by one," she said, wrapping her arm through his. "That's how we do it, starting with the one we passed back there."

"One what?"

"The Wal-Mart."

"It's not up for discussion," Seth said, sitting up from his sleeping pad. "No one is going back."

"In that plaza," Bren said, ignoring her father. "When we were drawing the Wraiths away from the temple. Remember, when we cut through the parking lot?"

"Stop it, Bren!" Jonah said. "Your father's right. We can't go back. Look, Finn, as much as I want to help you find your brother, at this point I think you're just grasping at straws." He shook his head resolutely. "Going back would be more than insane, it would be suicidal. That place is crawling with Wraiths, and we've riled them all up. Besides, even if he was there, there's no way he is anymore. Adrian would have taken him and left. They're long gone by now."

Finn glanced at Bix, hoping at last for some support from his best friend. But all he got was a defeated look.

"I don't need you!" he cried at all of them, and threw his hands into the air. "I'll do it on my own, then."

"No, you won't," Bix said, though he didn't sound too sure.

"And I'll help," Bren added.

"You're not going anywhere, young lady!" her father snapped. "This foolishness ends now!"

"You made a deal!" Finn shouted, whirling around to face Mister Abramson. "You said you'd go along with whatever we agreed to until we got Harper back. It's your fault we even have to have this discussion!"

"That's right. I said I would help *as long as we all agreed*," Seth replied. "I don't see the others agreeing. In fact, they're telling you to stop. But why should I be surprised? You've always been just like your father, too stubborn to accept when you're wrong."

"Daddy, no!"

"It needs to be said, honey. We submitted to Abraham's demands for three years, and where did it get us? Look at us now. Most of us are dead. If we had simply let someone else make the decisions for once, we—"

"Like who?" Jonah interrupted. "You? My father? As I recall, it was my dad's decision to challenge Mister Bolles that caused problems in the first place. And it was your choice to murder Doc Cavanaugh and Rory and make it look like Eddie was a Wraith."

Silence filled the room. They had all privately come to terms with what had happened back there in the bunker in their own different ways, had even accepted their friends' deaths and Seth's role in them as something to be set aside for the sake of their need to survive. In some sense, they supposed they could understand why he had done it, even while they hated the man for it. They had to, if they were going to continue to accept Bren as part of their group. To shun him would be to shun her and, by extension, Finn. The teenagers were guilty of nothing except, maybe, a certain idealistic naïveté.

Heavy footsteps sounded in the hallway, and they turned toward the door, steeling themselves when it opened.

Eddie stepped into the flickering light, his face pale and glistening with the accumulation of road grime, ash, and sweat, as well as the flaking spackle of his own dried blood.

The gaping tear in his shirt exposed one of the sites where he had been bitten. The skin was completely clear now and the gouged wound beneath it was nearly fully filled in again. He stood in the doorway like a hulking monster, a man with superhuman strength and abilities, and the same thoughts and fears crossed the minds of most of the people inside that room: How long before the thing he's become turns on us?

Because it seemed not a question of *if*, but *when*.

"You all need to keep it down in here," he said, speaking in a low voice. "On a night like this, when there's no wind, sounds carry. We can't afford to attract anything to us, whether infected or otherwise." He frowned. "Besides, you should be resting. Kari and Harrison's shift is almost finished, and they're eager to get to bed."

Bix snorted.

Eddie threw him a dark look. "You think this is funny?"

"Well, sorta. I mean—"

"Don't waste your chance to get some sleep. You don't know when you'll get another."

Bix looked like he wanted to say something, but Finn gave him a quick shake of the head.

Eddie wagged a finger at them, then turned to Finn. "No one's going anywhere tonight, so you might as well leave the discussion about it until morning."

He tapped the imaginary watch on his wrist and pointed to Jonah and Bix. "You two have the next shift. Two hours on. Then Finn and Seth."

All four of them groaned.

Eddie spun around and left them without saying another word.

Bix let out a low whistle through his pursed lips. "Ain't nothing wrong with Eddie's hearing, that's for sure. But he's blind as a bat, if he can't see what's going on with Dad and Kari."

CHAPTER

EDDIE JUMPED OFF THE BACK OF THE TRUCK AND TRIED the door, but it wouldn't open. He could see that the latch wasn't engaged, but someone had shoved a bent metal rod into the push bars to prevent anyone from getting inside, and while he knew he could break it, he didn't think it was prudent, especially given the large splotch of dried blood at his feet. It was relatively fresh, and it smelled human.

"Someone's been here recently," he said, bending over and picking up a couple water bottles. They were still full.

"See anything inside?" Finn asked.

"You just keep watching for Wraiths."

He moved over to the bank of windows beside the door. Holiday wrapping paper had been taped over them, most of it sun bleached to a uniform yellow, their former printing rendered into ghosts. He found a spot where a corner of one had come away, and he cupped his hands around his eyes and pressed his face into the glass to see inside. "Too dark."

"Told you," Bix whispered to Finn. "Can't even see what's right in front of him."

"Oh, I can see just fine," Eddie said. "Just like I can hear you, Bix. I meant it's too dark inside. If anyone was in there, they'd want more light."

"Unless they heard us coming. The truck's not exactly quiet."

Eddie stepped back and surveyed the line of storefronts. Over the years, the wind had blown trash and leaves into discrete mounds against the buildings, and the rain and snow had compacted them into semi-rigid drifts that nestled into the corners where sidewalk met wall. Most of the piles were undisturbed, but the one right in front of the door had been pushed away.

"Maybe we should try in back," Finn called.

"You're supposed to be watching for Wraiths."

"Red's on it."

Red turned from where he stood on the other side of the truck bed and nodded. He seemed perfectly content to do the job, one of the rifles cradled in his arms. Eddie frowned, not because he considered the man much of a threat to them anymore, but because his loyalties had been so easily switched. It rubbed him the wrong way.

He sighed and realized he'd better get used to it. This was apparently the new reality, a world where individual survival was paramount and the threats innumerable, where at any given moment you professed fealty to whomever offered you protection.

He waved at Kari, who was again at the wheel. Harrison was seated beside her. Mister and Missus Abramson had refused to come, as did Jonah. And Finn had vetoed Bren's wish to accompany them, despite her protestations.

"Let's check in back," Eddie said, and hopped lightly onto the back bumper.

"You haven't checked all the doors out front."

"Feels too exposed out here. There was a fence around the back lot. Limited access means fewer points to worry about."

Kari pulled away, circling in the same direction they had taken the day before. They approached the first corner moving slowly so they could check around the building. When it was clear, they proceeded to the next and repeated the process.

"Stop," Harrison murmured, putting a hand on her arm. "Wraiths. At least a dozen."

"Are they dead?" Kari asked.

Eddie jumped off and walked to the corner and peered around it. "Looks that way. I think you should back it up."

"But—"

"Do it. We can't go this way anyway. It's blocked by that lamppost we knocked down yesterday. We'll back in from the other side so we're pointed in the right direction in case we need to make a quick getaway."

The boys crouched in their respective corners at the back of the bed, ready to shoot at anything that moved. Eddie and Red took their positions at the front corners.

"You know I always got your back, right?" Bix told Finn. "Whatever you decide, I'm there. I just didn't want to be the one to pressure you into doing something you hadn't thought through."

"It's my brother," Finn grumbled. "Nothing to think about."

"Maybe, but it's been three years since you've last seen him. Are you really sure you want him back in your life?"

"What the hell is that supposed to mean?"

"I don't know. Never mind. Forget I brought it up."

Finn avoided Bix's eyes, though he made sure his friend could see his scowl. He was still sore about last night, and the unwelcome reminder of how much Harper had overshadowed him before the Flense only made it worse.

"I just don't like seeing you get your hopes up," Bix pressed. "It's been like a rollercoaster ride for you these past few days. Sometimes you just need to step off and take a break, get yourself a funnel cake or something."

Finn swallowed dryly. He hated when Bix came up with corny stuff like this. In his own way, it made sense. "Yeah, it's been a little like that," he admitted. "Up and down. But no matter how bad it is for me, all I can think about is how much worse it must be for Harper."

The bed rocked from side to side as they reentered the main road, then turned onto the side street at the corner. Kari stopped once more before backing a few feet into the parking lot, giving them time to survey the scene from the new perspective.

It was the same spectacle— a jumble of dusty vehicles, many on flats; lots of debris; weeds; the broken post and the vehicles it had crushed coming down. And a dozen or so bodies scattered about.

Finn studied them, searching for signs of life. Given the state of their clothing, which was mostly rags, they were obviously Wraiths. Some were bloodied, but others showed no evident signs of trauma.

"Did we do that?" Bix asked.

"Someone did," Eddie said behind them, and sniffed the air. "Lots of fresh blood here, too. Get a little closer, Kari."

She slowly guided the truck deeper into the lot. Both Bix and Finn braced themselves on their knees, but kept their weapons propped up on the side rails. They couldn't tell if this was some kind of trick. After the stunts Adrian had pulled before, it seemed almost certain this was another of his traps.

You're assuming he's here.

Finn tried to push the doubt away, but it refused to be ignored. If he only had a sign . . . .

"Stop for a moment," Eddie said. "Red, keep watch over our escape route."

They were still a good hundred feet away from the first body. Eddie walked back from the front of the cab and peered out between the boys at the bodies.

"See anything?"

"One of them might be breathing." He turned back. "Okay, a little more, Kari. Slowly. Watch yourselves, boys."

The truck lurched as she put it into gear again. Broken glass and other debris crunched beneath their tires. Finn, who was on the side closest to the stores, pressed himself against the rail and stared out at the buildings, his nerves primed for the slightest movement. He felt lucky that most of the ache from yesterday was now gone, but that infernal itching was still there. He'd thought it might drive him nuts, but now that he was here, it actually felt like it was fading away.

It's the adrenaline again. You know they're here. And Harper might—

He nearly squeezed his trigger when something dropped heavily onto the bed of the truck right beside him. He spun around and froze, confused by the sight of Eddie's quivering body.

"Kari! Stop the truck!" Bix shouted. "Stop the truck now!"

"I heard you! What is it?"

Red dropped to his knees behind the cab and peered out over the rooftops. "Where are they?" he said in a harsh whisper. "Who shot?"

"I didn't hear a gunshot," Finn replied. "Did anyone see anything?"

No one moved for several seconds. Finn shimmied over to Eddie and checked his breathing. "He's alive! But I don't see any wounds. Eddie, can you hear me?"

"Look at his eyes," Red whispered. "Shit, look at his eyes! It's happening! He's finally turning into one of them!"

Finn looked, and his heart nearly froze. Eddie's eyes were wide open and rolled back.

But they weren't black. What Finn saw was the whites, just like he'd seen back at Adrian's compound.

He jumped to his feet. "He's here! Adrian's here, and he's close by! He's got one of those devices turned on!"

"Get down, Finn!" Bix whispered.

"There's no shooter!" Finn snapped. He slid back to the end of the truck bed and scanned the buildings again. The doors were all nondescript, none yielding any hint which of them Adrian was hiding behind. "Harper!" he shouted.

Bix grabbed the waist of his pants and tried to pull him down. *"Get down! You'll get shot!"*

Finn's knee buckled and he nearly fell. "Stop, Bix! It's the device! Just like what happened back— Look, there! Jesus! That's Adrian's truck! How could we have missed it yesterday?"

"You know how many gray trucks there are—"

"There's no dust on it! It's his!"

He pulled away and was over the rail before Bix could stop him again. He heard Harrison's door open, followed by the scuff of footsteps on the pavement. The engine revved and whined as Kari backed the truck up.

He ran over to Adrian's Chevy, though now that he was sure they were here, it felt like he was swimming through mud. The roof was crumpled beneath the lamppost, the doors crimped shut. He peered in through one of the broken windows and saw the device on the floor, just out of reach.

"Help me move this, guys!" He tried to raise his arms, but they felt like lead weights. With a grunt of effort, he braced his hands beneath the lamppost and lifted, but he couldn't get it to budge. His knees buckled from the effort.

"Out of the way, Finn!" Kari said. She stuck her head out the window, waving. She edged the truck back until the tailgate contacted the top of the post. The metal squealed, and more glass popped out from the strain on the crushed frame. The truck yielded to the pressure with a loud groan. Then, with a sharp snap, the post flipped up out of the crease and bounced onto the hood with a loud crash.

Finn wasted no time sweeping the glass out of the window frame on the driver's side. He suddenly felt energized, but the pain of his injuries was back with a vengeance. Nauseous, he hoisted his body through the tight opening and tumbled into the cab.

Outside, the truck engine coughed into silence. Kari's door creaked open, and she jumped out. The world turned quiet once more, save for the gentle wind.

And the metallic crick of an old loose sign swinging at the end of the parking lot.

And then the first hisses of waking Wraiths.

"WE LIED TO HER, SETH," **KALEAGH** **ABRAMSON** **SAID.** "Her own parents. We've been lying to her nearly her entire life. Bren will never forgive us when she finds out."

"Keep it down. She'll hear you."

"I sent her upstairs to keep watch with Jonah."

"You let her go up there? In the dark?"

"Are you actually worried about her and Jonah? Of all the boys from the bunker who—"

"That's not what I meant, and you know it. I just mean she could fall off the roof. Can we not do this right now?"

But Kaleagh refused to drop the subject. She wanted to hurt him, to make him understand the pain she felt inside. "You know she and Finn were having—"

"Kaleagh!" Seth crossed his arms over his chest and scowled. He didn't want to hear it. "Enough."

They didn't speak again for several minutes. She stared into the dying embers in the fireplace; he leaned against the frame of the closed door to the hallway.

At last, he cleared his throat. "She's only seventeen — and a young seventeen at that — and she still has a lot of growing up to do. We tell her what she needs to hear. If we have to lie, so be it."

Kaleagh turned and looked at her husband— really looked for the first time in as long as she could remember. *When had he changed*, she wondered. What had happened to make him be like this?

"Honey, listen, we have to stick together on this," he said, pushing away from the wall. "Stay on message. Once we have—"

"Stay on message?" she parroted. "How can you still think like that? After all that's happened, how can you still believe this is for the best? Can't you see? Everything's changed. The world isn't the place you remember from before. Look at what happened to Eddie yesterday! You can't even explain that, can you?"

He stepped over and knelt down by her side, and for a moment she thought he might wrap his arms around her and pull her close, like he used to do, back before the Flense. Back in the time before they worked for that horrid company. Back before they'd sold their souls to the devil. Before all the lies and secrets.

It was so much harder for her, since her lies were secrets of omission. As far as any of them knew, she was entirely innocent of it all. That's how Seth had insisted it should be, but she didn't know how long she could keep up the charade. And he was so blind he couldn't see how it was killing her.

But he didn't touch her. She thought she might actually shiver with revulsion if he did. She still loved him. He was still the father of their daughter. But he had done things she could never forgive. And he had made her do things that made her hate herself.

"I didn't cause this," he quietly told her, perhaps sensing the true nature of her feelings. "*We* didn't make this . . .

happen." He stood up again and waved his arms in a wide circle. "We were trying to help humanity. You know that, right? In fact, we *were* helping. So many diseases, so many genetic defects and pathogens and cancers, and all we had to do was put these tiny machines inside of people and make them better. You saw the results yourself with your very own eyes. What we did was miraculous. Look at Eddie. And what about all those other places, Chili and Africa and Russia? We eradicated Zika and chikungunya. We stopped cancer, mended injuries and—"

"*We* didn't do any of that. Not you. Not me."

"We were a part of it, even if it was after the fact."

"You're making excuses for what we should never have agreed to do. The flu shots—"

"Were sanctioned by the government!"

"The government?" She sniffed in disgust. "Look around. Open your eyes, Seth. Do you think this invention helped humanity? Because from where I'm sitting, it looks pretty damn clear it didn't."

"The government—"

"When did they ever have the best interests of mankind in mind? Certainly not in our lifetimes."

"Governments don't survive by killing off the people they govern, honey. Successful people. Taxpaying people."

"And where are the taxpayers now?"

"They didn't want this to happen."

"They should have known it would!"

"How?"

"You should have known!"

He didn't respond to her right away. A vein pulsed in his forehead, and the muscles in his neck throbbed as he chewed the inside of his cheek, a habit he'd developed many years ago, long before he'd started working in the Valley. It was a horrid thing, the chewing, and it had caused him to suffer from terrible canker sores for much of his adult life. But after an administration of nanites pre-programmed with epithelial biocodes cleared him right up, he'd been completely sold on the technology.

"They weren't our invention," he finally said, and managed to sound offended that she would imply such a thing. "The company brought us on because of the security issues. We fixed them."

"Really? Then how do you explain the Flense?"

"Faulty product was already in the marketplace because of the flu epidemic. We had nothing to do with that. I tried to fix it, but the Flense hit a lot sooner than we thought."

"Wait, you knew it was coming?"

He stammered for a moment. "Another day and we would have had the new protocols in place. One day was all we needed."

She sneered at him. "One day, one hour, one minute. Does it matter? We could have stopped it long before that point."

"How? By going public? You signed the same non-disclosure agreement I did. If we breached it, the financial penalties alone would have destroyed us, not to mention the impact on our professional careers."

"Good thing *that* didn't happen. The world is dead, but at least we're still hirable."

He sighed. "No one is more upset at our failure than I am, honey. But that doesn't mean we should stop now. Even as the Flense was spreading, we kept trying. We were close when the internet collapsed."

"The internet was still running — spotty, but running — when we were at the evacuation center, Seth. We didn't have to run away to the bunker. We should have stayed and kept working on it!"

"And what? Would you have us die there? We had to leave!"

"Yes, Seth, you saved us, but you let the world die."

"That's not fair. I kept trying, even after we were inside the bunker. I thought it could still work. Cellular data networks were still transmitting. There was satellite. We still had some communication capabilities, the phone in the monitor room—"

"Everyone else was dead!"

"How could I have known it would happen so quickly, so completely?"

"We should have told the others in the dam! The stupid NDA no longer mattered anymore! Instead, you let Gia and Abraham stumble around in the dark for three years with their homemade microscopes and their guesses."

"How would Doc Cavanaugh have been able to help? How would Abraham? They couldn't. All they would have done is strung us up from the railing on Level 5 if they knew we had a part in what happened. And then what would happen to Bren? We had to keep it a secret for her."

"That's always been your problem, Seth. You never really saw the big picture, only how it affected you personally. That's why you did what you did. It's why you handed over Finn's brother to that evil man."

"I wish I hadn't, but I had no choice. He would have taken him anyway and killed us for it. If I had known about the phone, I would have—"

"You sacrificed an innocent kid."

"All isn't lost."

Her eyes narrowed. "What do you mean? What haven't you told me, Seth?"

"A cure. The things that have happened to Eddie over the past few days, they've given me some insights. We just need the right equipment. And samples from his blood."

"Is that all, just blood samples?"

His face pinched. "Maybe the nanites in his brain, too."

CHAPTER

FINN COULD SEE THE WIRES POWERING THE BOX. HE traced them in the shadows from the current inverter to where they disappeared up into the underside of the console, and he realized that Adrian was running the device directly off the truck's battery beneath the hood.

"Finn! Get out of there! We've got company."

He wasn't surprised by Bix's shout. He'd expected Adrian to come out and challenge them by now. But he had to see they had him outnumbered and outgunned, and it did no one any good to kill each other at this point. Besides, he should also have figured out by now that they weren't going to give up until he handed Harper over.

A gunshot rang out, and he froze. "Stop shooting!" he shouted, but his voice sounded trapped inside the enclosed space.

He felt someone reach in through the window and grab his leg, fingertips slipping over the fabric of his jeans. They hooked onto the tops of his sneakers and pulled. He turned his head to see who it was. The morning sun was directly behind them, and all he could make out was the shape of someone's head and shoulders.

It hissed and started to crawl into the truck.

Finn cried out and scampered toward the other window, but another figure rose up and blocked it.

Gun! Crap! Where's my gun?

More shots rang out, followed by panicked shouts.

The Wraiths were climbing in from both sides now, so he went the only place he could, over the seat into the cramped space behind. His feet fumbled over the toolbox, upending it and spilling the contents out. Without lowering his gaze, he reached down and groped through the tools, hoping to find something hefty enough to defend himself with.

The biggest thing he could find was a heavy socket wrench. He swung it at the head of the closest Wraith, connecting just as it looked up and opened its mouth. The thick metal sunk deep into the creature's eye socket, and it flopped lifeless to the seat, still dangling halfway through the window.

A hand grabbed his arm through his jacket and squeezed. The second Wraith's face was a nightmare of blackened teeth and dried blood. Its eyes were tarry pools. It clacked its jaws and bared its lips.

"No!" Finn screamed and pulled his arm away, but all he succeeded in doing was dragging the monster further into the cab. "Get away! *Help!*"

He let go of the wrench handle — it was too stuck to pull free — and kicked at the seat until it sprang forward, trapping the other Wraith against the steering wheel. Keeping his feet pressed against the seat, Finn retreated deeper into the back. The monster still tried to reach him, its fingers pawing at the air near his leg, and Finn saw with horror the exposed skin on his calf barely inches away from its fingers.

"No! Get away!" he sobbed.

He groped through the pile of tools again, fingers fumbling for something, anything. He came up with the tray, smaller tools spilling out and onto the floor, and rammed one end of it at the Wraith's face.

Blood exploded from its crushed nose and spurted into the air. Finn twisted away to avoid the spray. He didn't know if it was contagious.

The Wraith seemed to shake off its daze. The spurting stopped, reduced to a thick oily flow. The creature pushed back, harder this time, and began to free itself. Once more, Finn rammed the end of the metal tray at its head. This time it ducked and grabbed for it, yanking it from his grip.

He drew back again, one foot still on the seatback. The other slipped off and fell into the gap toward the dash. He tried to pull it away. The toolbox overturned beneath him again and he lost his traction. The seatback jerked upright. Finn reached down again, shouting for help. If he could just break the window behind him, he could—

But out of the corner of his eye, he saw several more Wraiths in the bed of the truck. They pawed at the glass, prying at the cracks with their bloody fingers. He threw whatever he could wrap his fingers around at the monster in the cab, but it all bounced off with little effect.

With a loud tearing noise, its snagged pants ripped free of the shards of glass in the window frame, and it fell the rest of the way inside, slipping into the foot space beneath the steering wheel, where it became momentarily wedged in the tight space.

Finn squeezed himself into the far back corner, but he had nowhere else to go. The Wraith grabbed the seatback and pulled itself closer, hissing and smacking its cracked lips.

A gunshot blast tore through the tiny space. The side of the creature's face disappeared in a crimson cloud, and it flopped to the seat, then slumped into the other foot well, its arms and legs sticking stiffly up into the air.

"Get out of there, Finn!" Eddie screamed, yanking the door open and pulling the corpses out.

Finn kicked at the seatback, then ejected himself, doing his best to avoid touching any of the blood. It seemed to cover everything.

"There's more coming!" Bix screamed. "Get to the truck!"

Kari was already in the driver's seat again, desperately trying to start the engine. Finn could hear her cursing, but the motor wouldn't catch.

"Pump the gas! Pump the gas!"

"No, you'll flood it!"

"It won't start!"

"We need to get inside the building! We can't hold them off much longer! There's more coming!"

"The device!" Finn screamed, but Bix grabbed him and pulled him away from Adrian's truck.

Harrison led the charge to the doors, but each one they tried was locked. Eddie pushed his way through them and, with a grunt of effort, wrenched the closest one free. Splinters of wood and masonry exploded from around the frame. "Not yet!" he warned, and vanished inside while they fired at the Wraiths coming at them from behind. He reappeared a moment later and told them it was safe.

"Go!" he roared, stepping back into the sunlight and spraying the approaching Wraiths with the machine gun. "Get inside! NOW!"

Kari entered first, her own pistol now in her hand and aimed into the darkness.

"Finn, go!" Bix yelled.

"No, you go! I need to find Dad!"

The two men were still on the back of the truck firing at the Wraiths. Harrison jumped off first and stumbled as his ankle twisted on the curb. Red was right behind him, pulling him up.

Their feet tangled and they both went down. There was a blur as the nearest Wraith swept into view. Someone screamed. Finn spun around and fired once before Bix stopped him. "Dad!" he cried again. "Don't shoot, Finn!"

The Wraith bowed its head over the two men and opened its mouth. Another shot rang out. This time, the creature flopped over and didn't move. The boys ran over.

"Don't touch it!" Finn warned. But Bix was beyond hearing him. He grabbed the Wraith by a wrist and yanked it off.

Skin on skin! Finn silently screamed in horror.

But the Wraith wasn't dead. It twisted around, baring its teeth, and lunged. Bix ducked away as it snapped, its mouth finding only empty air. A moment later, Eddie was there. He grabbed the monster by an ankle and hurled it halfway across the parking lot.

"Go!" he shouted.

Harrison disentangled himself from Red and stood up. But Red remained where he lay, trembling. "Don't . . . touch . . me," he hissed.

"Red?"

The transformation was swift. A terrible black scrim swept over the man's eyes, and his skin lost all hint of color.

"It's too late for him!" Eddie shouted. "Leave him! Everyone inside!"

"But it touched me, too!" Harrison raised his arm, which was covered in blood. "It bit me!"

"No! Harrison!" Kari screamed. "Oh, my god, why?"

"It's okay! He's immune!" Bix shouted, and grabbed his father and pulled him toward the door. "Dad's immune! Go!"

"You don't know that for sure, Bix!" Eddie yelled. "We can't—

"We're not arguing!" Finn said. He grabbed Red's pistol off the ground and fired it at the closest Wraith, but the bullet ricocheted off the truck. "They're coming!"

They slipped into the darkened building with Eddie at the rear. Before shutting them in, he tore off a metal downspout hanging beside the entrance and jammed it into the push bar, twisting it around until it locked against the frame.

They could still hear Red fighting the creatures with the last shred of his sanity, his cries growing weaker and less coherent. They all knew it was futile, and the Wraiths showed him no mercy in the face of his defiance. His screams cut straight through the cinderblock walls. But all too soon they faded away, leaving only the sounds of feeding and the angry hisses and groans of the other monsters trying to get inside.

CHAPTER

45

THEY BLOCKED THE DOORWAY WITH ANYTHING THEY could find in the immediate vicinity, pushing shelves and desks into place until the entry was jammed from floor to ceiling.

Most of the rooms opening up on either side of the corridor appeared to have once been offices. There was a restroom, the door slightly ajar. The stink emanating from it suggested it had been used fairly recently. They shut it and moved on.

"There's a body in here!" Kari called from another room further along the corridor.

Eddie approached the corpse with caution, then nudged it with the toe of his boot. "Jesus," he whispered. "He's just a kid."

"Harper?" Finn whimpered.

"Give me some room."

He flipped the body over, revealing the fatal gunshot wound to the head. The boy's eyes were still open, frozen in a death mask of shock. But they weren't black like a Wraith's. Nor did they belong to Harper.

"Not him," Finn said, his voice breaking with relief.

"Body's still in rigor," Kari noted, "so he hasn't been dead long. Skin's cold. A day, maybe. Not more than two." She glanced up at Eddie, who nodded.

"Leave it," he said, before turning around and exiting.

They made their way toward the double doors at the other end of the hallway, which Eddie had earlier blocked with a board through the handles. Once more, he told them to wait a moment while he checked the warehouse beyond.

Many of the shelves were still stocked with unopened boxes, their contents labeled on the outside. The items were useless to them, relics of a world where children's toys, office supplies, and toilet plungers were once essential survival items. Light filtered in from filthy skylights in the ceiling, just enough to prevent them from stumbling into one another.

"Smells like at least two more people were here, maybe three," Eddie said. "They're all mixed up. And fading."

Finn growled in frustration. He hated that they had come so far and gotten so close to rescuing his brother, only to miss them once again.

They came to another set of double doors at the front end of the warehouse, but this time Eddie did not ask them to wait. They gathered around him as he stood in the open doorway and listened to the silence and sniffed the stale air. Once more, he shook his head and announced it was all clear.

Many of the display shelves in the store had been dismantled or moved around to form discrete living spaces for as many as a couple dozen people. All of them had collections of filthy bedding, as well as stacks of well-worn books and magazines. Crayon and pencil drawings were tacked up everywhere, depicting scenes of a world long since dead by people who probably were as well.

If they're lucky, Finn mused.

There was trash everywhere. Broken glass, too. And in a couple different places, thick, dark stains that looked like blood.

"Kari, stay with Harrison here," Eddie instructed. "Keep an eye on him. Let him rest while me and the boys search the rest of the store."

"I'm fine, Eddie."

"I'd rather you rested while you can. Finn and Bix, spread out. Look for medicine and any clean fabric you can find to use as bandages. Also, food and water."

Finn placed a hand on Kari's arm before he left. "I think he'll be fine," he quietly said. But his eyes flicked down to the firearm in her hand. She nodded grimly.

When he turned, Bix was there, watching him. Nobody said anything. They all knew the stakes. Nobody had to explain what would need to be done if Harrison started to change.

At the far end of the store was a pair of gas grills, used but empty cooking pots stacked up on top and thousands of disposable plates and utensils dumped to the side. Someone had long ago rigged up a ventilation system with flexible plastic tubing to guide the poisonous gasses into the ceiling space above. Soot and dust drifted down when Finn shook one.

Dozens of empty propane tanks lay scattered nearby. Both of the grills were now cold, but there was evidence that one of them had been recently used to cook something. All around were piles of empty cans on the floor, their lids torn open. Finn found a couple where the residue was still tacky.

He tossed them away in disgust.

He knew they wouldn't find anything of any use to them here. The place had long ago been abandoned because all sources of food and water had been depleted. Every single nook and cranny would have been scoured many times over.

"Not a scrap to eat or drink," Bix confirmed. He seemed more upbeat than before, clearly relieved that another twenty minutes had passed without bad news from the other side of the store. "No water, soda, beer, or liquor. I checked it all, even the cough medicine, mouthwash, and baby formula. Anything that could be eaten or drunk already has been. Not even a bottle of rubbing alcohol, hydrogen peroxide, or eyewash saline left. It's all gone. Nothing useful."

"That's not true," Eddie said, handing him a box filled with items.

"Fish food and blocks of birdseed?" Bix asked, sorting through it.

"Protein. It'll serve in a pinch."

"And Halloween costumes? We need new clothes, but, seriously?"

"As long as they're sealed inside their packages, they'll be clean. We can use them for bandages. And here's a bottle of window cleaner. It's got alcohol in it and will sting like crazy when it goes on, but it'll disinfect your father's wound. Plus," he said with a wry grin, "it's eco-friendly. Got to protect the environment, right?"

"As long as it doesn't leave any unsightly streaks," Bix added. It was his first attempt at humor since the tragic encounter outside, and the banter helped relieve some of the tension they were feeling.

"Guess we can safely say your dad is immune, too," Finn said, squeezing his friend's shoulder. "Congratulations. That now makes three of us."

Bix looked immensely relieved. "Sorry, bud. It's an exclusive club."

"How do I become a member?"

Eddie slowly exhaled and shook his head. "Wish I knew, but I have a feeling Seth might. It's time he told us everything."

They returned to the others with the items, then sat in a semi-circle to discuss what they knew. Eddie mentioned that he'd found another of the interference devices by one of the front entrances, but added that it had been smashed to bits.

"Adrian would rather destroy it than let us have it."

"Then why would he leave the one in his truck?" Bix asked.

"That was probably unintentional. He couldn't get to it and was counting on us not being able to either."

"Is it possible he left it as a trap? I mean, what if he was waiting for us to come back?"

"No," Eddie said. "I'm convinced he believes we're dead. The smell tells me he left this place hours ago."

"Then how did the Wraiths wake up?"

"When Kari pushed the lamp post off the truck," Finn said, "I think it knocked one of the battery connections loose."

"I agree," said Eddie. "I remember losing muscle control soon after we entered the lot. But then it was suddenly gone and I could move again. I remember sitting up and seeing Finn crawling inside the truck right before the Wraiths woke up."

Finn jolted in surprise at his own memory of those few moments. He had actually felt something then, too, an odd combination of sensations— generalized weakness, but with pain focused in his injured shoulder and thigh, a faint cloudiness in his mind. He hadn't given it much thought at the time, especially since the situation shifted so quickly and he had more important things to occupy himself with, like staying alive and uninfected.

Had he really sensed it? Or was he misremembering?

"Really sucks about Red," Bix said, shaking his head. "I mean, we really didn't treat him very nice."

Eddie stood up and walked off, clearly upset over what had happened as well. It hardly seemed possible that just a couple days ago they would gladly have left the man for the Wraiths. He had done some awful things before, but he hadn't been a bad person. If anything, it was a sobering reminder of how vulnerable they all were to losing their humanity.

"It's a shame," Harrison quietly said. "But we move on. Let's not allow his sacrifice to be in vain."

Kari sighed. "Well, until we can get the truck running again, we're sort of stuck here."

"I suggest we take advantage of the daylight then," Eddie said, "and do a more thorough search for anything else that might be of use to us. Think outside the box. Look for anything adhesive. Also fire extinguishers, matches, lighters, camp fuel, even aerosol cans that might be used to produce shooting flames."

"Anything we can use as a weapon or to trade," Finn added with a nod.

"And clean clothes," said Bix.

They all frowned at him.

"What? You all reek." He reached into Eddie's box and withdrew a package, which he tossed over to Finn. "This one's for you."

"Lumberjack?"

"I was saving the French Maid costume for Jonah."

Eddie chuckled and walked back over. "In that case, you'll want this, Bix," he said and pulled out a spray can with a scene of a forest on it.

"Insect repellent?"

"It's pine scented. I recommend you apply it liberally, especially around the pit and butt regions."

* * *

Bix found Finn on his knees near the front entrance some time later. "You okay, Finn-meister? Find something interesting?"

Finn stood up. "Blood. Just a few drops, and it's not very old. It's still tacky."

"Don't assume it's Harper's, man. Could belong to that kid in the back."

Finn sighed. "I know. But the pattern is too . . . not random. I think this spot might've been where Harper was kept." He pointed to a nest of ratty pillows, empty water bottles with droplets still inside, and several long strips of fabric that might have been used to tie him up. "The blood trail forms a circle between here, the front window, and the broken device over there. No blood leading into the back."

"If you're trying to figure out where Adrian took him—"

"What if Harper's already dead?"

"He's not dead, Finn. We'll find him."

"How?"

"We have the maps."

"Ten of them. We don't know anything else. If Harper figured out where Bunker Twelve is and that's where they're going, then we're screwed."

They were quiet for several moments, each not voicing what was in their thoughts. Neither wanted to be the first to admit defeat.

Bix's fingers played absently over the surface of the linoleum tile, his nails catching on some deep gouges. He picked up a metal fork lying next to him and began to dig into the surface.

"Stop."

"What, I just—"

"These scratches. I need light."

Bix withdrew a book of matches from his pocket and lit one. Finn leaned in closer, gesturing for Bix to do so as well. "What does that look like to you?"

"Letters. Caca? Cocoa? I can't tell."

"It looks like Ca . . . cob."

"Jacob? So?"

Finn plucked a tiny corkscrew of plastic off the floor and held it up for Bix. "These are fresh scrapings. See? They're not filled in with dirt like the rest."

"Maybe the dead kid's name was Jacob."

"That's not a J. I think it's a C. And that's a little A. And another C."

"C-A-C-A spells poop."

Finn ran his palm over the surface of the floor, feeling for more scratches. "There's more. It goes under the pillow. Get up."

"Eight hundred and ten?" Bix read, after he moved out of the way. "What is it, a date? August tenth?"

"It's too hard to see. I need more light."

"I'll do you one better," Bix said. He tore a page out of an old road atlas lying nearby and lit it with another match.

"Not much help way over there, buddy."

"Just wait a sec."

He let it burn about halfway, then blew it out and rubbed the ash into the scratches. "Hand me that water bottle over there."

"It's empty."

Bix sprinkled the last few drops onto the soot and smeared it around, adding a little spit to the mix. Then he pulled off his shirt and wiped the floor clean. When he was finished, the scratches stood out against the lighter tile.

"That's not an 8, that's a capital B."

"Bio? Or is it Blo? Blo Jacob? Congratulations, we've just found Adrian's secret erotic fantasy porn stash."

"Get your head out of the gutter for a moment, Bix. What do you see?"

"It's either an 8 or a— It's Bunker Ten?"

Finn nodded excitedly. "Harper just told us where to go."

"You don't know that he left this. Anyway, the cure is supposed to be in Bunker Twelve."

"But we don't know where that is. And Harper knows we don't, either."

Bix shook his head. "Blo Jacob sounds just as plausible, Finn. Maybe even more so."

Finn whistled the others over for a look.

"It's a chemical symbol," Kari guessed, after studying the scratches from several different angles. She agreed that the first part looked like it could refer to Bunker Ten, and scowled at Bix when he suggested his alternative interpretation. Harrison snorted, then quickly chastised his son.

"Or it's just someone's random doodling," Eddie said.

"What chemical?" Finn asked Kari.

"C-a-c-oh-three," Kari replied. "Calcium carbonate. From seashells. It's also what they used to give for upset stomachs."

"Great, it's a prescription. Take a couple Rolaids and call me when you're no longer contagious and hungry for human flesh."

"It's also a constituent in marble and limestone," Kari added.

"Certainly a lot of that in this area," Harrison remarked. "There are several mines west of here, which means if it's a clue, it doesn't give us much to go on. You'd think your brother would give you something more definitive, Finn.

Have you considered how unlikely it is we'd actually find this in the first place?"

"We don't know the circumstances he was under. Maybe he had to hide it."

Kari shook her head. "Or maybe we're chasing rabbits down rabbit holes, Finn."

"What about the triangle?" Eddie asked. "Could that mean something, too?"

Bix jumped up with an exclamation. "Gaah! Stupid. It's not a triangle! I mean it is, but it's proof this was meant for us!"

"How do you know?"

"Because look at the window there! What do you see in the dust?"

"Another triangle . . . and an arrow!"

"Pointing right to this spot here. And the door, the blood spots! It all points here."

"I still don't get it," Finn said. "What does any of it mean?"

"It's your name, doofus!" Bix cried.

"My name's not doofus."

Kari burst out laughing. "Of course! It's a fin!"

Bix slapped his friend on the back. "Awesome name. Bet you're glad it's not Dick."

CHAPTER

JONAH RAPPED HIS KNUCKLES ON THE DOOR FRAME AND waited for the others to start stirring from their sleep. "There's a vehicle coming from the south," he announced. "It might be them."

The Abramsons sat up from their makeshift beds by the unlit fireplace. They'd run out of chopped wood from the pile in the yard that morning, so Seth ripped out pieces of cabinetry from the kitchen downstairs. But the boards were varnished and produced a thick, black smoke that could be easily seen outside, and Jonah had put it out. Once night fell, no one bothered to stoke it, leaving the room cold and dark.

"What?" Seth asked. He fumbled around before finding his flashlight and flipped it on.

"Turn it off!" Jonah hissed. He went over to the window and covered it up again, repeating what he'd said a moment earlier. "Can't be sure if it's them or not."

"Can I turn on the flashlight now?"

"No, I don't want to ruin my night vision."

Seth flicked it on anyway, but covered the lens with his hand, letting only a thin shaft out.

"They're back already?" Bren murmured. She stood up and stretched, and the blanket fell off her shoulders. "Is Harper with them?"

Her mother picked it up and wrapped it around Bren's shoulders. "Are they okay?"

"I don't know. The vehicle's still a ways out. Assuming they stay on this road, they'll reach us within the half hour. Hard to say without any other reference points."

They accompanied him up to the third floor attic and carefully climbed out onto the gently sloping roof, where they huddled tightly together to conserve heat. The elusive dot of light, undiminished by pollution, was still very small and very far away, perhaps as much as twenty miles.

The stars overhead were dazzlingly bright and uncountable, but the celestial light was too weak to reach the ground. And as there was no moon, it made them feel like they were afloat on an ocean of ink.

Each exhale clouded the air around them, so they sat without speaking, and simply watched the tiny twinkling spark make its way across the vast dark ocean. Sometimes it disappeared for a few seconds, as if breached by a wave; other times it vanished for much longer periods, and they waited with bated breath wondering if it would surface again. But each time it reappeared, the light seemed closer, yet it still took forever.

At last, one light resolved into two. Then, at long last, they could hear the distinctive rattle of the truck's engine and knew it was them.

They went down and waited in the shadows on the porch, but remained out of sight.

Just in case.

At last the truck pulled into the yard, sat idling for a moment, and extinguished the lights. The engine knocked and coughed before wheezing into silence.

Jonah was ready. He handed the unlit flashlight to Bren and fingered the trigger on his rifle. "Eddie?" he called out.

The driver's side door opened.

"Kari?"

"F-finn?" Bren stammered. "Is that you?"

"Yeah, it's us," Eddie responded. He sounded beyond tired. "Finn's okay."

"Did you find him? Did you get Harper?"

Harrison appeared out of the darkness, flicking on a flashlight to guide his way over the uneven ground. His arm was wrapped and in a sling. Bix followed behind, his face drawn. Finn and Eddie brought up the rear.

"Where's Kari? And Red?"

Eddie gestured for them to go inside.

"Come on," Jonah said, turning to Seth and Kaleagh. "Food first. They're probably hungry. And let's get the fire going again."

Bren caught Finn by the arm as he made his way up the steps. "Kari?"

"She's gone," he said, choking back a sob. "We had to fight our way out. She didn't make it. Neither did Red."

CHAPTER

EDDIE DISAPPEARED INTO THE ROOM WHERE THEY'D unloaded their remaining supplies the previous day. The others went upstairs to warm up and get something into their stomachs.

He could hear Jonah through the floor asking what happened, but no one seemed willing to volunteer an explanation, not at least while Eddie was absent and couldn't defend himself against the second guessing that would inevitably follow.

He found them seated beneath blankets, the fire still small but licking at fresh planks. Seth turned to him as he walked in and repeated Jonah's query.

"We found where they'd been keeping Harper," Eddie began. "Bren was right. It was the plaza we'd driven through yesterday."

"Were they there?"

He shook his head. "He was definitely there, but we found it empty. Except for the Wraiths." His gaze flicked to Finn, who sat shivering beneath his blanket and staring into the cup in his hands. "Red was taken first, within minutes of us arriving. We managed to get away by locking ourselves inside the store. Kari was . . . ." He cleared his throat. "She died as we were trying to escape."

He didn't mention how it was Finn's reckless actions that caused the Wraiths to wake and attack them in the first place, nor did he explain how Kari's death had come as a result of his own choices. They had already assured him he wasn't to blame, just as they had all told Finn Red's death wasn't his fault. But neither of those things was exactly true. Every decision they made had consequences, and it was paralyzing to know that their next one might get someone else killed.

For the first time since sending Hannah with the Caprios to the army base did Eddie seriously believe he might not see his daughter again. It pained him more than the attack yesterday to imagine her carrying on in this world without his protection.

"That's it?" Seth asked, incredulous. "That's all you're going to say about that? What happened?"

"There's nothing more to tell," Harrison said. He slumped in his seat in one of the overstuffed chairs, his head in his hands, and refused to look up.

Seth spat in disgust. "So, all of this was for nothing. We've lost them."

"Are you more upset over losing Adrian and Harper or Red and Kari?" Finn demanded.

Seth glared at him but didn't answer.

"So, what do we do now?" Bren asked. "Do we keep looking for Bunker Twelve? Or do we just return to the army base?"

"Adrian and Harper are still in play," Eddie finally said.

"Excuse me? How?"

Eddie popped the plastic cap off the cardboard tube under his arm and tapped the thick roll of maps out. "Get that stuff off the coffee table. And bring over a couple candles for light." Then he nodded over to Finn and Harrison to join him, once more asking for some space to spread out.

"Tell me what's going on?" Seth demanded.

Harrison rose from his chair with a heavy sigh and placed a hand on Seth's arm. "Be patient. We've discussed this at length and decided—"

"I never decided anything. I wasn't consulted!"

"Dad! Please," Bren cried. "Just stop it! Can you just stop talking and listen for once? Let's see what they have to say."

"Finally, a voice of reason," Finn muttered.

They thumbed through the stack of papers until they found the right one. Like the rest, it was a topographical map with very few details, and almost no text, just a few odd words and nonsensical codes. None of the grid lines was labeled to denote coordinates.

"Figures nothing's circled on this one," Finn said, clearly disappointed. "The bunker could be anywhere on here, and we have no clue where." He sat back and ran his hands through his hair. "How are we even supposed to know where in the world this map is from? It could be South America, for all we know."

"It's gotta be somewhere close," Bix said.

"That's only a guess."

"Harper wouldn't have directed us to Bunker Ten otherwise."

"Harper?" Seth exclaimed, confused. "Bunker Ten?"

"He left Finn a clue," Eddie said. "Listen, boys, let's not despair before we've even started." He leaned over and scrutinized the paper. His shadow fell over the map, but he had no trouble seeing it. "Let's start with these features. What can we discern from them?"

"They look like ridges, three of them running roughly north-south. At least, I think up is north."

Eddie nodded. "Each is flanked by a relatively flat area."

"Three ridges that could be anywhere," Jonah pointed out. "And what's the scale of the map? We could be looking at a million square miles and mountain ranges ten thousand feet tall or mounds of dirt covering barely a hundred square feet."

"My guess is it's somewhere in between."

"Great."

"What about these words?" Bren asked, pointing to a notation between the middle and right ridges. "What's *tad*?" Then she slid her finger to the left between the middle and left elevation features. "And *sdmc*?"

"We're not going to get much from those, I don't think," Eddie said. "They look like acronyms. But these other ones might be promising. We've got *pyrite* on this flat area along the left edge of the map; *aragonite* at the top of the first ridge; *halite* at the tip of the third ridge; and *silicon* on the right edge."

"Well," said Harrison, "we know they're minerals."

"Yeah, but can anyone guess what they might mean?"

"Pyrite is fools' gold. Halite is salt. Silicon is sand." He shrugged. "No idea what aragonite is."

"Gold, salt, sand and . . . . Still not helpful."

"Can someone please explain to me why we're looking for Bunker Ten?" Seth asked.

"Because Harper—"

"Stupid!" Bix exclaimed, jumping up off the floor. "I'll be right back!"

They could hear him pounding down the steps, stomping through the rooms, then out the front door and across the porch.

While they waited, Finn used the time to describe what Harper had left behind and why they believed it was a message left specifically for him. He pulled out a drawing Bix had made of the scratches. Both Seth and Jonah were skeptical, but they had no time to press the issue before Bix returned, his face flush from the cold.

"Sorry it took so long," he said. "Should have taken a flashlight." He triumphantly held up the road atlas he'd found earlier. "Brought this from the store. I know, I forgot the milk and eggs, honey, so sue me."

He flipped through the pages, muttering the names of states that no longer existed: " . . . South Dakota, Tennessee, Texas, Utah, Ver—" He stopped and flipped back. "Utah!"

"Great," Finn said, his shoulders drooping in disappointment. "Except you tore out the one page we needed."

Bix flipped back and found another missing page. "Actually, it was New Jersey. If half of Utah's missing, then my guess is Adrian took it. That means we're on the right track!"

"Anyone could have torn that page out at any time for any reason," Eddie pointed out.

"Why tear it out?" Jonah asked. "Why not just take the whole book?"

"Okay, I'll give you that. But what if they wanted the map for eastern Texas instead? That's what would be on the other side of the missing page."

Seth pushed his way back into the circle with an impatient huff. "Look, these maps were intentionally left as vague as possible, in case they ever got into the wrong hands. That's to discourage the average person from understanding their significance, identifying the bunkers' locations, and publicizing them."

"What's your point, Seth?"

"My point is, to be of any use, they still have to contain enough information if you know what to look for. One of these notations is the bunker's identifier. The rest simply provide help with the map's region, orientation, and scale."

"Still not helpful."

"This line here? That's a road, probably the one servicing the bunker."

"That's a big assumption."

He pulled out the map for Bunker Eight. "This squiggly line is the river. See how it intersects with this other line right in the middle of the circle? That's the road we arrived on."

He thumbed through the other maps until he found the ones for Bunkers One and Two. In both cases, the circle designating the location of the bunker was positioned over a line that looked like a road.

"Okay, but we still don't know where this road is."

Finn pulled the remaining half of Utah out of the atlas and set it beside the topo map for Bunker Ten and spent the next few minutes comparing them. "It looks like this line might be Highway 80. See how this little squiggle here as it passes through Salt Lake City roughly matches up here on the right side of our map?"

"And halite is the mineral name for salt!" Eddie exclaimed. "As in Salt Lake! Your brother must have figured that out!"

"Are you saying the bunker's in the lake?"

"Harper didn't write the chemical symbol for salt. It was calcium carbonate, remember? Neither *pyrite* nor *silicon* fit, because pyrite is an ore of iron oxide — iron pyrite — and silicon is, well, it's a silica-based mineral. Which leaves aragonite. And that's on the road, just as Seth said."

"What about *tad* or *sdmc*?"

"They aren't minerals. They may be other landmarks, place names or locations of some relevance to the bunker. Maybe evacuation centers?"

"But is the chemical symbol for aragonite calcium carbonate?" Finn asked.

No one replied.

"Anyone?"

"I honestly don't know, Finn," Eddie quietly said. "Kari was our resident scholar."

"It has to be that. Nothing else makes sense."

"It only makes sense if we're right," Harrison pointed out. "We don't know that we are. Are you willing to bet your brother's life on a guess, Finn, especially one as flimsy as this?"

Finn didn't answer. He looked around at the rest of them, hoping for help. Mister Blakeley was right, of course. It was wishful thinking to assume aragonite was the location of the bunker.

And yet it felt right.

"As far as Harper's concerned," he finally said, "a wrong guess is no worse than no guess at all."

CHAPTER 48

IT WAS STILL DARK WHEN THEY SET OUT AGAIN, THIS time leaving no one and nothing behind. If their assumptions were correct, then the target site was only about seventy miles away due west of the city.

Eddie had argued that, for safety reasons, only a small group should go— smaller, even, than those who had gone the previous day into the city. Finn couldn't tell if it was because of his general dislike for Seth or his reluctance to put more people at risk.

But Seth insisted on going, as did Jonah, and everyone agreed they'd all be safer together. So it was settled.

Besides, if it turned out Bunker Ten really was where they thought it was on the map, then they all wanted to be there to find it.

The hour or so before dawn was bitterly cold, forcing those in the back to burrow beneath several layers of blankets and a tarpaulin in order to avoid freezing. They managed to get some warmth directed to them from the heater in the cab after Jonah punched out the window. He volunteered to drive, claiming he didn't like the way the engine sounded and wanted to keep a close eye on it. Bix teased him about it, saying he was a wuss and just wanted to be close to the heater, but it was halfhearted ribbing. The truck was clearly having mechanical issues.

In the end, however, Eddie drove, because he could most easily see without needing the headlights. They didn't want Adrian to know they were coming.

As for the noise of the engine, there was nothing they could do about that.

"Starting to get light," Eddie announced about an hour and a half in.

"How will we know what to look for?" Finn asked, sticking his head out from underneath the covers. Bix burrowed out to join him and groaned in delight at the blast of heat hitting his face. Someone underneath complained he was letting in the cold air.

"Street sign up ahead," Eddie replied, and pointed down the road.

It was another minute or so before the boys could make out what it said.

"Exit 56," Bix read, squinting through the pre-dawn gloom. "ARAGONITE 4 MILES. TOOELE WASTE MANAGEMENT SITE 17 MILES. NO PUBLIC SERVICES."

"Sounds like the boonies," Jonah said. He sounded distracted. The engine rattle was getting worse.

Eddie guided the truck onto the exit ramp, and they coasted to a stop at the bottom. Leaving the engine on, he applied the parking brake and got out.

"What are we stopping for?" Bren asked.

"Checking for tire tracks."

He returned a minute later, nodding. "Someone's been here very recently. Sand's loose, and there's fresh tracks in it. Lucky the wind hasn't picked up and erased them yet."

They all looked at one another, not believing their luck. Finn felt a surge of pride for his brother. If the roles were reversed, he doubted he'd have the presence of mind to leave clues like Harper had.

Eddie put the transmission into gear, then cranked the wheel to the left. The truck bucked once and coughed. To compensate, he gave it more gas. The engine stalled.

Five minutes later, after diving beneath the hood with a flashlight, Jonah announced he had bad news. "Fuel line's done for." He held up the offending object and peeled it open. "Completely caked shut."

"Can it be reamed out?"

"Already tried with some wire. Tore a hole in it. The rubber's brittle."

"Anything else we can use?"

He shrugged. "Even if there was, the fuel pump and filters are probably in just as bad shape, which would explain the engine light." He sighed and shook his head. "We were lucky to make it this far."

"So, we walk. It's only four miles."

Eddie nodded. "Pack what you can carry. Prioritize. Food, guns, ammo, and as much water as you can manage." He turned to Seth. "That means everyone."

"Are you sure this is a good idea?" Kaleagh asked.

"We know someone came this way, most likely within the past few hours. My guess is it was Adrian and Harper."

"But it's four miles across the desert."

"A two-hour hike, max. One and a half, if we hustle. Waiting won't help."

"And if there's nothing when we get there?"

He shrugged. "We can't very well sit here. Eventually, the Wraiths will find us. And we can't go back. It's fifty miles to the city and not much between here and there. It's too far to walk. We have to keep going."

Dawn was breaking when they emerged from the other side of the underpass and climbed the sandy incline to ground level. The vista opened up before them, a stark, flat, barren landscape with a smattering of brush in a kaleidoscope of browns and grays. The wind blew, a bitter thing that pried relentlessly at their clothes with its polar fingers. It was like the Wraiths themselves, searching for access to bare skin.

Within a hundred feet, the tire tracks beneath their shoes vanished, erased by the drifting sand.

There were no lights, no buildings, no signs of life. And the road, little more than a shallow rut that the desert wind was slowly erasing, extended on in a straight line before finally diminishing out of view many miles away.

CHAPTER 49

"I THINK Y'ALL NEED TO EXPLAIN TO ME AGAIN WHY you think this is the place," Adrian demanded as he directed Harper toward the next building. They had already spent hours searching through the smaller structures scattered about the compound in northwestern Utah and found nothing to suggest any part of it had been designed to hold hundreds of survivors for any length of time. "Y'all ain't lyin to me, are ya?"

"No, sir."

There was a large parking area in the middle of the yard with a few ratty-looking cars in it, plus a single solitary bus, its door propped open and drifts of sand filling the corners of the steps. Like the half dozen buildings they'd already inspected, the long abandoned vehicle was just another empty shell, with only the wind to fill it like the spirits of the dead.

Most of the heavy machinery was parked in a main-tenance lot behind a wire fence. But it was all bulldozers and trucks.

"Cause I ain't seen nothin makes me believe this is one of them famous bunkers. It's a dump. No water, no visible source of power."

They came to the door of a new building, a warehouse by the looks of it, although they had learned that outward appearances weren't always very informative. The previous large structure they'd searched had looked the same from the outside. Inside, however, the space had been divided up into offices, all of them fully carpeted and filled with dusty machines and computers. Rat-eaten electrical wires and spider webs dangled from water-damaged ceiling panels. There was also a kitchen, a shower, and a locker room. Posters of safety practices were tacked or stapled to the walls. Another sign bragged that it had been 713 days since the last accident, while yet another reminded them that the site could be inspected at any time: *So remember your training. Wear eye and head protection at all times on the worksite. And report unsafe incidents to your supervisor.*

They expected to be attacked through each door they opened, but it didn't happen. And they found nothing of use inside, whether supplies or any sign of a bunker entrance. No clue that the place had ever been anything other than what it had built to be— an industrial site.

"Just a few more to go," Adrian noted. He craned his head up to the windows near the eaves of the tin roof. The panes of glass were small and dusty. A few were broken out. "Y'all better not be yankin my chain, boy."

He banged on the door, and the knocks echoed hollowly inside. There was a soft, scuffing sound, like bare feet on concrete, and they all stepped hurriedly back.

"Hold up!" Adrian whispered. He stepped to one side of the door and leaned against the wall gripping his pistol in both hands. He nodded at Charlie, who positioned himself directly in front and raised his rifle.

He could shoot me now, Adrian thought. But the look in Charlie's eyes, told him everything he needed to know about the man. He was a coward, always had been, always would be. That's why he'd shot his own brother in the head back there, because he didn't have the guts to face what Adrian would have done to him if he had lived. Killed his own damn brother to keep from having to watch him being sacrificed.

Some might call it heroic. But in Adrian's mind, it was cowardice.

And the good Lord does not suffer cowards.

Nor did he. He waved at the boy, instructing him to open the door.

Harper reached up for the knob with both hands — still bound together at the wrists — and turned it. The door made a crackling sound as it broke away from its foam weather stripping seal.

"Do it."

Harper tugged the door wide and stepped back. At the same time, Charlie stepped forward and aimed the rifle into the darkness.

Nothing happened at first. They waited, neither hearing nor seeing anything. Charlie started to relax.

Then there was a sudden loud fluttering and an ear-piercing shriek. A dark shape burst through the opening. The rifle jumped in Charlie's hands, a flash of light and an explosion of sound. Blood spattered Harper's face as he spun away, tripping over his feet and sprawling to the ground.

"Just birds, you fool!" Adrian shouted. "Stop shooting! It's just birds!"

But Charlie was too hyped up to hear. He fired off another round, and more blood and feathers rained down on Harper.

He was yanked to his feet and shoved brutally toward the dark entrance. Blood dripped off Adrian's face as well, making him seem even more evil. A bitter anger passed through Harper directed at Charlie. He'd had the perfect chance to kill the madman, yet he didn't take it. But then he felt guilty for thinking it. No one deserved to die. And no one had any right to take another person's life.

"Get in there!" Adrian growled.

Tiny bones crunched beneath Harper's feet as he stepped in. Several more bodies lay scattered across the threshold.

It took his eyes a few seconds to adjust to the gloom, but by then the other two had stepped in and already reached the same conclusion.

"This is it, sir," Charlie said excitedly. "It has to be."

The building was full of buses, enough to carry several hundred people, maybe even a thousand.

"Yes, I do believe it is," Adrian said, and the tone in his voice sent a shiver down Harper's spine. "Now, go find me a way inside."

CHAPTER
50

EDDIE STOPPED IN THE MIDDLE OF HIS SENTENCE AND grabbed Finn by the arm before turning to shush the others. The crunch and scrape of their tired feet on the road ceased all at once, leaving only the lonely whisper of the wind as it wandered over the desolate landscape.

The quiet was a welcome reprieve. The sound of their footsteps had been chafing at his thoughts, eroding his concentration.

He'd unconsciously picked up his pace in order to get away from them, but at some point Finn had caught up with him. He was going too fast, Finn said, leaving the rest of the group behind. It wasn't safe. The pace was stressing them, both physically and emotionally.

"Missus Abramson and Mister Blakeley especially," he'd added.

So Eddie agreed to slow down, but he wouldn't cede the distance separating them. Finn remained by his side, despite Eddie's reluctance to talk. Before long, the kid dredged up the dreaded subject of Kari's death.

"I know it's bothering you, Eddie," he said.

"And why shouldn't it? If I had just let you pull that device out of Adrian's truck as we were leaving, we would have had protection and she would still be alive."

"And if I had done it, you wouldn't have been able to help fight off the attack that saved the rest of us," Finn countered.

"Lot of good that did. I thought I could defend us. I overestimated my abilities once again, and this time Kari paid the price. I'm not sure Harrison will ever forgive me."

"He doesn't blame you."

"Not sure I believe that."

"It doesn't change anything to beat yourself up about it. It happened, we move on."

"You call beating yourself up over what happened to your father moving on?"

"I'm not—"

"Finn, stop. I've seen it. Everyone's seen it. Whether you're aware of it or not, you've been punishing yourself for his death."

"Yeah, well. Why shouldn't I? We weren't exactly on the best of terms when he died. I hate myself for not trying harder. Or for being a better son."

"You're not your brother."

Finn sighed.

"And since we're being so honest, Finn, there's also the way you've been treating Bren."

"Wow, this just keeps getting better."

"You two were the best thing to happen to us inside that bunker. Seth and Kaleagh may have hated it. Not surprising. No parent likes to think about being replaced in their child's life. I feel the same way about Hannah."

"Are you talking about Bix?"

Eddie chuckled. "Bix is . . . oblivious. Thank goodness for that. Anyway, the point is, the rest of us got a real thrill seeing how you two treated each other. It gave us hope for the future, hope that we could restart again someday with some sort of foundation of decency. But after everything went down, all you've done is push her away."

"I think I deserve a little distance," Finn grumbled.

"But does she? Bren's not responsible for what happened, Finn. Even the things her father did, she had no hand in it. You can't blame her."

It was quite some time before Finn responded. "We were talking about you, not me."

"Nothing more to talk about. Kari's gone. It's my fault. Like you said, we can't change it, we can only learn from it and move on. Now, if you'll excuse me, I'd like to—"

That's when he'd heard the bang and told everyone to be quiet.

They all remained motionless while Eddie listened, his head tilted slightly into the wind. "That! Did you hear that?" he asked, after the second report reached his ears. "It sounded like a gunshot."

They shook their heads.

He waited several moments more, expecting to hear it again, yet dreading he would. The sound was long gone, carried away by the wind. Not even the echoes of it remained. Yet he was determined to trace its source, as if the air contained a remnant of the sound, a memory of the vibration, and that he would be able to track it as he would a lingering smell.

The road they were on continued straight for miles, undulating over the barren landscape. Its shoulders eventually merged to a sharp point, seemingly no closer now than when they'd started out from the truck over an hour earlier.

He turned to the left, where the ground sank sharply away a quarter mile distant. Far beyond the blind drop rose a hazy line of mountains, worn down by a million years of erosion, the easternmost line of elevation on their map.

There. That's where it came from.

Before he realized it, he was running. He could hear the others shouting after him, but he ignored their calls. The view quickly opened up as he approached the lip of the depression, and he realized by the appearance of the wound in the earth, perhaps three miles wide and several hundred feet deep, that he was looking at an open pit mine.

Down to his right, he could barely make out what used to be a road, and he guessed that it joined up with the one they were on. A line of railroad tracks intersected it, angling off to the left before veering southward. Sections of it were erased from view by the drifting sands. And there, off to his right and partially hidden from where he stood, was a cluster of buildings.

The entire place looked utterly devoid of life.

But then there came another bang, and this time he was certain the mine was the source of the sound.

Jonah was the first to reach him, followed soon after by the other teenagers. The adults alternately jogged and walked over the rough terrain, bringing up the rear. They were quite winded by the time they arrived.

"It's a mine," Finn observed. "Aragonite?"

"That would be my guess. Looks like some kind of open pit operation. Or it was before the Flense, anyway."

"See anyone?"

Eddie shook his head. "Heard another gunshot, so someone's down there."

"Smell anyone?" Bix asked, then objected when he received a half dozen frowns and eye rolls.

"We should be able to go down from here," Jonah said, testing the stability of the slope. He descended about thirty feet, then turned. "It levels out a bit further down. This first part is the steepest. It'll be faster than going back out to the road."

"Faster still if we all just slide down on our asses," Bix said.

"Language," Harrison warned, stepping up to the edge. He wiped the sweat from his forehead onto his sleeve. "If we go down here, we risk being seen out in the open."

"I don't think there's any way to get down there unseen," Eddie remarked. "The road's even more exposed." He pointed across the compound to where the rough gravel track wound its way up the sides of the mine to ground level.

"So, this is it?" Bren asked. "Bunker Ten is down there?"

"Has to be," Eddie replied. He stepped gingerly forward, following Jonah's lead. Some of the loose gravel rolled away. "Be careful, keep your heads down, and be quick."

* * *

They reached the perimeter fence a half hour later, taking their time to stay as much within the shallow erosion dikes and mining cuts as much as possible. They had, by then, heard several more bangs, but they eventually concluded they weren't gunshots. Instead, they sounded like something banging in the breeze. The reports were too random and too varying in intensity, while being too consistently from the same point in the compound.

They heard nothing else— no shouts, no vehicles, no footsteps.

For the last hundred feet to the fence, they were forced to wade through deep drifts of loose blown sand, which further slowed their progress. They angled for a corner behind the closest building, and there, as silently as possible, they helped each other climb over the barbed wire.

"There's your gunshots," Jonah said, pointing at a pile of debris at the end of a nearby building. On top was a large section of corrugated steel, its corner wedged beneath a rusty piece of machinery. Every so often the breeze lifted it up, then released it to slam back down again.

"This place gives me the creeps," Bix whispered.

Finn hopped down off the fence, grabbed his pack, and almost immediately went sprawling when he tripped over a loose rock. Both Jonah and Bix laughed at him. "Have a nice fall?" Bix asked. "See you next spring," Jonah finished, which elicited more laughs and warnings from the others to be quiet.

Finn reached forward to brush the sand off his pants before yanking his hand away with a surprised yelp.

The rock he'd tripped over was a human skull. With his heart in his throat, he dug it out of the sand. It was white on top, where it had been exposed, gray underneath. Bits of dried flesh and hair clung to it. He flung it away with a disgusted grunt.

Thirty feet to his right, Bren let out a bloodcurdling scream. Eddie was with her in a flash, covering her mouth, but the damage was already done. They all froze, expecting someone, or something, to appear and challenge them.

"What is it?" Eddie whispered.

Bren pointed into the sand, then kicked at it, exposing another skull. More were quickly uncovered. Then, around the corner, they found dozens, if not hundreds, more skeletons.

"What the hell happened here?" Jonah asked.

"Wraiths," Harrison said, holding up a long curved rib bone. "It's covered in teeth marks. Most of them are."

"Looks like it was a massacre."

"Must have been a long time ago," Jonah said. He unearthed another skull with the toe of his boot. It, too, was bleached nearly white and deeply scored.

"I guess we know why they called it the Flense," Bix whispered. He looked a little green around the gills.

"But who were they? Miners? Bunker survivors?"

"We still haven't found a bunker."

"Not yet."

"Well, whoever they were," Eddie said, "let's hope the things that got them are long gone."

CHAPTER

ADRIAN FLEW INTO A RAGE AS SOON AS HE REALIZED the entrance to the bunker was not behind the last door. Instead, they found only a small utility closet draped with cobwebs and the corpses of a thousand flies trapped in the delicate strands. Sand had blown in from a vent in the back. "Y'all lied to me!" he screamed at Harper, ejecting tiny projectiles of spittle through his dust-caked lips. He shook his fist at them. "We've been through this whole goddamn place and ain't found nothin! Y'all lied! I ought to just kill both of y'all right now!"

"I d-didn't lie!" Charlie stammered. "H-he did!"

"Shut up!"

"B-but the buses, sir. What about the buses? You saw them! How else would they bring all them people—"

"I told y'all to shut up!" He whirled around and slammed the butt of his pistol against the man's face. A fountain of blood arced through the air and splattered onto the floor. The man fell, clutching his shattered nose and mewling incoherently. "It's a goddamn junk yard, you idiot!"

He turned back to Harper, who threw up his hands against the expected blow. *This is it*, he thought. *He's finally lost it. I've pushed him too far, and now he's going to kill me.*

"Well?" Adrian screamed.

"It was a guess," Harper cried. He didn't like lying and wasn't good at it, but the circumstances had called for deception. His survival depended on it. "I told you all along it was just an educated guess."

"Educated?" Adrian shrieked. "I shoulda known better than to listen to a damn kid who ain't never even graduated high school! Because of yer so-called educated guesses, we done wasted all this time in this here dump! Hopeless! Goddamn hopeless! I'm done with y'all!"

"It has to be somewhere close by!" Charlie squeaked. "The map matches up!"

Adrian slapped the scrap of printed paper from Charlie's hand with a growl, then grabbed him by the arm and jerked him to his feet. "Get moving! Every minute my Jenny suffers because of yer stupidity is another minute I'm gonna enjoy watchin her havin her way with the both of ya."

He spun back to Harper. "And if she dies before that gunshot heals, I will personally make sure y'all spend the rest of yer miserable lives wandering this place the same way she is now!"

"Maybe we should check that place up the road," Charlie stammered. He turned to Harper. "That could be it, right? That was on the map, too, wasn't it?"

"I said I wasn't sure." Once more, he hoped Adrian wouldn't see the deceit in his eyes.

But he knew he'd failed when Adrian's face twisted with sudden realization. "You little shit! Yer tryin to buy time! That's it, ain't it? Y'all still believe yer brother's comin for ya. Well, he may be one persistent little prick, but this time he ain't comin. He ain't got the phone. He ain't got a clue about this place. He's dead."

"You don't know Finn like I do. He'll come, like he's been doing. He won't stop. He's smart and strong and—"

He didn't see Adrian's hand before it was too late to duck out of the way. It slammed into his face, all burly knuckles like a chunk of knotted wood, the black steel of the pistol barrel adding to the force of the blow. For a moment he thought he would pass out from the pain. The world spun around him, and his stomach lurched. Somehow, he managed to stay on his knees.

"Yer brother has been an almighty thorn in my side for too long, that's for sure," Adrian spat. He leaned down over the boy. "Him and his cocky boyfriend. Them and their dirty lies and tricks. I should have let my sister have them both when I had the chance. Could have sicced her on Finn just t'other day, like a dog to a bone. Well, that ain't never gonna happen now, but I can still let her have you instead."

"You need me. If you're going to figure out what the rest of those files mean, if you're going to find the cure—"

"There ain't no cure!"

"You want it for your sister!"

The hand flashed into view again, but Harper expected it this time. He ducked. Nevertheless, the fist caught him a glancing blow. He fell backward onto his hands.

"You want the cure to bring her back!" he shouted defiantly.

"Tain't no cure!" Adrian growled. He barked out a laugh. "Nothin but a lie, weren't it? All of it. Y'all ain't no good to me no more."

"It's real," Harper whispered. He could feel his chances of survival slipping away. He needed the man to believe he was still of some value. "Maybe Charlie's right. I was wrong. We should check up the road."

"Naw, we're done." Adrian reached into his pocket and drew out the phone. "Without this, it don't matter. Without this, ain't no one ever gonna find nothin, no matter if'n it exists or not. Without this, there ain't never gonna be no cure."

He dropped the phone to the cement floor, slammed the heel of his boot onto it, and ground it into pieces.

Harper gawped in surprise. Everything Cheever had shown him, including the coded list of the bunkers, the maps, the keys to figuring out where the cure had been was on there.

Now they were all gone.

Adrian wrenched Harper to his feet. "To hear yer brother talk about it, I'da thought y'all were the smart one of the pair. But yer not very smart at all."

"Finn's the smart one. He's coming."

He flung Harper back to the floor and kicked him in the ribs. Harper coughed and looked up to find the pistol pointed at his head. The madman's finger was on the trigger, and he was squeezing it.

But then there came a bloodcurdling scream through the open door at the other end of the building, and he hesitated. Charlie spun around with a panicked gasp. Adrian simply frowned and shook his head in irritation. The beast that had once been his sister uttered a second hungry cry, and a smile crept over his face.

"Naw," he said. "Shootin's too good for y'all. I got somethin else in mind."

CHAPTER

"GOT A FLASHLIGHT?" JONAH ASKED, AS THE BEAM flickered out and left them in darkness. "Mine's dead."

"Gave mine to Missus Abramson," Bix replied.

"Great," Jonah grunted, slamming the offending instrument futilely against his palm. "Remind me again why Eddie thinks it's a good idea to keep pairing the two of us up?"

"Because he knows you need someone big and strong to protect you. You know, being such a frail little flower and all."

"You saying you're my Prince Charming?"

"Ugh, hell no! That's just creepy!" There was a scratching noise, then the flare of a tiny flame, and Bix's face lit up. "But it's also sorta true. Bix to the rescue again."

"Great, he's starting to refer to himself in the third person."

"And you're addressing people who aren't there."

"You know you're not supposed to play with matches. You'll start wetting your bed again."

"Hey, at least I stopped."

Jonah chuckled and gestured for Bix to continue on.

"You know, speaking of matches," Bix said, "I got one for you." He cupped his free hand in front of the tiny flame to keep it lit and edged toward the door at the far end of the dark hallway. After a moment, he stopped, bent over, and plucked some paper off the floor and lit the corner before the match could burn itself out.

"I'm afraid to ask," Jonah said.

"Your face, my ass. Get it? It's a match."

"Uh huh. That's so funny I forgot to laugh."

"Oh, come on. You know it's hilarious."

Bix turned around when Jonah didn't answer. "What are you doing?"

"Was just wondering that myself," Jonah replied. "I mean, what *are* we doing? Why are we even here? Look at us. We got no transportation. We've left all our food and water behind where someone can make off with it. This mission is . . . I'm just not sure we're doing anything but keeping ourselves busy."

"We're looking for Harper. Remember?"

"You know we're not going to find him. We all know that. He's not here, Bix."

Bix stepped back to the older boy. "I think it's time you shut your mouth."

"You know it's true. Why are we chasing ghosts? Is it because we don't know what to do with ourselves? I think that must be it."

"We're going to find Harper for Finn. And then we're going to find Bunker Twelve."

"You mean Bunker Ten."

"Twelve, Ten, what's the difference?"

"So, you admit it? We're just keeping busy."

"We're looking for the cure!"

"And what are we going to do when we don't find it or anything else? How long do we keep up this charade?"

"As long as it takes. Finn is my best friend. I'll do whatever he thinks is best."

"And what if it gets you killed? Or your father?"

"You really are a coward, Jonah, you know that?"

"You're the coward for not telling him what he needs to hear. Come on, Bix, I saw you having doubts back there. If you were truly his friend, you'd be challenging him instead of letting him fool himself like this. There is no bunker, no cure. And Harper is long gone. He's probably dead. Or worse. Do you want Finn to find his brother turned into a Wraith? It's time to go back."

"I can't believe you're saying this. No wonder no one likes you."

Jonah didn't react. He didn't deny it or get angry.

"I am not giving up on Finn. And neither should you."

"He's living in a fantasy world, Bix. Reunions with long lost family members are a quaint but silly idea. Chasing it is going to get everyone killed."

"Ah, I finally understand what this is about," Bix said. "You're jealous of Finn because he's out here looking for his brother. You feel guilty that you're not doing the same."

"Don't you dare— Hey, get back here!"

"I'm done having this discussion with you, Jonah."

Bix cast the burning paper to the floor before the flame could scorch his fingers. It went out and submerged them once more into darkness.

Jonah heard him shuffling away, the sound of his hands sliding along the walls and his feet scuffing the tiled floor. After a moment, he heard the jiggle of a door knob and the metallic pinging of the tumblers as they fell into place.

Then there was light, blinding light. He shielded his eyes and started to move forward.

"Bix? Hey, Bix?"

"Um, Jonah?"

"What'd you find? An exit?"

"I think you'd better get the others."

"Why? What is it?"

"We found it, Jonah. We found Bunker Ten."

CHAPTER

"HOLD UP, FINN. HARPER'S NOT HERE," JONAH SAID, stepping over to stop him when he and Bren came running in.

Seth and Kaleagh were right behind, followed by Eddie, who had found the four of them at the other end of the compound.

Finn pushed his way past. The large, brightly lit room looked like some sort of staging area, with benches along the walls and open cubbies underneath. Set into the walls were small lockers, hundreds of them stacked three high. Most of the numbered doors hung slightly ajar. Loose items of clothing lay about on the floor or spilled out from inside the cubbies— jackets, sweaters, boots. A dusty stuffed animal sat in one corner, a handbag in another. A sneaker lay on its side nearby, its partner nowhere to be found.

"What is this place?"

"Some kind of changing area," Jonah said. "We think the bunker inhabitants had to change clothes before entering."

"Why?"

"No idea."

"Where's Bix and his dad?"

"They went looking for you, too."

At the opposite end of the room was a pair of gray panel doors. Stenciled on the left was a large white capital letter B. On the other was the number 10.

Jonah held him back. "Just wait a minute."

"But he might be in there!"

"And we haven't figured out how to open them."

Finn brushed his hands aside and went over to the doors. Jonah was right. There were no knobs or handles. He turned to the others in confusion.

"I don't think they're here, Finn" Eddie said. "I haven't detected any trace of smell, not from Adrian. Not from anyone. Neither in here, nor in any of the other buildings we searched. Nobody has been here in a very long time."

"They could have just passed through quickly without stopping or leaving any trace. Maybe the doors were open then."

Eddie shrugged. "I'm sorry, Finn. I don't know what to tell you."

"But we saw the tire tracks! Where else could they have gone? And this has to mean Bunker Ten! You can't tell me that's a coincidence!"

"I'm not arguing with you on that point. I'm just saying that if we manage to get inside, you should be prepared for them not to be in there."

"But we'll find someone, right?" Bren asked. "Someone had to turn on these lights."

"They're automatic, just like they were in Eight," Eddie said. "It's all on motion sensors." He pointed to a camera mounted above the door. "If they're monitoring us, they haven't bothered to make contact."

Finn placed his ear against the door but couldn't hear anything inside. He ran his fingers along the edge to pry it open. It wouldn't budge.

"If it's any consolation," Eddie said, "I think I heard voices earlier. Be patient. They're not going anywhere."

At last, the outer door at the other end of the hall slammed open and the two Blakeleys hurried in. Both appeared flushed, but while Bix was animated by the find, his father was subdued. He went over to one of the benches and sat down, coughing lightly into his hand.

"Any contact yet?" Bix asked.

Jonah shook his head.

"Has anyone tried banging on the door?"

"No, but—"

Finn slammed the butt of his pistol against the panel and shouted Harper's name. The sound echoed inside, but elicited no response.

"We could try and force it open," Seth suggested.

"Probably not a good idea," Harrison said. "And, if I recall correctly, you were one of the people who *didn't* want to let Williams in when he showed up at the dam."

"That was different!"

"How?"

"Because we were inside then," Jonah said mockingly. "And now we're not."

Seth scowled at him, but didn't reply.

Finn stepped away from the doors and slowly circled the room, swinging open lockers and checking inside. Most were empty, but in one he found a small dark blue duffle, the fabric stiff with age. It contained several packets of compressed protein bars and water, the plastic chewed through by mice, as well as an emergency kit.

"Did anyone else find another set of doors on the compound?" he asked, rotating around to face them. "Anything else marked B10?"

They all shook their heads. "Why, what are you thinking?" Bix asked.

Finn held up the duffle. "This is a survival pack. I think I saw a few outside in the sand with those skeletons. I just didn't bother opening them up to see what was inside."

"So, you think those were bunker residents who never made it in?"

He shook his head. "These are meant to be for when the survivors got out, to give them a bit of a head start." He dug through it and pulled out a flashlight radio, some batteries, iodine pills.

"How come we didn't have survival packs?" Bix asked.

"We did," Seth replied. "They were in one of the locked rooms on Level Four."

"You knew about them and you never offered to let us have them when we left?"

"Never mind that," Finn said. "This door isn't the entrance to Bunker Ten. It's the exit. Those people who died out there? They were leaving."

"Why? It obviously wasn't safe out there. They had to know that."

"Maybe it wasn't safe inside, either."

A stunned silence followed, but it lasted only a moment before a loud buzz and click made them jump.

"Um," Bix whispered, as one of the two doors slowly swung open. "Is anyone else getting a really bad feeling about this?"

ADRIAN COULD SEE THAT HIS JENNY WAS REGAINING her strength, but with her recovery came restlessness. She was hungry and would need to feed soon, and the proximity of food was making her angry. "Not much longer," he whispered to her. "Be patient."

He couldn't let her eat out here in the middle of the desert, nothing but miles of emptiness in which to run and no device to sedate her. This was neither the place nor the time to indulge her.

It pleased him to see that the gunshot wound to her chest had finally stopped bleeding and the hole was sealed up. Gone was that terrible whistling sound coming through it when she breathed. In fact, from what he could see, the wound was healing up nicely.

He knew she had been extremely lucky the bullet missed her heart. He doubted she'd have been able to recover from that serious of an injury. Maybe, but probably not. He suspected, however, that the slug might have nicked a major artery, given the amount of blood she'd lost.

He was grateful the boy hadn't put the bullet into her brain instead. Not like his brother had done to him. Head shots were just about the only guaranteed fatal injury. He'd seen ferals recover from other trauma that would kill a man— amputations, falls from great heights, terrible burns. But never a shot square to the head.

That was just about the only wound they couldn't recover from.

Those, and drownings, which was probably why they avoided water.

He looked into the rearview mirror and frowned with disgust at the two in back.

Soon, he thought idly.

He thought the sanctuary would be an apt place to do it. The device in his ruined truck would still be operating, providing him again with some measure of control over her.

As if knowing his thoughts, she lurched toward him, straining against the bindings and grunting with effort. But she could do little more than that at the moment. He'd made damn sure she couldn't get free.

"Shhhh," he placated her. He could understand the torment she was suffering. He let the resentment he felt blossom inside of him. It focused him.

The tires of the Silverado rattled over the washboard road as they made their way back toward the main highway. Much of the actual surface was buried beneath drifting sand, the rest caked with dried mud deposited by the seasonal heavy rains. He could still make out the road's edges by the parallel humps running along each side. It was best to remain between them than to risk snapping an axle. And he didn't want to risk getting the truck stuck in the sand.

The landscape to his immediate right disappeared as it yielded to the old mining operation. The rim of the dig skewed toward him until some of the facility's buildings came into view far below. When he reached the empty guard shack at the drive leading down into the dig, he stopped and got out to take a look, just in case.

The drifts here were deep, though not enough that a large truck would have any problems. They were also undisturbed, save for the tracks he had left hours before.

"Yup, this ain't it neither," he said, stepping back to the truck bed to address the boy. "Ain't nobody been this way lately."

Adrian saw something flicker in the boy's eyes — fear, disappointment, it didn't matter — and he shrugged. "Sorta feels anticlimactic, don't it?"

Harper didn't answer.

"Too bad. I was really hopin y'all were right."

"He'll come."

"Naw, if'n he's still alive, I think he's given up on y'all." He flashed a grin, then walked back to his seat and shut the door.

A rooster tail of sand sprayed into the air as he pulled back onto the road and drove off.

CHAPTER 55

"SETH, YOU AREN'T ACTUALLY THINKING ABOUT GOING down there," Missus Abramson said, holding him back by the arm. "You, too, Bren. I did not give you permission to go!"

Bren paused a few steps down the concrete stairwell and turned back to face her parents. "We need to stick together, Mom."

Seth nodded grimly. "We should at least find out what happened here. We'll be safer with the group."

But still she resisted. "You heard what Finn said. Those people were trying to get away from this place, and now you want to go in there?"

"We don't know for sure what happened here," Seth countered. "For all we know, those could be the remains of the people who worked here before the Flense."

He placed his hands on her arms, hoping to reassure her. "Do you remember the guards at the dam, how they defended us when we arrived? What do you think happened to them after we sealed the doors? They sacrificed their own lives so we could—"

"I don't think those people out there were guards, Seth. Or miners. I think Finn was right. They were people trying to get away from the bunker. They had those survival packs."

"Which the guards could have taken."

She squeezed past Seth and onto the landing to address the others. There was some kind of control console beside the door, just like they'd had on Level 10 in their own bunker, but what it did was a mystery to them. The switches and knobs didn't seem to have any effect when manipulated. A thin layer of dust, undisturbed, covered the surface and informed them it hadn't been touched in a long time.

On the other side of the landing was the narrow opening to a steep stairwell, which the others were now descending. They had stopped, waiting for her to make up her mind. Eddie was in the lead, already maybe fifty feet ahead. Although his large body filled the space from one side to the other and prevented her from seeing past him, the odd angle made him seem tiny and vulnerable.

"How far down does this go?" she called. Her voice sounded dead, as if there was something about the concrete walls and ceiling that absorbed it.

Eddie turned for a moment to gauge the distance. "There's a landing about another eighty feet or so down. Probably puts us close to a hundred feet underground at that point. Seven or eight stories, I'd say. It's angled away from the dig, into the intact bedrock."

"Can you see anything, any . . . ?" She wanted to speak the words *bones* or *bodies* or *blood*, but they caught in her throat. "Any people?"

He shook his head. "Nothing but these steps. A few random items. Just garbage, nothing alarming."

"Any sounds? Smells?"

"Aside from the buzz of these lights, no."

"Look honey," Seth said. "Someone's down there. Someone's alive and uninfected. Must be if they opened that door for us. And they wouldn't have done that if they thought we were a threat."

"The only thing we know for sure is that *we* aren't a threat," she replied.

"What could we possibly have to fear from other survivors like us?"

"Look, we're going down," Eddie said. "We have to. If you're worried about safety, then my advice is to spread out, give each other enough room so that we can pull back in a hurry if we need to. The strongest of us are at the front, where the risk is the greatest. If we sense any threat, we'll signal a retreat."

Kaleagh glanced behind her at the stuffed teddy bear Jonah had toed into place to prevent the door from shutting and sealing them in, since there was similarly no knob on the inside as well. While it ensured they would be able to get out should they need to, it also left them vulnerable from anyone — or anything — coming in from outside.

Harrison seemed to sense her thoughts. He edged his way back up the steps, pulling on the railing and puffing as he squeezed past Bren. "I'll bring up the rear then," he said, lifting the rifle in his hand. He tilted his head behind him. "Go on. It'll be safe."

"Just hold onto the rail and watch your step as you come down," Eddie called up. "You don't want to slip and fall."

* * *

"Anyone else feel like we're inside a tomb?" Bix whispered.

"You know, you don't always have to say everything you think," Jonah muttered.

"You don't want to know what I'm thinking right now."

Like Missus Abramson, Bix had had reservations about entering the bunker. But after seeing the determination in Finn's eyes, he'd kept quiet. Besides, he was curious. They all were. Even if Finn was right about the bones outside, there could still be more people alive inside, people like themselves, survivors.

At the bottom of the steps, they found their way blocked by another locked door and no obvious way to open it.

"I remember seeing a documentary in school once," Bix said, nervously pacing around the edges of the small landing. "It was about the pyramids in Egypt. You had to go down this long, steep tunnel—"

"Shut it, Blackeye," Jonah snapped.

At last, his father stepped into the landing. "All here."

Eddie gestured at the camera in the corner of the ceiling. A red light blinked patiently at them, itself seemingly alive and aware.

To their surprise, the door buzzed and clicked, then swung open a couple inches.

"That definitely did not happen in the pyramids."

"We can still go back, Seth," Kaleagh whispered, an unmistakable tremor in her voice. "It's not too late. We don't need to do this."

They all looked to Finn, who pressed his lips together and didn't offer an opinion.

"I hear . . . something," Eddie said. He wrapped his fingers around the edge of the door and slowly pulled it open. The hallway beyond was dark, but lights flickered on before they even set foot inside.

Doorways lined both sides of the corridor, which extended a significant distance away before disappearing in the gloom where the lights had not yet come on. The floor was littered with discarded items— bits of clothing, empty cardboard and plastic packages, sheets of paper, trash.

"Housekeeping must have taken the week off," Bix muttered.

"Is that . . . . Is that music I hear?" Bren asked. A few melodic strains reached their ears, but it was too faint for them to be sure.

"Christmas music," Eddie said, nodding. "*Silent Night.*"

They crowded forward to hear, but he held them back, warning them yet again that they needed to be cautious. Then he turned and called out into the open hallway: "Hello?" He curled his finger into the trigger guard of his pistol and shifted the weapon to the front, but didn't raise it. "Anybody here?"

No one answered.

"Stay put," he murmured to the others, and slipped into the hallway, edging his way forward as cautiously as possible. He had the gun in both hands now, ready to aim and shoot if necessary. He stopped at the first room and knocked gently. "Hello?" he said, his mouth close to the door.

He glanced back at the group, then reached down with one hand and wrapped his fingers around the knob and turned.

The door clicked open.

"Hello?"

Using his foot, he nudged it wide.

"Anyone here?"

"What is it?" Seth whispered.

"Some kind of storeroom, I think. Shelves filled with boxes." He frowned and stepped backward, a look of confusion on his brow.

He shut the door, then moved over to the next one down the hall and tried again. "More supplies," he announced. "Can't be sure, but it doesn't look like anyone's been in them for quite a while."

He gestured for them to follow, reminding Harrison to chock the door open with something to prevent it from closing, then repeated the check of each room they came to. Most appeared to be used for storage, and by the ratio of space to supplies remaining on the shelves, they guessed that less than half of what was originally stocked remained unused.

They found a kitchen, mostly clean save for a few dishes in the large metal sinks, the food on them dried hard as cement. There was even water pressure in the faucets, and after letting the tap run for several minutes, it turned clear and steam began to rise.

"Home sweet home, folks."

"Yeah, but to who? Wraiths?"

"Hush, Bren."

"How is this place even being powered?" Bix wondered.

"No idea."

The working pantry beside the kitchen had been ransacked.

The library farther down the hall was well used but not messy.

The television in the game room was off and silent. Bix powered it up, before shutting it down again. "Anyone up for a movie tonight?" he asked. "I'm thinking a *Ghost Busters* marathon."

They found a chess board abandoned mid-game, the pieces arranged like a still-life puzzle. White appeared to be winning.

Some of the doors were locked and required a key to gain access.

"Anyone notice something odd about this place?" Bix whispered.

Several of them nodded. It was too obvious not to. It was set up almost exactly like Bunker Eight.

As they drew deeper into the complex, the music grew stronger, though it was still very faint.

They passed a stairwell. Jonah pushed the door open, listened for a moment, then guided it quietly shut. They continued on down the hall.

At the end of the hallway, they reached the elevator. The doors were already open, but there was no car, just an open shaft extending down a long ways. The music was drifting up to them from somewhere far below.

"Well, I'm complaining to the safety officer about this."

Eddie punched the button and glanced up at the thirteen lights arranged overhead. None of them was lit, and there was no sound of a bell or motor.

"Okay," he said. "Looks like we're taking the stairs."

CHAPTER
56

HARPER DUG IN HIS HEELS, SEARCHING FOR TRACTION. Sand poured into his boots. It covered his legs to mid-calf and threatened to drag him down into the drift. With a grunt, he pushed against the back of the truck with all of his might.

"Bet he's glad he has us now," Charlie grumbled from the other corner. He squeezed his eyes shut and ducked his head as the tires spun, spraying sand into the air. The wind blew it back into their faces. Adrian gunned the engine again, but it only mired them even more deeply.

"Push harder!" Adrian yelled out the window. The shout was punctuated by an inhuman shriek of fury from the other seat, making Harper's skin crawl.

Charlie looked over, his face red with effort and plastered with sweat and sand. "If you know anything about this other bunker or cure or anything about anything," he said, "please just tell him. Maybe it'll make him change his mind."

"I've told him everything I know," Harper replied, and grunted as he put his back into it again. The bumper lifted slightly, and the truck slued a few inches to the right. But then it settled in again, just as deep as before.

The engine shut off and fell silent, leaving nothing to mask the grunts and hisses of the Wraith in the passenger seat. Adrian stepped out to assess the situation. Both Harper and Charlie straightened up and backed away to do the same.

It was clear they weren't going to be able to drive out. They could try and dig enough of the sand away to free the tires, but they'd have to repeat the process several times over before they were out of the drift. It was simply too large, too deep, too soft, and it was a wonder they hadn't gotten stuck in it on their way in.

Adrian turned his attention from the tires to the two standing with their hands on their knees and scowled. "Y'all are useless."

"Please, sir," Charlie begged, "we're trying."

The man seemed undecided for a moment, then turned his gaze back in the direction they had come. The guard shack for the mine was still in view, perhaps an eighth of a mile back. The rim of the dig was now farther away from the road, hiding the compound from where they stood.

They were stuck in the middle of nowhere with little food and water, four miles from the main road, which might see a passing car once every few days, and perhaps fifty miles from any reasonable chance of scavenging supplies. The only positive was that the area had been so sparsely populated before the feral that they ran little chance of encountering any of the deadly creatures out here.

Little, but not negligible.

The more immediate risk was from dehydration. And wolves.

"This is why I prefer horses," he grumbled, and slapped the side of the truck. He pulled Charlie's rifle from behind the seat and slung it over his shoulder, then gestured at them with the pistol to start walking.

"Where?"

"Where the hell do y'all think?"

"What about her?"

Adrian glanced back at his sister. "Y'all want me to bring her?"

"No!"

He chuckled sourly. "She ain't goin nowhere. Now move! That way."

They reached the inner gate at the edge of the compound a half hour later, where Adrian ordered Charlie to check the vehicles scattered about the lot. "Them buildings there look like maintenance bays," he said. "Check inside for anything we might use to drive outta this place or dig the truck out. The kid and I will go lookin for food and water."

He tossed the rifle over to Charlie, which he nearly fumbled. It surprised him that Adrian would trust him with such a long leash, especially after everything that had happened over the past couple days.

"Find us a working vehicle," Adrian cajoled, "and all will be forgiven. Heck, I'll even make y'all my right-hand man, if'n you do."

"Y-yes, sir," Charlie stammered. He hesitated a moment, then spun around and headed for the closest building, glancing back every so often to make sure Adrian wasn't pointing the pistol at his back.

"He ain't gonna leave me," Adrian said, after seeing the incredulous look on Harper's face. "He had a chance back there at the church and he didn't take it. He had more chances at the dump. It's because he knows he'll die out here on his own. Only reason he's even still alive after all these years is on account of bein with the people at the army base."

Harper's face revealed nothing.

"As for y'all, wouldn't trust ya as far as I could throw ya." He grunted and gestured with the gun toward a separate cluster of buildings near the back, then gave him a shove in the back. "No way I'm lettin y'all outta my sight."

They searched an office building and found nothing that hadn't already been ransacked. A candy machine had been smashed and the food removed. A soda machine lay on its front, too heavy to overturn, taunting them with promises of something sweet hidden away in its bowels. The water jugs in a small cafeteria were dry, as were all the toilets.

The next set of structures ran along the fence close to the rail line. Cranes towered into the sky like silent, slumbering giants, ready to wake and resume moving the mined ore from truck to conveyor tipple to hopper car. But the tracks were empty, and no ore trucks waited. All was silent and still.

Adrian wiped a bead of sweat from his forehead and peered around, nostrils flaring at the dust that hovered constantly in the air. A few nondescript buildings sat in the farthest corner from the gate, across a deeply rutted apron of bare earth. The ground slumped away on the right into the mine proper.

He turned around. Behind them was the main compound, and no sign of Charlie. For a moment, he felt uncertain he had made the right decision. What if Charlie decided to betray him? Perhaps it hadn't been such a good idea to let him go off on his own.

A gust of wind blew across the pit, and from the cluster of buildings, he heard the slap of metal against metal, drawing his attention back. The place had such a look of utter desolation that he had no hope of finding anything useful.

The banging noise repeated. *Loose roof panel*, he thought, and decided to return to the main part of the compound and find Charlie before the imbecile had time to realize the opportunity he'd been given. "Come on," he told the boy, but Harper didn't seem to hear him. Adrian tracked the direction of his gaze until he saw what had distracted him.

There, nearly invisible against the white sky, rising out of a pipe in the roof of one of the buildings, was a thin puff of steam.

"Well, I'll be damned," he mumbled. "Looks like someone's here after all."

CHAPTER 57

"MAYBE FINN WAS RIGHT," BREN WHISPERED, AS THEY completed their search of the bunker's dedicated living space on Level 3. They found all of the doors ajar, but not a single soul inside. Clues that the residents had abandoned the sanctuary in a hurry were evident in the scattered belongings left behind. Some appeared to be sentimental in nature. "But why did they leave?"

The arrangement of the bunker continued to bear a disturbing resemblance to their own, down to the barebones nature of the simple living quarters— unfinished walls, concrete floors, thin bed mats, harsh lighting. Except for the common rooms upstairs, there were no televisions, bathroom facilities were shared, and there was very little to make the place welcoming.

The first major distinction between the two bunkers was that this one contained so many more units. The corridor on this level was intersected by another across the hall from the stairs, providing room for as many as five to seven times the number that could fit in the dam.

"What I'm wondering is where's the person who let us in?" Bix murmured. "Why haven't they come out to meet us?"

"Because they're observing us," Finn replied glumly. He seemed to have accepted, at least for the moment, that they wouldn't find Harper, but each minute that passed only soured his mood all the more. "They're studying us, making sure we're not a threat to them."

"I'm telling you, we should've broken into the control room upstairs and checked the monitors," Jonah said. "I'd feel better knowing what we're heading into before we actually, you know, head into it."

"Sure, if you're looking for a good way to piss off our hosts," Bix said.

"We're not going to start breaking doors down," Harrison advised, leaning weakly against the wall. "Not yet, anyway."

"You okay, dad?" Bix asked, troubled by how pale and haggard his father appeared. Harrison was favoring his injured arm, splinting it tight against his side.

Eddie frowned. He had known the bite wound had become infected — he could smell the sickness, not the nanites, but the bacteria — and had mentioned it that morning before leaving the house. But Harrison had brushed off any advice and insisted he was fine. He clearly wasn't.

"I think we better just keep looking," he said. "If the similarities hold, there will be a med bay two levels down."

"Should be one regardless," Jonah added, also giving the injured man a worried look.

The others shifted uneasily, uncertain what to say or do. Most of them had dismissed the Wraith bite from their thoughts when it became clear he wasn't going to turn into one of them. And as he'd suffered in silence since then, they had mostly forgotten about the incident.

But now, their ignorance about the nature of the Flense and how it worked fed into their fears.

"If we're lucky, they'll have some drugs down there and clean bandages," Eddie said.

"Nothing a little aspirin won't fix."

Kaleagh Abramson went over and placed the back of her hand on his cheek. "You're burning up. You need antibiotics."

Seth looked like he wanted to pull his wife away from him.

They made their way down a level, but instead of finding dedicated storage and access to a loading bay, as they would have in the dam, they found even more living spaces. As before, these were also empty.

"Christ, how many people did this place hold?" Finn asked, as they reached the end of the hall. He paused to glance down the unsecured elevator shaft. He guessed that the car was stalled near the bottom, perhaps one or two floors up. The distance made him dizzy, and he teetered for a moment on the edge before drawing back.

"We haven't seen any blood," Bix said. "If there had been a breach, we would have seen something."

"Come on, Finn," Bren said, and gestured. The others had already headed for the stairs. She ran a hand through her tangled and greasy hair, and for the first time in a long while, Finn noticed how ragged she looked. Dark bruises circled her eyes, and her pale cheekbones seemed sharper than usual. He felt a pang of guilt in his belly. What Eddie had said was true. He had neglected her, and she was suffering emotionally, as well as physically.

"They're heading down," she said. "We shouldn't get separated."

Finn glanced at Bix, who nodded in agreement, and he was startled to see how pasty his friend appeared, too. They were all undernourished, dehydrated, exhausted. And it was all because of him, all because of his selfish obsession with finding his brother.

And the cure.

Except, if he was really being honest with himself, the promise of a cure had never been at the top of his list. He wasn't even sure he believed it existed anymore. All he wanted was to find Harper.

And it was killing him that he didn't really understand why.

* * *

Just as Eddie had predicted, the med bay was located on Level Five, to the left of the stairs as they exited them and at the opposite end of the hallway from the elevator.

The clinic appeared clean and was, incredibly, still well-stocked with medical supplies and equipment. Even the refrigerator still ran, though there was mold on the seal and it was in need of defrosting. Bix stuck his head into the freezer and let out a contented sigh, at least until Bren scolded him to shut the door.

"Too bad there's no soda," he complained. "Or beer. I could use an ice cold brew right about now."

He glanced over, but his father didn't seem to have heard.

"Be serious for once," Bren whispered.

Eddie tossed Kaleagh a plastic bottle filled with a viscous orange-pink fluid in it. "Oral amoxicillin. Should still be good."

"This says it's for children."

"Just double the dosage," Seth snapped. "He'll be fine."

"You really think you should be handing out medical advice?" Jonah said, pacing near the door to the triage area. The deeper they went into the bunker, the edgier he'd become. And he wasn't the only one.

"What's that supposed to mean?"

"It means if it weren't for you, we'd have a real doctor with us!"

The room fell silent.

Finally, Harrison cleared his throat. "We need to put that behind us, move forward. We all need each other to survive."

"Doesn't mean I have to like him."

"Perhaps not, but we do need to trust one another," Harrison pressed. "Seth has contributed enough to earn his spot among us. Just as Red did. He died helping us."

"I doubt Mister Abramson would be so willing to do the same."

"Let's focus on what we need to do to survive, shall we? He's earned the right—"

"Are you kidding me?" Jonah yelled. "He hasn't earned anything! He hasn't done a damn thing but mooch off the rest of us and complain and get in our way. Open your damn eyes, Harrison!"

"Hey!" Bix shouted. "Don't talk to my father like that!"

"Well, someone has to say something!"

"Why?"

"Why? Because you won't! Because we're all trying so damn hard not to hurt each other's feelings. What the hell are we doing here? There's nothing to find in this place! Nothing!"

"The cure—"

"There's no cure! This place is empty! Whoever was once here left!"

"Then who let us in?"

"No one let us in, Finn. Come on. You know it, just like everyone else knows it. No one opened that door because it was automatic."

"You don't know that!"

"Stop it!" Bix screamed.

"Why are we blindly following Finn? Why are we letting Seth, this . . . this murderer, come with us?"

"Jonah," Finn quietly said, "Seth has a family to protect."

"At least he has a family! What about my family, huh?"

"Enough!" Eddie shouted, stepping between them. "Jonah, you need to calm down. Now is not the ti—"

"I won't calm down!"

"Go take a walk."

"No, that's all right," Seth said, stepping over to the door. "I can tell I'm not wanted. I know you all hate me for what I did back there. You just don't understand why I had to do it. It was for our protection." He looked at them all in turn. His eyes lingered the longest on Finn's face.

"Dad, please . . . ." Bren said, stepping forward.

Seth ignored her and squeezed past Jonah, who refused to budge out of the doorway. With a pained look on his face, he nodded once more at them, then pulled the door open and stepped through.

"Dad, where are you going?"

"No, Bren," Finn said, pulling her back. He handed her his pistol to hold onto. "Let me go talk to him."

CHAPTER 58

*"**K**EEP YER DAMN FOOL MOUTH SHUT, BOY,"* **A**DRIAN warned in a harsh whisper, as they made their way toward the shouting voices. They were still too distorted to unravel what was being said, much less identify who was speaking, but it didn't matter. Whoever it was, the longer they continued to fight amongst themselves, the better it was for him. He jabbed the pistol into the boy's back and urged him onward.

It seemed to be coming from the other end of the hall, but before they reached the open elevator shaft, he realized the argument was taking place on one of the lower floors. For some inexplicable reason, the elevator doors were open, but there was no car.

Well now, he thought, as he prodded Harper forward. *That ain't very safe, is it? Someone could fall down and get hurt.*

They returned to the stairwell and descended, stopping only long enough to poke their heads out on each level to confirm it was empty before continuing on. The argument had shifted from shouting to something a bit more civilized, but the voices were still indistinguishable, a tangle of sharp words and muttered interjections.

Arriving on Level 6, he had Harper silently pull the door open, then held him back as he looked carefully out.

At the far end of the hallway, off to the right, two men stood illuminated in the glow from the elevator shaft. They were still speaking, though the sharp edges had softened. Their body language, however, bespoke of the lingering tension between them. The rest of the hallway was empty.

"Not a word," Adrian whispered. With a hand on Harper's neck, he guided him toward the speakers, making sure to keep them in view over the boy's shoulder.

They were more than halfway there before he recognized the clothes on the taller of the two, and his pulse quickened. How could they have found this place? He'd taken their maps away. And why hadn't he seen any tire tracks?

Well, it didn't matter anymore.

The second figure, much to his surprise, wasn't Bix, but the man who had betrayed the boys.

No wonder they're arguing.

He paused and glanced back the way they'd come, wondering where the others might be.

All dead.

They had closed the gap by half again before he felt Harper tense up beneath his hand and knew the boy finally realized it was Finn standing there. His brother's name spilled from his lips, no more than a whisper, but it was enough to cause the two to turn.

"Harper?" Finn said. "Is it— Oh my god!"

Adrian felt the boy step forward, but he yanked him back. He pressed the pistol hard into Harper's spine until he twisted in pain. "No one move," he growled. "Stay right there. And no shouting for help, or I'll put a bullet in poor Harper's little brain."

"I can't believe it's really you," Finn whispered.

"Shut up and tell me who else is here."

"No one."

Adrian's eyes flicked to the pistol shoved into the front of Seth Abramson's waistband, the grip peeking out from the bottom hem of his untucked denim shirt. Just the one; the boy didn't seem to have a gun.

"Slowly take that out," he said gesturing. "Fingers only! Set it on the floor. I said slowly! Good, now kick it over to me."

The gun slid to a stop a few feet in front of him. He pushed Harper forward. Then, using his foot, he slid the weapon behind them and out of reach.

"Boy, lift up yer shirt and turn around."

Finn did as instructed.

"I-is Dad with you, Finn?" Harper asked.

Finn's gaze flicked over to Seth. "You didn't tell him? Back there at the bunker, you never said what happened?"

Mister Abramson didn't reply.

"He's dead, isn't he, Finn?"

"Enough chit chattin," Adrian growled. He took another quick glance behind him. The hallway was still empty. "You there," he said, jutting his chin out at Seth. "Move away from the boy. Other side of the hall, up against the wall there. Now sit. This don't involve you no more. And as I am a man of my word, I will allow y'all to leave, despite the trouble y'all put me through."

Something flickered in Seth's eyes. He hesitated a moment, then stepped in front of Finn, blocking him from Adrian. "Listen to me," he said, "it doesn't have to be like this."

"I said move away."

"You got what you wanted. We gave you the phone—"

"Y'all mean I took it."

Finn could see the muscles rippling on Seth's cheek. This was a side of him he hadn't seen before— strong, resolute. Unselfish. It was the first time he'd seen him actually risk his life for anyone but himself.

"Mister Abramson, please," he murmured. "Adrian's right. This is about me and him." He tried to push Seth away, but the man reached back with both hands to block him from moving.

It took Finn a moment to realize Seth was doing more than simply shepherding him out of Adrian's sightline. He was also fumbling at the small of his own back, where Kari's pistol lay hidden beneath his shirt.

"Listen to the boy," Adrian growled.

"I can't let you have him."

"Y'all ain't got no choice in the matter. One of them's got to die. Heck, I'll even let y'all have this one in exchange, just like I said before."

"You lied then. Why should I believe anything you say now?"

Adrian shrugged.

"Everyone, please, just calm down," Finn said. "Don't do anything stupid."

Seth pushed him back again. He had finally extracted the gun from his belt and had his finger on the trigger, but was still hiding it.

"Don't, Mister Abramson," Finn whispered. He couldn't let him use it, not with Adrian using Harper as a shield. They'd come all this way and endured too many hardships to lose each other now. "We can talk about this, Father Adrian. I think we all want the same thing here."

"And what is it y'all think I want?" Adrian demanded.

"The same thing your sister wanted: the cure."

"Ain't no cure. And if'n there were, I'd aim to destroy it."

"You could bring her back. She could be just like she was before."

This seemed to rattle Adrian. His face flushed red.

Finn slowly extended his hand and placed it over Seth's fingers. He could feel the older man stiffen at the touch, but he didn't try to wrest the gun free.

"That ain't God's will, boy."

"And what about your will? Don't you want her back?"

Another flicker of self doubt.

"We can at least try," Harper said, picking up on Finn's cue. "We can bring her back for you. There's still a chance."

"It's the devil speakin through y'all, boy. Ain't no person can come back from such a thing. She's already in hell. Ain't no comin back from that."

"How can you say that?" Finn growled. "After all your talk about salvat—"

Harper's shout startled him. He tried to duck away from Adrian, but the man was too quick.

At the same time, Seth yanked the hand with the gun in it out of Finn's grip.

"No!" Finn cried, and tried to grab it back. "Don't shoot!"

Everything happened all at once then. Harper dropped to his knees, leaving Adrian fully exposed for half a heartbeat. Seth spun around, wrenching Finn's wrist at an awkward angle. A shot rang out, filling the hallway with the blast. And at the opposite end of the corridor, Bren and Eddie burst through the door of the medical clinic.

Finn tried again to grab the gun, but Seth brought his other elbow up, catching him below the ear. His head rocked backward, and his knees buckled. With a shout of fury, Seth yanked the gun away with one hand while shoving Finn away with the other. Already off balance, Finn tripped over his own feet and stumbled backward, flailing his arms to try and regain his balance.

But there was no floor beneath him. He tilted backward into the open shaft, and it was like time slowed almost to a stop.

Bren screamed.

Harper reached out as Adrian aimed the pistol.

There was another gunshot, and the last thing Finn saw before he dropped below the edge of the landing was a spray of blood.

Then it was all gone and he was falling.

CHAPTER 59

JONAH JERKED UPRIGHT FROM THE CHAIR WHERE HE'D been dozing, startled awake by the sound of Eddie's alarmed cry that something was wrong. Over Harrison's drowsing form on the treatment table before him and through the open doorway into the triage area, he saw the big man burst through the outer door into the hall, Bren right on his heels. Then came the distant sound of a gunshot.

"Finn!" Bix cried.

"Son!" Harrison yelled, sitting up. He tried to grab Bix, but was too slow.

"Stay here!" Jonah ordered him and Missus Abramson.

He followed Bix out the door, then down the long corridor. At the far end, he could see three people in front of the open elevator shaft screaming at each other, two of them wrestling. Eddie was nearly there already, and Bren was a hundred feet back.

He's here! Jonah realized with a jolt of surprise. *Adrian's here!*

And he was fighting with someone who looked like Finn, except it wasn't him.

Harper?

He saw Seth, too, standing with a pistol in his hand.

But he didn't see Finn.

Bren screamed his name. She was sobbing as she ran.

Where is he? Where did he go?

And then it hit him, the realization that something terrible had happened to Finn, immediately followed by the knowledge of what that thing was.

He pivoted and slammed his body into the stairwell door, ignoring the pain in his hip as it scraped against the push bar. He took the stairs three, four, at a time, gripping the handrail hard enough to burn the skin off his palm. Down he went, spiraling ever deeper into the heart of the bunker, toward whatever mysteries it had yet to yield. He didn't know who or what might be waiting there, whether friend or foe, but he didn't care.

All he could think of was Finn at the bottom of the shaft, and he hoped and prayed that somehow, by some miracle, he was okay.

He grabbed onto something. He's not hurt. He's okay.

But there was an undeniable truth in the echoes of Bren's anguished shrieks, and he knew that he would not find what he prayed for.

Rage filled him, rage and despair. His feet slammed into the eleventh landing. His ankle twisted, throwing him off balance. He stumbled hard into the wall, then exploded out the door and into the hallway. A scream of agony rose in his own throat. How had Adrian found them? Had he been waiting for them? Was he the one who let them in?

Eddie didn't smell him.

But Eddie's abilities weren't infallible.

Adrian did it. Adrian pushed Finn over the side.

His thoughts were a jumble as he raced toward the elevator. The doors were open, but no car filled the space behind them.

Please, please, please, he silently prayed, trying to ignore the wails of grief drifting down from above.

He was blinded by his own tears. Yet he careened on, bouncing off the walls toward the square of light, which seemed forever out of reach.

He barely managed to catch himself on the edge of the opening, and he hugged himself to it before his momentum could drag him into the hole.

He turned and looked down.

There, not six feet beneath the floor level, was the top of the broken elevator car. And just as broken, was Finn staring glassily upward at the ceiling high above. Beneath him, a pool of blood grew with inexorable slowness.

CHAPTER

60

By the time Bren reached her father, he had already lost a massive amount of blood through a hole in his abdomen. He was dying, and yet he still had the strength and presence of mind to pull her away from the edge of the elevator shaft. He couldn't let her fall.

She was hysterical — beyond all reason — and as she battered him with her fists and screamed that he had pushed Finn over the side, he tried to tell her it was an accident.

He tried to speak, but he seemed incapable of expelling any air from his lungs. Nothing seemed to want to work. Barely a whisper left his lips.

"I saw you!" she screamed. "I saw you push him! How could you do it? How could you kill my Finn? I loved him! I loved him! *WHY?*"

He didn't try to stop her from beating him. He couldn't even feel it anymore. He couldn't feel anything. Just this odd sense of floating now. And warmth.

And peace.

He was outside of himself. He saw Eddie lift her away, and he wanted to yell at him to let her stay by his side, even if she hated him. He saw Harper by the opening, finally free of Adrian's grip. The boy collapsed to his knees and sobbed.

He shouldn't lean so far out. He's going to fall, if he's not careful.

He wondered if Finn would have reacted in the same way as his brother was doing now, crumbling to pieces like that.

Maybe three years ago. Maybe he would have fallen apart then. But not now.

And he finally appreciated how much the boy had changed, not so much during the time they had spent together inside the bunker, but in the handful of days since leaving it. He realized how much the bunker had held him back, kept him from reaching his full potential.

Or maybe it was his father who did.

Harper was supposed to be the strong one. But he was weak, falling apart when there was still work to be done. Seth doubted Finn would be so fragile.

How could I have been so wrong about him?

He saw Bix tackle Adrian, beating him like a wild beast, and Seth almost laughed at how uncontrolled, how unthinking he was, acting purely out of instinct and hatred. His fists were a blur, pummeling the man about the face and shoulders.

He sensed Bren had returned to his side again, except she wasn't beating at him anymore. He tried to look at her, to see her through his corporeal self rather than the amorphous presence now floating near the ceiling. He felt his chest shake as he took in another impossible breath. Eddie again tried to pull her away, but Seth reached up and grabbed her arm and opened his mouth.

They all stopped, waiting, and again he thought he might laugh at the looks on their faces. He thought he could start spouting gobbledygook and they'd probably think it was the most profound thing they had ever heard, his last dying words.

Tell her, Seth. Don't screw it up. You only get one chance to make this right.

But then he realized he didn't know what to say to them, only that it had to be the truth. But would he even know the truth if he saw it? He'd been keeping it hidden away for so long, even from himself, that it had become this slippery amorphous thing, squirming through his fingers whenever he tried to grasp it.

He coughed, and florets of blood sprouted on his daughter's face where there had been none before. She didn't bother to wipe them away. Instead, she bent down lower over him, still furious, still crying, waiting for him to atone for his sins.

He knew his chance was slipping away. The truth of his dying had forced her to temporarily forget Finn's own death, but it wouldn't last for long. He opened his mouth again.

"What is it?" Eddie asked. It was an odd thing, the way the overhead lights shone off the man's bald pate, blinding him. Seth wanted to reach up and touch it, like if he could just make that connection, it might save him, save them all. "What are you trying to say, Seth?"

Another crimson bubble burst from his lips. But no sound accompanied it.

He felt the man's hands on him, jostling his body, shaking him back into consciousness. They were rough and pitiless.

Seth closed his eyes. He expected nothing but blackness, but it was all white now. And it dislocated away from him, the whiteness. Now it floated apart, like a white sheet flapping in the wind just beyond his reach. And the space between them, this dark moat, was filling up with a thick, inky mud.

Tell them. Tell them about the book! It's all in there.

"Dad? Daddy!"

But instead of slipping back into that warm, enveloping whiteness, he felt himself slipping back into the darkness. Not death, not yet. Maybe not ever. This was . . . . It was something else.

The nanites!

He could feel them now, hard at work inside of his body, repairing the damage the bullet had wrought in its passage through him, replacing the missing blood, sealing shut the shattered blood vessels and repairing the organs the slug had tried to destroy.

He sucked in another breath, and this one actually seemed to come much easier.

He opened his eyes, and the view before him was from his own body. Bren was there, above him, her face streaked with tears cutting runnels through the dirt and spots of blood. He saw Eddie straighten up in surprise. And he saw Bix rise up over Adrian, who cowered beneath him with a hand raised in supplication.

Seth whispered his wife's name. And this time his words were strong enough to reach his own ears, as well as theirs.

They were all looking at him now, waiting. All except Harper, who sat crumpled and sobbing at the edge of the opening.

He saw Adrian push himself off the floor with the other hand. He saw the glint of black in it and recognized Kari's Ruger. A burble of air escaped Seth's lips as he tried to shout a warning.

He heard the bang, though it suddenly seemed so far away. And he saw the blackness suddenly retract from him, exploding in a flash. But instead of white, this time it was only a curtain of red.

And it grew until it swamped all else out.

Until that, too, faded away into nothingness.

CHAPTER 61

CHARLIE KNEW HE'D WAITED TOO LONG. HE HAD known it for the past twenty minutes. And yet he'd been too scared to run.

He'd almost done it a half dozen times already, his body twitching in anticipation of the flight. But each time, he'd frozen in fear. And each time, once he realized his failure, he cursed his cowardice and knew that Adrian had been right about him. That's why he'd trusted him enough to let him go off on his own. He was just a worthless little chickenshit piece of shit.

I AM NOT!!!

He was off and running before he realized it. His feet pounded the hard earth until he reached the sand drifts at the edge of the compound and threatened to drag him down. Then he was at the bottom edge of the slope, where it suddenly steepened into a wall, and he thought it might be too much for him to climb. But he couldn't risk the road. The road was too exposed. If he took it, Adrian would surely see him before he could get out of range. And he was a good shot, even at a distance.

He scrambled up, using his free hand to keep himself from falling before realizing he could use the rifle in the other to greater effect. His lungs burned. He had sand in his eyes, in his mouth and nose. Sand in his shoes, weighing his feet down.

But then he was scrambling over the top and running over level ground again.

Free!

He chanced a look over his shoulder, half expecting to see Adrian right there, right behind him, pointing his pistol at his back. He could even feel the spot where the site would be, the soft divot of flesh at the base of his skull. And there would be a flash and a puff of smoke coming from the end of the barrel, which would tell him it was already too late to duck. And he would feel the bullet enter his brain between his eyes a moment before the report of the gunshot reached his ears.

But Adrian wasn't there.

So Charlie Bolton ran, laughing at himself, laughing both at his cowardice and at the spontaneous and wholly uncharacteristic bravery he had suddenly developed. He hadn't known he'd had it in him. Adrian didn't believe he had, but he did.

The truck was still there, sitting in the road, its tires sunken deep into the soft sand, and he laughed again, relishing the sound of it, even though the wind came and tore it from his lips.

He laughed because he knew Adrian was a creature of habit and superstition. He would have left the keys in the ignition like he always did, ready for a quick getaway.

He reached the truck and stopped, pausing with his hands curled over the edges of the back bumper so he could catch his breath. He'd need his wits about him, his strength. Because there was one thing he needed to do before he dug himself out and drove away. One thing before he was truly free of that maniac back there.

He dropped to his knees, gasping for air and wishing he had some water. His lungs burned.

A minute.

Two.

He couldn't afford to wait any longer. He had to move.

He made his way to the passenger side door and yanked it open with one hand, the rifle in the other, finger on the trigger, ready to fire a bullet into the head of the monster Adrian had brought with him.

Sick man sicko what the fuck is wrong with him and why would he—?

The first thing he noticed was that the key wasn't in the ignition.

The second, was that the seat was empty.

And the seatbelt had been chewed through.

Then, last of all, he heard the soft hiss of air passing through the infected monster's lips behind him, brushing the hair at the base of his neck like the loving caress of his mother's fingers.

JONAH LIFTED FINN'S HEAD AND CRADLED IT IN HIS arms. Waves of uncontrolled grief wracked his body. He was a roiling ocean in a storm, his sobs breaking pitilessly against the shores of his soul.

Finn was still alive. His body was broken, joints pulled asunder, arms and legs bent and broken. Bones shattered beyond repair. Blood leaked from his mouth, his nose, his ears. The sound of his agonized breathing was a torment far greater than any Jonah had ever known. It was more than he could bear.

"Don't die," he wept. "Please, Finn, don't die. Oh, god, please no."

Just make it quick. Please, no more pain. No more suffering. Just take him.

Finn shuddered. Then all tension fled from his body at once. He sighed, and Jonah knew that it would be his last. Yet Finn defied him and opened his eyes once more. And from somewhere deep inside, he found the strength to speak: "She . . . . She's . . . ."

"What, Finn? Bren? What about her?"

The boy's head sank into Jonah's grieving arms, and his eyes slowly closed. He sucked in one final hitching breath, then let it out.

"She's . . . coming."

If you like the BUNKER 12 series, then check out
the companion series THE FLENSE

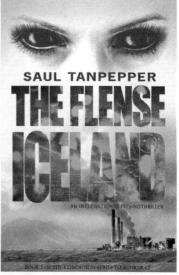

This four-book epic pre-apocalyptic technothriller follows the
exploits of French biomedical investigative reporter, Angelique de
l'Enfantine, as she scrambles to uncover the cause of a series of
mysterious and deadly global tragedies. But the closer she gets to
uncovering the terrifying truth, the greater the risk grows, both to
herself and to all of Humanity.

Book One: *China*
Book Two: *Iceland*
Book Three: *Africa*
Book Four: coming soon!

And look for *Shelter in Place*, a thrilling standalone short story set
between the worlds of THE FLENSE and BUNKER 12

AVAILABLE IN DIGITAL AND PRINT

http://www.tanpepperwrites.com/gameland

SAUL TANPEPPER is the creator of the acclaimed cyberpunk dystopian series, GAMELAND. A former army medic and PhD scientist, he now writes full time in several speculative fiction genres, including horror, apocalyptic, science fiction and paranormal. A frequent world traveler, his works are heavily influenced by these experiences and his background as a biotechnology entrepreneur. He currently resides in California's Silicon Valley with his wife of more than twenty years and his two children. He is the author of the story collections *Insomnia: Paranormal Tales, Science Fiction, & Horror* and *Shorting the Undead: a Menagerie of Macabre Mini-Fiction.*

To receive updates, subscribe to Saul's e-newsletter,
Tanpepper Tidings

https://tinyletter.com/SWTanpepper

For more information about this and his other titles, visit
www.tanpepperwrites.com